Workbook to accompany

A Biography of the English Language

Second Edition

C. M. Millward

Boston University

THOMSON

WADSWORTH

Australia Canada Mexico Singapore Spain United Kingdom United States

Workbook to Accompany
A Biography of the English Language, Second Edition
C. M. Millward

Printed in the United States of America
9 10 11 — 08 07 06 05

For more information contact Thomson Wadsworth, 25 Thomson Place, Boston, MA 02210 USA, or you can visit our Internet site at http://www.thomson.com

ISBN: 0-15-501647-4

PREFACE

The organization of this workbook parallels that of *A Biography of the English Language*. It can, however, be used with other textbooks of the history of the English language because most of the exercises are self-contained or presuppose access to material that will appear in most college-level textbooks on the subject. As in the first edition, the exercises vary in length, difficulty, and approach. Some are very simple, others much more challenging. All are intended to encourage students to think about earlier stages of English and the relationship of earlier stages to their own language as well. All are based on the assumption that a hands-on approach is the most effective one for understanding the structure of a language.

Users of the first edition of the *Workbook to accompany A Biography of the English Language* will recognize the format and many of the exercises in this edition. Several new exercises have been added, and some changes have been made to clarify instructions, correct minor errors, and improve felicity of expression.

Most of the exercises use actual, unedited examples of English rather than highly edited or manufactured ones. Although variant spellings and other irregularities may sometimes make an exercise slightly more complicated, I feel strongly that students should be allowed to see the English language in its natural state, weeds and all, rather than as a product of a compulsively tidy grammarian.

Because access to earlier texts suitable for linguistic analysis by relative novices can be a problem, additional supplementary illustrative texts for both Old English and Middle English have been included, along with glosses, for instructors to use as they like.

Instructors will find that most of the chapters here contain too many exercises for them all to be assigned each semester; this is especially true for one-semester courses in the history of the language. My intent has been to provide a selection from which instructors can choose materials best suited to their particular needs. Further, some instructors may want to assign the exercises in an order different from that of the workbook itself. This will be the case for those who have organized their own course topically rather than chronologically.

The materials in this workbook have been drawn from a wide variety of sources ranging from unpublished medieval manuscripts to contemporary television commentary. I am particularly indebted, of course, to the *Oxford English Dictionary* and the publications of the Early English Text Society. Extensive excerpts from other specific sources receive individual acknowledgment.

C. M. MILLWARD

Contents

Holt, Rinehart and Winston, Inc.

Holt, Rinehart and Winston, Inc.

CHAPTER 1

INTRODUCTION

1.1 Important Terms

1. abstraction
2. affix
3. allomorph
4. amelioration
5. analogical change
6. bound morpheme
7. concretization
8. conditioned change
9. connotation
10. denotation
11. derivational affix
12. Early Modern English (EMnE)
13. external (outer) history
14. fission
15. free morpheme
16. function word
17. fusion
18. generalization
19. grapheme
20. graphics
21. inflectional affix
22. internal (inner) history
23. lexical morpheme
24. lexicon
25. Middle English (ME)
26. morpheme
27. morphology
28. narrowing
29. Old English (OE)
30. pejoration
31. phoneme
32. phonemics
33. phonetics
34. phonology
35. Present-Day English (PDE)
36. principle of least effort
37. reflex
38. semantics
39. strengthening
40. syntax
41. unconditioned change
42. weakening

1.2 Questions for Review and Discussion

1. Do animals have language? Provide evidence both for and against your answer.

2. Give three or more examples of the systematic nature of English other than those mentioned in the text.

3. Imagine and describe a language based solely on touch (as opposed to sound or sight). Describe how it might work and list some of its disadvantages as well as advantages it might have over sight- or sound-based language systems.

4. What is the difference between phonetics and phonemics?

5. What is the difference between a morpheme and a word in English?

6. Give two examples in which syntax alone distinguishes two English utterances (i.e., the phonemes and morphemes are the same, but the word order is different).

7. Why is redundancy essential in natural language?

8. In what ways does the written version of a language affect the spoken version?

9. List possible explanations for *why* languages change.

10. Why is the principle of least effort unsatisfactory as an explanation for all changes that occur in language?

11. What are some of the external pressures that have led to changes in American English?

12. Summarize the reasons for the terminal dates of OE, ME, and EMnE.

13. What are the primary sources of information about earlier stages of English?

14. Summarize the problems associated with using texts as a source of information about earlier stages of a language.

15. Why are translated texts less than satisfactory as a source of information about earlier stages of a language?

Holt, Rinehart and Winston, Inc.

1.3   Onomatopoeia

Onomatopoeia, or the formation of words by imitating the natural sounds associated with the object or action being referred to, is inadequate as an explanation for the origin of all human language. Nonetheless, all languages have at least a few onomatopoeic (or echoic or imitative) words, especially for animal sounds and environmental noises. Such words are often similar across languages, as is the case, for example, with the word for the sound made by a cat: Spanish *miau*, Afrikaans *miaau*, Chinese *miao*, French *miaou*, Swedish *mjau*, and so forth. On the other hand, such words must fit the sound system of the language; if there should be a language with no *m* sound, the speakers' cats could not "say" *miao*.

A.   Listed here are the words for several noises or things that tend to be represented by onomatopoeic words in many languages, though not every word is necessarily onomatopoeic in origin. Match the words with their meanings by writing the appropriate number of the meaning beside each set of words.

1. bark of a dog
2. crowing of a rooster
3. cuckoo
4. hiccough
5. noise made by a horse

6. snore
7. sound of a bell
8. sound of a clock
9. sudden loud noise

_____ French *hoquet*	_____ French *hennir*	_____ Chinese *dīngdāng*
Russian *ikota*	German *wiehern*	French *dingue-din-don*
Scots Gaelic *aileag*	Irish *seitreach*	German *kling-klang*
Swahili *kwikwi*	Russian *rzhat'*	Irish *ding deang*
Swedish *hickning*	Swedish *gnägga*	Russian *din'-din'*
Turkish *hiçkirik*	Tagalog *halinghíng*	Swedish *bingbång*
_____ Chinese *wāngwāng*	_____ French *coucou*	_____ Chinese *hānshēng*
French *ouâ-ouâ*	German *Kuckuck*	French *ronfler*
German *wauwau*	Russian *kukushka*	German *schnarchen*
Irish *amh-amh*	Spanish *cuco*	Irish *srannaim*
Russian *am-am*	Swedish *gök*	Swahili *koroma*
Swedish *vov-vov*	Turkish *guguk kuşu*	Swedish *snarka*
_____ Chinese *dīdā*	_____ Chinese *wō*	_____ French *boum*
French *tic-tac*	French *cocorico*	German *bums*
German *tick-tack*	German *kikeriki*	Irish *plimp*
Irish *tic*	Swahili *wika*	Lao *bpa:ng*
Swahili *ta-ta-ta*	Swedish *kuckeliku*	Swahili *bomu*
Tagalog *tumik-tak*	Tagalog *tilaok*	Swedish *pang*

B.   Make up new onomatopoeic words for the following sounds.

Typewriting on an old manual portable ___clikety click click___

A toenail clipper in use ___bick bick___

A dogfight ___bow rowe___

A washing machine with an unbalanced load ___pow tom powtom___

Plastic bottles filled with liquid rolling around in the trunk of a car
___plish splish splish___

3. (a) We'd do anything for you.
   (b) For you we'd do anything.

_____

4. (a) Paula rooms with Myrtle.
   (b) Myrtle rooms with Paula.
   (Why is this different from A. 1.?)

_____

C. Contextual Meaning. Sometimes a particular word order can be interpreted in two very different ways. Explain how each of the following sentences is ambiguous.

1. Samuels had his books audited. _____

_____

2. Jane called her dog a caretaker. _____

_____

3. I don't enjoy drawing rooms. _____

_____

4. Those soldiers are too young to kill. _____

_____

D. Cultural Meaning. Sometimes the meaning of a given word order varies according to the lexical items used. Explain how the choice of the final word in each of these sentences affects the meaning.

  1. Janet made him a good dinner.
  2. Janet made him a good husband.
  3. Janet made him a good wife.

_____

_____

_____

Would the sentence *Janet made him a good spouse* mean the same as sentence 2 or sentence

3 above? Explain. _____

_____

_____

Which meaning (1, 2, 3) would *Janet made him a good agachiceron* have? Explain. ____

_____

_____

_____

_____

Holt, Rinehart and Winston, Inc.

Name _____

1.7   The Systematic Nature of Language

All languages are systematic; otherwise we would not be able to say anything new in them. All natural languages also have irregularities in their systems that must be learned item by item. Still, more often than not, we can predict the correct form of something we have never heard or seen because we have learned the rules of the system.

A. Morphological Systems

1. Listed below are the demonstrative adjectives/pronouns of the Turkish language. By examining the complete forms given, fill in the blanks with the correct endings of the remaining forms. There are no irregularities.

	"this"		"that"		"that yonder"	
	Singular	*Plural*	*Singular*	*Plural*	*Singular*	*Plural*
Subject case	bu	bunlar	şu	şunlar	o	onlar
Possessive case	bunun	bunlarin	şunun	şunlarin	onun	onlarin
Dative case	buna	bunlara	_____	şunlara	_____	onlara
Objective case	_____	bunlari	şunu	şunlari	onu	_____
Locative case	bunda	bunlarda	_____	_____	onda	onlarda
Ablative case	bundan	bunlardan	şundan	şunlardan	_____	_____

2. What is the plural ending (affix), regardless of case? _____

3. Which is attached to the base word first in Turkish, the plural affix or the case affix?

_____

4. Which is attached first in English, the possessive case ending or the plural ending? (Big hint: Think of the words *child* and *alumnus*.) _____

B. Syntactic Systems
Listed here are several sentences in Scots Gaelic, together with their English translations. The translations are English equivalents of the Gaelic sentences, *not* word-for-word glosses of them.

1. Tha each agam. — *I have a horse.*
2. Tha tigh agad. — *You have a house.*
3. Tha peann aige. — *He has a pen.*
4. Tha ad aice. — *She has a hat.*

5. Tha an cu agad. — *You have the dog.*
6. Tha an sgian agad. — *You have the knife.*
7. Tha am bàta aige. — *He has the boat.*
8. Tha an sgian aig a'ghille. — *The boy has the knife.*

9. Cha'n eil sgian agam. — *I don't have a knife.*
10. Cha'n eil ad agam. — *I don't have a hat.*

6. Look up the term *Turkish towel*. How do the dictionaries indicate capitalization? Is *Turkish towel* preferred over *turkish towel*? _____

_____

7. Look up the word *mercenary*. How is major stress on a word indicated? How is secondary stress indicated? _____

_____

8. Look up the word *magazine*. What is the difference between the two pronunciations listed? What determines the order in which the variant pronunciations appear? _____

_____

9. Look up the word *coral*. Where in the entry is the etymology listed? How does the dictionary distinguish between immediate source and ultimate etymology? How does the dictionary distinguish between source words and cognate words? _____

_____

_____

_____

_____

10. Look up the words *joy* and *joie de vivre*. How does the dictionary distinguish between loanwords and unassimilated foreign words? _____

_____

11. How is the order of the definitions under each entry determined? By preferred meaning first? Historically earliest meaning first? _____

_____

12. Look up the word *level*. Are the different parts of speech (adjective, noun, verb) all under the same main entry? _____

_____

Within the entry, where are inflected forms given (e.g., *leveled*)? _____

_____

Where are idioms involving the word located (e.g., *level best*)? _____

_____

13. Find the discussion of usage labels in the introductory material. Which labels are used?

_____

_____

_____

14. Look up the word *doubt*. How does the dictionary handle words with many closely related synonyms? _____

_____

Holt, Rinehart and Winston, Inc.

15. No native speaker planning to leave her apartment simply because she is moving to another city would be likely to write to her landlord, ''I will *evacuate* the apartment by August 25.'' Why? Look up the words *evacuate* and *vacate* as transitive verbs in the dictionaries. Which one would best help a nonnative speaker avoid this error in usage?

Explain. _____

_____

_____

_____

If neither is satisfactory, rewrite the definition of *evacuate* to distinguish its implications

from those of *vacate*. _____

_____

16. You would be unlikely to say, ''Though she's not a true beauty, she has a lovely *grin*.'' Look up *grin* (noun) and *grin* (verb) in the two dictionaries. Is either definition

adequate to explain why the sentence is unacceptable? _____

Look up the word *grin* in the *Oxford English Dictionary*. Comment. _____

_____

_____

Holt, Rinehart and Winston, Inc.

CHAPTER 2
PHONOLOGY

2.1 Important Terms

1. affricate
2. allophone
3. alveolar
4. alveolar ridge
5. apex
6. articulator
7. aspiration
8. bilabial
9. blade
10. consonant
11. dental
12. diphthong
13. dorsum
14. epiglottis
15. esophagus
16. fricative
17. front, central, back vowels
18. glottal stop
19. glottis
20. hard palate
21. high, mid, low vowels
22. interdental
23. labial
24. labiodental
25. larynx
26. lateral
27. lax
28. liquid
29. nasal
30. palatal
31. pharynx
32. phoneme
33. plosive
34. point of articulation
35. primary stress
36. prosody
37. reduced stress
38. resonant
39. retroflex
40. schwa
41. secondary stress
42. semivowel
43. spirant
44. stop
45. tense
46. trachea
47. uvula
48. uvular trill
49. velar
50. velum (soft palate)
51. vocal cords
52. voiced
53. voiceless
54. vowel

Name _____

2.8   **Multiple Vowel Phonemes for One Spelling**

Put the following words into phonemic transcription.

bit	_____	verb	_____	scarf	_____
sign	_____	we	_____	chalk	_____
police	_____	had	_____	judge	_____
pretty	_____	was	_____	flu	_____
tell	_____	hate	_____	bull	_____
mother	_____	gym	_____	head	_____
do	_____	myrrh	_____	heard	_____
go	_____	city	_____	meat	_____
mob	_____	try	_____	blow	_____
soft	_____	rear	_____	how	_____
double	_____	foul	_____	weird	_____
soup	_____	dried	_____	their	_____
soul	_____	sieve	_____	vein	_____
should	_____	thief	_____	conceit	_____
course	_____	friend	_____	stein	_____
again	_____	beauty	_____	been	_____
plaid	_____	chauffeur	_____	free	_____
maid	_____	exhaust	_____	matinee	_____
Caesar	_____	plateau	_____	does	_____
Gaelic	_____	laugh	_____	shoes	_____

Name _____

2.9   Multiple Consonant Phonemes for One Spelling

Put the following words into phonemic transcription.

beige	_____	exist	_____	reason	_____
carry	_____	extra	_____	schism	_____
cedar	_____	genius	_____	social	_____
cello	_____	ghetto	_____	sure	_____
chaperon	_____	geese	_____	Thailand	_____
chip	_____	lesion	_____	though	_____
chemistry	_____	noose	_____	thought	_____
cough	_____	of	_____	wife	_____
dizzy	_____	pizza	_____	xylophone	_____

3.1 Important Terms

1. alphabet
2. cuneiform
3. Cyrillic
4. futhorc
5. grapheme
6. ideogram
7. logogram
8. petroglyph
9. pictogram
10. rune
11. syllabary

Holt, Rinehart and Winston, Inc.

3.2   Questions for Review and Discussion

1. For what purposes was writing apparently first developed?

2. Under what circumstances is writing a more suitable means of communication than speech?

3. What is the difference between a pictogram and an ideogram?

4. What is the difference between a syllabary and an alphabet?

5. What is the difference between a logogram and a grapheme?

6. Name several ideograms familiar to native speakers of English.

7. Would a syllabic writing system be more or less suitable than an alphabet for writing English? Why or why not?

8. What phonological characteristics of a language make it *best* suited for a syllabic writing system?

9. What are the advantages of a logographic writing system? The disadvantages?

10. Cumbersome as it is, the Chinese logographic writing system is perhaps the best system for writing Chinese today. Suggest reasons why.

11. What are the advantages of an alphabetic writing system? The disadvantages?

Holt, Rinehart and Winston, Inc.

Name _____

3.3 Pictograms and Ideograms

A. Many of the graphemes used in the various writing systems of the world today were once pictographic, though they have been so altered and simplified over the millennia that their pictographic origins are no longer obvious. For example, the Latin letter *a* is derived from the Semitic *aleph* 'ox', and we can still see the head of an ox if we invert the capital form of the letter: ∀. Pictograms are still widely used today, especially for brevity and in situations where speakers of different languages are to be addressed; road signs such as (I-30) are obvious examples.

Many other familiar ideograms are also pictographic in origin, but the association between picture and meaning may be obscured. For example, ↗ is a symbol for November because Sagittarius, the archer, is the astrological sign for November; the arrow, of course, represents the archer.

Explain how each of the following ideograms is ultimately pictographic.

1. ♉ (sign for April–May) _____

2. ⬎ (music: *diminuendo, decrescendo*) _____

3. ✝ (biology: hybrid) _____

4. ♆ (astronomy or astrology: Neptune) _____

5. ↑ (chemistry: gas) _____

6. † (preceding a date = ''died'') _____

7. ♈ (vernal equinox) _____

8. ♒ (sign for January) _____

9. ✳ (weather) _____

B. Some ideograms are ultimately based, not on a picture, but on a word or another written form. What is the word or other written form underlying the following ideograms?

1. @ _____	4. π	_____
2. & _____	5. £	_____
3. ¢ _____	6. %	_____

C. Still other ideograms are seemingly completely arbitrary; that is, they do not derive from either a picture or a word. What do the following ideograms mean?

1. √ _____	4. ∴	_____
2. # _____	5. ∞	_____
3. ♀ _____	6. ÷	_____

Holt, Rinehart and Winston, Inc.

Name _____

3.4   Ideograms: Chinese

In the Chinese writing system, many characters contain both a semantic and a phonetic element. Frequently, the semantic element is represented by a **radical** that is itself an independent word. For example, the radical 田 *tián* 'field' appears in words such as 畴 *chóu* 'farmland' and 畜 *chù* 'livestock'.

For the following items, guess the meaning of each semantic radical by examining the meanings of the characters that contain it. Write this core meaning in the blank beside the radical.

1. 女 *nü* <u>woman</u> _____

奴 *nú* 'slave'; 奶 *nǎi* 'breasts'; 她 *tā* 'she'; 妍 *yán* 'beautiful'; 姊 *zǐ* 'elder sister'; 姻 *yīn* 'marriage'; 妖 *yāo* 'evil spirit'; 妈 *mā* 'mother'

2. 目 *mù* _____

盹 *dǔn* 'doze'; 眨 *zhǎ* 'blink'; 看 *kàn* 'see'; 眉 *méi* 'eyebrow'; 眺 *tiào* 'look into the distance'; 眸 *móu* 'pupil (of eye)'; 睇 *dì* 'look askance'; 瞄 *miáo* 'take aim'

3. 火 *huǒ* _____

灯 *dēng* 'lamp, lantern'; 灼 *zhuó* 'burn, scorch'; 炎 *yán* 'inflammation'; 炜 *wěi* 'bright'; 炝 *qiàng* 'boil'; 炽 *chì* 'ablaze'; 炮 *pào* 'cannon'; 烟 *yān* 'smoke, tobacco'

4. 虫 *chóng* _____

虻 *méng* 'horsefly'; 蚁 *yǐ* 'ant'; 蚤 *zǎo* 'flea'; 蚌 *bàng* 'clam'; 蛀 *zhù* 'moth'; 蛇 *shé* 'snake'; 蛟 *jiāo* 'flood dragon'; 蛙 *wā* 'frog'; 蛛 *zhū* 'spider'

5. 石 *shí* _____

矿 *kuàng* 'ore, mineral deposit'; 矽 *xī* 'silicon'; 研 *yán* 'pestle, grind'; 砺 *lì* 'whetstone'; 砾 *lì* 'gravel'; 硬 *yìng* 'hard'; 碣 *jié* 'stone tablet'; 礁 *jiāo* 'reef'

6. 山 *shān* _____

岌 *jí* 'lofty, towering'; 岗 *gǎng* 'hillock'; 岩 *yán* 'cliff'; 岬 *jiǎ* 'promontory'; 岭 *lǐng* 'mountain range'; 峙 *zhì* 'stand erect'; 峰 *fēng* 'peak'; 巅 *diān* 'summit'

7. 气 *qì* _____

氕 *piē* 'protium'; 氖 *nǎi* 'neon'; 氙 *xiān* 'xenon'; 氛 *fēn* 'atmosphere'; 氡 *dōng* 'radon'; 氢 *qīng* 'hydrogen'; 氟 *fú* 'fluorine'; 氧 *yǎng* 'oxygen'

8. 弓 *gōng* _____

引 *yǐn* 'draw, stretch'; 弛 *chí* 'relax, slacken'; 张 *zhāng* 'stretch, spread'; 弦 *xián* 'bowstring spring'; 弧 *hú* 'arc'; 弩 *nǔ* 'crossbow'; 弹 *dàn* 'bullet, bomb'; 弹 *tán* 'to shoot, pluck'

9. 歹 *dǎi* _____

死 *sǐ* 'die, death'; 歼 *jiān* 'annihilate'; 殁 *mò* 'die'; 残 *cán* 'savage, furious'; 殃 *yāng* 'disaster'; 殆 *dài* 'danger'; 殒 *yǔn* 'perish'; 殨 *huì* 'festering'

10. 车 *chē* _____

轧 *yà* 'run over'; 轨 *guǐ* 'path, track'; 转 *zhuàn* 'turn, revolve'; 轮 *lún* 'wheel'; 轴 *zhóu* 'shaft, axle'; 轸 *zhěn* 'carriage'; 轿 *jiào* 'sedan chair'; 挽 *wǎn* 'pull, draw'; 辋 *wǎng* 'rim of a wheel'

3.5 Syllabaries: Japanese

Modern Japanese uses three writing systems: (1) the *kanji*, based on and usually identical to Chinese logograms; (2) the *hiragana*, a syllabary used for native words other than nouns, verbs, and adjectives; for inflectional endings for all words written in *kanji*; and for some nouns, verbs, and adjectives for which the formerly used *kanji* have become obsolete; and (3) the *katakana*, a second syllabary used for foreign loanwords and foreign proper names, onomatopoeic words, names of plants and animals used in a scientific context, and a few other special contexts. (In contemporary Japan, there is a fourth de facto system: romanization, or the Latin alphabet, although it is not officially recognized.)

The *hiragana* and the *katakana* are presented in the following charts, together with their syllabic equivalents. The only additional information you need to know for this exercise is that the voiced sounds [g z d] are indicated in both kanas by two short diagonal strokes at the upper right corner of the symbol for the corresponding voiceless sound [k s t]. Thus, for example, in *hiragana*, く is [ku], and ぐ is [gu]. Similarly, in *katakana*, テ is [te], and デ is [de]. In both kanas, all syllables beginning with [p] are formed like syllables beginning with [h], but with the addition of a small circle at the upper right corner. For example, in *hiragana*, ひ is [hi], and ぴ is [pi]; in *katakana*, ホ is [ho], and ポ is [po]. In both kanas, [b] is treated as the voiced version of [h]; for example, ヒ is [hi] and ビ is [bi] in *katakana*. In *katakana*, long vowels in loanwords are indicated by a following horizontal stroke: ー, as in コーヒー ([kōhī] 'coffee').

The Katakana

	ア a	イ i	ウ u	エ e	オ o
k	カ ka	キ ki	ク ku	ケ ke	コ ko
s	サ sa	シ shi/si	ス su	セ se	ソ so
t	タ ta	チ chi/ti	ツ tsu/tu	テ te	ト to
n	ナ na	ニ ni	ヌ nu	ネ ne	ノ no
h	ハ ha(wa)	ヒ hi	フ fu/hu	ヘ he(e)	ホ ho
m	マ ma	ミ mi	ム mu	メ me	モ mo
y	ヤ ya	—	ユ yu	—	ヨ yo
r	ラ ra	リ ri	ル ru	レ re	ロ ro
w	ワ wa	—	—	—	ヲ o
					ン n

The Hiragana

	あ a	い i	う u	え e	お o
k	か ka	き ki	く ku	け ke	こ ko
s	さ sa	し shi/si	す su	せ se	そ so
t	た ta	ち chi/ti	つ tsu/tu	て te	と to
n	な na	に ni	ぬ nu	ね ne	の no
h	は ha(wa)	ひ hi	ふ fu/hu	へ he(e)	ほ ho
m	ま ma	み mi	む mu	め me	も mo
y	や ya	—	ゆ yu	—	よ yo
r	ら ra	り ri	る ru	れ re	ろ ro
w	わ wa	—	—	—	を o
					ん n

Holt, Rinehart and Winston, Inc.

Name _____

1. Transliterate the following Japanese words from *hiragana*.

よく   _____ 'well, often'

できる   _____ 'can, be able'

うれしい   _____ 'happy'

あそこ   _____ 'there'

2. Write the following Japanese words in *hiragana*.

kono ('this, these') _____

isu ('chair') _____

hashi ('chopsticks') _____

3. The following words, written in *katakana*, mean *beer, Beethoven, bus, cream, knife, taxi, table,* and *whiskey* in Japanese. Match the *katakana* with the meaning by writing the correct meaning to the right.

タクシ   _____

バス   _____

ナイフ   _____

ビール   _____

テーブル   _____

ウイスキー   _____

クリーム   _____

ベートーベン   _____

4. Write the following words in *katakana*.

tabako ('tobacco') _____

Amerika _____

tenisu ('tennis') _____

Toyota _____

Name _____

3.6   A Syllabary for English?

Invent a syllabary for English to write the following words.

1. pie _____	12. spy _____	23. strength _____
2. buy _____	13. spry _____	24. shopped _____
3. tie _____	14. sky _____	25. rubbed _____
4. die _____	15. sly _____	26. haunted _____
5. guy _____	16. snow _____	27. sill _____
6. vie _____	17. slow _____	28. silly _____
7. sigh _____	18. shrill _____	29. slowly _____
8. try _____	19. spill _____	30. usual _____
9. thigh _____	20. still _____	31. major _____
10. thy _____	21. expend _____	32. decide _____
11. shy _____	22. stronger _____	33. cheap _____

A. How many *different* characters did you need for the words in the list? _____

_____

B. What problems did you encounter in devising your syllabary? _____

_____

_____

C. Would there be any advantages to a syllabic writing system for English? Why or why not? _____

_____

D. What would the major disadvantage be? _____

_____

Holt, Rinehart and Winston, Inc.

Name _____

3.7   Syllabary or Alphabet? Devanagari

Hindi, the most widely used of the modern Indic languages, is the native language of about 40 percent of the population of India. Its writing system is the Devanagari (or Nagari) script. Hindi has a complex phonological system with forty consonant phonemes and eleven vowels. For simplicity's sake, we will limit our illustration of the script to eleven consonants and seven vowels.

Consonants

क	/k/	प	/p/
ग	/g/	ब	/b/
त	/t/	म	/m/
द	/d/	र	/r/
न	/n/	ल	/l/
स	/s/		

Vowels

अ	/a/	उ	/u/
आ	/ā/	ऊ	/ū/
इ	/i/	ओ	/o/
ई	/ī/		

A few complete words written in the Devanagari script follow.

अब	/ab/	'now'	बीस	/bīs/	'twenty'
आग	/āg/	'fire'	पानी	/pānī/	'water'
इतना	/itnā/	'this much'	दाल	/dāl/	'lentil'
उनतीस	/untīs/	'twenty-nine'	सन	/san/	'year, era'
कब	/kab/	'when?'	सिर	/sir/	'head'
कम	/kam/	'little, less'	रोग	/rog/	'illness'
कि	/ki/	'that'	रूप	/rūp/	'form'
तू	/tū/	'you' (intimate)	लाल	/lāl/	'red'
बस	/bas/	'bus'			

1. Does the script go from left to right or right to left? _____

2. How is /a/ written after a consonant? _____

3. What is unique about the writing of /i/ when it appears (in speech) after a consonant?

_____

_____

4. Transliterate the following words written in Devanagari.

a.	तब	'then' _____		f.	लोग	'people' _____
b.	सो	'so' _____		g.	गीत	'song' _____
c.	बुरा	'bad' _____		h.	सूती	'made of cotton' _____
d.	पति	'husband' _____		i.	उदास	'sad' _____
e.	मन	'mind' _____		j.	कुली	'porter' _____

5. Write the following Hindi words in the Devanagari script.

   a. /pīlā/ 'yellow'   _____

   b. /din/ 'day'   _____

   c. /nal/ 'pipe, tap'   _____

   d. /sās/ 'mother-in-law'   _____

   e. /gap/ 'gossip'   _____

6. In what way(s) is the Devanagari script like a syllabary? _____

   _____

   _____

7. In what ways is it like an alphabet? _____

   _____

Holt, Rinehart and Winston, Inc.

Name _____

3.8   Related Alphabets

Though they have diverged over the centuries, the Greek, Latin, and Cyrillic (Russian) alphabets are closely related—both the Latin and Cyrillic alphabets are derived from the Greek. Using the table of alphabets to be found in any good desk dictionary, transliterate the following words into the Latin alphabet. Then give an English version of the words, all of which exist in English, though the usual English spelling may vary slightly from the transliteration.

Greek Word	Transliteration	English Spelling
ἀκμή	akmē	acme
ἀκροβᾰτέω		
γεωγραφία		
καταστροφή		
κόσμος		
κρῐτήριον		
σύνταξις		
φαρμᾰκεια		
ψῡχή		

Russian Word	Transliteration	English Spelling
борзой	borzoĭ	borzoi
Большевизм		
борщ		
водка		
Правда		
самовар		
степь		
тундра		

Holt, Rinehart and Winston, Inc.

3.9   Other European Alphabets

Although both the Latin and the Cyrillic alphabets are clearly based on the Greek alphabet, other alphabets not obviously connected with the Greek alphabet were used for writing Indo-European languages in the past.

A.   The Ogham alphabet was used for writing Old Irish, probably as early as the fourth century A.D. Though it was abandoned for the Latin alphabet after Christianity came to Ireland, the Ogham alphabet was still learned and occasionally used (for example, in marginal notes) throughout the Middle Ages. All the characters (''letters'') were written along a vertical line. Consonants were formed by one to five horizontal or diagonal strokes written to one side of or across this vertical line. Vowels consisted of one to five short strokes written on the vertical line. The symbol for *f* was also used for *v* and *w*. There was no symbol for *p* because Old Irish had no /p/ phoneme.

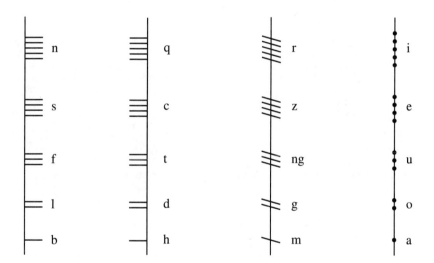

Holt, Rinehart and Winston, Inc.

Name _____

Transliterate the following into the Latin alphabet. (Although Ogham usually went from bottom to top or from right to left, this sample is written top to bottom.)

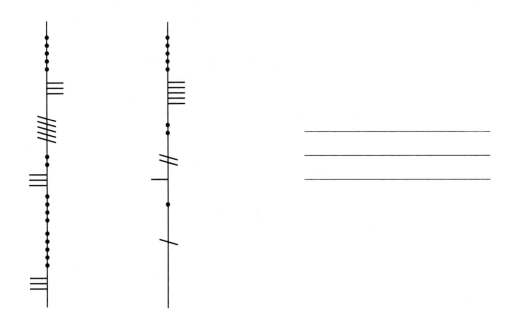

_____

_____

_____

1. What are the advantages, if any, of the Ogham alphabet over the Latin alphabet?

_____

2. What are the disadvantages, if any? _____

_____

3. Old Irish had neither /h/ nor /z/ in its phonemic system. Can you suggest a reason why symbols for these sounds were included in the Ogham alphabet? _____

_____

_____

Name _____

B.   The Glagolitic alphabet was an early Slavonic alphabet. There is some dispute over which came first, the Glagolitic or the Cyrillic alphabet, but, in any case, the Cyrillic eventually replaced the Glagolitic for writing Russian and the Slavic languages of other peoples following the Russian Orthodox Church.

Glagolitic	*Transliteration*	*Glagolitic*	*Transliteration*
(glyph)	a	(glyph)	t
(glyph)	b	(glyph)	u
(glyph)	v	(glyph)	f
(glyph)	g	(glyph)	x/ch
(glyph)	d	(glyph)	o
(glyph)	ε	(glyph)	št
(glyph)	z	(glyph)	ts
(glyph)	ǰ	(glyph)	č
(glyph)	z	(glyph)	š
(glyph) (glyph)	i	(glyph)	ŭ
(glyph)	i	(glyph)	y
(glyph)	g'	(glyph)	ĭ
(glyph)	k	(glyph)	æ
(glyph)	l	(glyph)	ju
(glyph)	m	(glyph)	ja
(glyph)	n	(glyph)	ē
(glyph)	o	(glyph)	ʒ
(glyph)	p	(glyph)	jē
(glyph)	r	(glyph)	jɔ̃
(glyph)	s	(glyph)	υ

Transliterate the following and then represent your transliteration into traditional English spelling.

(Glagolitic text line)

_____

_____

Suggest reasons why the Cyrillic alphabet replaced the Glagolitic alphabet.

_____

_____

Holt, Rinehart and Winston, Inc.

CHAPTER 4

LANGUAGE FAMILIES AND INDO-EUROPEAN

4.1 Important Terms and Names

1. ablative
2. ablaut
3. accusative
4. active voice
5. agglutinative language
6. Albanian
7. Anatolian
8. aorist
9. apophony
10. Armenian
11. aspect
12. Balto-Slavic
13. Britannic (p-Celtic)
14. case
15. Celtic
16. centum languages
17. Classical Latin
18. cognate languages
19. Common Germanic
20. Common Indo-European
21. dative
22. definite (weak) adjective
23. demotic
24. dental preterite
25. dialect
26. East Germanic
27. family tree
28. First Grammarian
29. First Sound (Consonant) Shift
30. futhorc
31. future
32. gender
33. genitive
34. Germanic
35. Glagolitic alphabet
36. Goidelic (q-Celtic)
37. Gothic
38. Jakob Grimm
39. Grimm's Law
40. Hellenic
41. High German
42. Hittite
43. imperative
44. imperfect
45. indefinite (strong) adjective
46. indicative
47. Indo-European
48. Indo-Iranian
49. inflectional language
50. injunctive
51. instrumental
52. isolating language
53. Italic
54. Sir William Jones
55. koine
56. Kurgan culture
57. labiovelar
58. language family
59. Linear B
60. loanword
61. locative
62. Low German
63. middle voice
64. mood
65. native word
66. nominative
67. North Germanic
68. number
69. Ogham
70. Old Norse
71. optative
72. passive voice
73. perfect
74. person
75. pluperfect
76. present
77. preterite
78. prosody
79. Rasmus Rask
80. Romance language
81. Sanskrit
82. satem languages
83. Second Sound (Consonant) Shift
84. *Stammbaum* theory
85. subjunctive
86. Tocharian
87. Bishop Ulfilas
88. Karl Verner
89. Verner's Law
90. vocative
91. voice
92. vowel gradation
93. Vulgar Latin
94. *Wellentheorie*
95. West Germanic

Holt, Rinehart and Winston, Inc.

4.2   Questions for Review and Discussion

1. What are some of the reasons why words with the same meaning may have the same or similar phonological form in different languages?
2. When seeking to determine the relationship between two languages, what kinds of shared vocabulary items provide the best evidence for relatedness?
3. What are some of the important language families of the world apart from Indo-European?
4. Explain the difference between the *Stammbaum* theory and the *Wellentheorie* of similarities among languages.
5. What do Basque and Etruscan have in common?
6. Is PDE best classified as an inflecting, agglutinative, or isolating language?
7. What are the principal subdivisions of Indo-European?
8. What are some of the features common to most or all Indo-European languages?
9. What evidence is used to determine the original home of the Indo-Europeans?
10. When did Indo-Europeans start to split into separate groups?
11. For which Indo-European languages do we have the oldest surviving written records?
12. Why is Hittite of particular interest to Indo-European scholars? Tocharian? Lithuanian?
13. What delayed recognition of Indo-European as a language family?
14. Why is Sir William Jones important to historical linguistics?
15. Where does Indo-European ablaut survive in PDE?
16. What is the difference between aspect and tense?
17. Apart from a marginally surviving subjunctive inflection, how does PDE express mood?
18. What major characteristics distinguish Germanic languages from other Indo-European languages?
19. Why is Gothic of particular interest to Germanic scholars?
20. What do the terms ''High'' German and ''Low'' German refer to?
21. Where did Germanic acquire its Common Germanic vocabulary not shared by other Indo-European languages?
22. Describe the operation of the First Consonant Shift (Grimm's Law and Verner's Law).

Holt, Rinehart and Winston, Inc.

CHAPTER 5

OLD ENGLISH

5.1   Important Terms and Names

1. ablaut series
2. abstraction
3. A.D. 449
4. A.D. 787
5. A.D. 878
6. A.D. 1066
7. Ælfric
8. affixing
9. alliteration
10. amelioration
11. Angles
12. Anglian
13. *Anglo-Saxon Chronicle*
14. back mutation
15. Benedictine Reform
16. breaking (fracture)
17. calque (loan translation)
18. case
19. compounding
20. concretization
21. connotation
22. denotation
23. Danelaw
24. dental preterite
25. dual pronoun
26. eth
27. Frisians
28. front mutation
29. functional shift
30. futhorc (runic alphabet)
31. gemination
32. gender
33. generalization
34. grammatical gender
35. Heptarchy
36. Insular alphabet
37. Jutes
38. Kentish
39. King Alfred
40. Mercian
41. mutated plural
42. narrowing
43. number
44. Old Norse
45. palatal diphthongization
46. pejoration
47. preterite-present verb
48. *punctus elevatus*
49. Ruthwell Cross
50. St. Augustine
51. Saxons
52. shift in connotation
53. shift in denotation
54. Southern
55. strengthening
56. strong (indefinite) adjective
57. strong noun
58. strong verb
59. thorn
60. Treaty of Wedmore
61. umlaut
62. variation
63. Venerable Bede
64. Vikings
65. weak (definite) adjective
66. weak noun
67. weak verb
68. weakening
69. wen
70. West Saxon
71. William of Normandy
72. Wulfstan

Holt, Rinehart and Winston, Inc.

5.2   Questions for Review and Discussion

1. What was the first Indo-European language spoken in the British Isles?
2. What was the second? Explain how it came to be used in England and when it ceased to be used.
3. Who were the Picts?
4. When did the first Germanic speakers come to England? Who were these people? Where did they come from? Where did they settle?
5. Where does the name "England" come from?
6. What was the Heptarchy? Name its members.
7. When was England Christianized? By whom?
8. Of what linguistic importance to England was Christianization?
9. Who were the Vikings? When did they first attack England?
10. What language did the Vikings speak?
11. What was the Treaty of Wedmore? What was its linguistic significance?
12. What was the Danelaw?
13. In what ways was King Alfred important to the history of English?
14. What three consonants did OE have that were not phonemic in Common Germanic?
15. What consonant *phonemes* does PDE have that were not phonemic in OE?
16. What is a long consonant?
17. What is breaking?
18. Explain why there is a difference in the vowels of OE *healdan* 'to hold' and *hylt* 'he holds'.
19. What was the first alphabet used to write Germanic languages?
20. Most surviving OE texts are written in what OE dialect?
21. What kind of affixes were most frequently used in OE inflections—infixes, prefixes, or suffixes?
22. Explain the difference between grammatical and biological gender.
23. What was the difference between OE "strong" nouns and "weak" nouns?
24. What is a mutated plural?
25. Under what grammatical circumstances were weak adjectives used? Strong adjectives?
26. Which pronouns had dual forms in OE?
27. How does the use of articles in PDE differ from that in OE?
28. What was the difference between strong verbs and weak verbs in OE?
29. How did OE preterite-present verbs differ from strong verbs? What are the PDE descendants of the OE preterite-present verbs?
30. How many inflected tenses did OE have?
31. How did OE form new adverbs?
32. In what ways did the placement of adjectival modifiers in OE differ from that in PDE?
33. Of all the possible word orders of subject (S), verb (V), and object/complement (O), what was the most commonly used order in OE for independent declarative clauses? For dependent clauses?
34. What was the major source of loanwords into OE?
35. Why were there so few loanwords from Celtic into OE?
36. List some of the processes by which speakers of OE formed new words by using the resources of their own language.
37. What was the metric basis for most OE poetry?

Holt, Rinehart and Winston, Inc.

Name _____

5.3   Phonology: Pronunciation and Spelling of Consonants

Though the match between spelling and pronunciation in OE was better than that of PDE, it was by no means perfect.

1. Long consonants were spelled with double graphemes. For example, *rīnan* 'to rain' was pronounced [rīnan], and *rinnan* 'to flow' was [rin:an].
2. The graphemes ⟨p b t d k m l r w⟩ corresponded well to pronunciation; they represented [p b t d k m l r w], respectively.
3. g   = [j] before or between front vowels and finally after front vowels*
     = [ɣ] (a voiced velar fricative) between back vowels or after [l] or [r]
     = [g] elsewhere
4. c   = [č] next to a front vowel*
     = [k] elsewhere
5. n   = [ŋ] before [k] or [g]
     = [n] elsewhere
6. h   = [h] before vowels and before [l r n w]
     = [ç] (a voiceless palatal fricative) after front vowels
     = [x] (a voiceless velar fricative) elsewhere
7. sc   = [š]
8. cg   = [ǰ]
9. f   = [v] when surrounded by voiced sounds
     = [f] elsewhere and when doubled
10. s   = [z] when surrounded by voiced sounds
     = [s] elsewhere and when doubled
11. ð or þ = [ð] when surrounded by voiced sounds
     = [θ] elsewhere and when doubled

A.   Transcribe the following words. You can transcribe the vowels as they are spelled here.

1. wita 'adviser' [wita]
2. limpan 'to happen' _____
3. biddend 'petitioner' _____
4. lāreow 'teacher' _____
5. ðūsend 'thousand' _____
6. kyning 'king' _____
7. heofon 'sky' _____
8. secga 'informant' _____
9. ranc 'proud' _____
10. cild 'child' _____
11. wrīþan 'to twist' _____
12. dimm 'dim' _____
13. prættig 'tricky' _____
14. sēoslig 'afflicted' _____
15. pæð 'path' _____
16. paþas 'paths' _____
17. æsc 'ash tree' _____
18. fyllan 'to fill' _____
19. fāh 'hostile' _____
20. mæsse 'mass' _____
21. brocc 'badger' _____
22. hnæpp 'bowl' _____
23. wlitig 'beautiful' _____
24. boga 'bow' _____

*Unless that front vowel was the result of umlaut. For simplicity's sake, no examples involving umlauted vowels are included here.

Holt, Rinehart and Winston, Inc.

B.   How would the following words, listed here in transcription, have been spelled in OE? (If the vowel spelling differs from the transcription, it is provided for you.)

1. [boduŋg] 'message' _bodung_

2. [hæərɣ] 'temple' _____ ea _____

3. [seǰan] 'to say' _____

4. [wil:īče] 'willingly' _____

5. [jerǽəvian] 'to rob' _____ ea _____

6. [kniçt] 'boy' _____

7. [θōxt] 'thought' _____

8. [mūða] 'mouth' _____

9. [pistol] 'letter' _____

10. [græf] 'grave' _____

11. [wašan] 'to wash' _____

12. [frēəzan] 'to freeze' _____ ēo _____

13. [moθ:e] 'moth' _____

14. [mōdrije] 'maternal aunt' _____

15. [sāɣol] 'cudgel' _____

16. [hæəvod] 'head' _____ ea _____

17. [θrǽšan] 'to crush' _____

18. [pliçt] 'danger' _____

19. [hraðe] 'quick' _____

20. [ābrazlian] 'to crash' _____

21. [čēpiŋg] 'trading' _____

22. [spirkan] 'to sparkle' _____

23. [myǰ] 'midge' _____

24. [θurx] 'through' _____

5.4 Phonology: Front Mutation

As is described on pages 85–86 of *A Biography of the English Language*, front mutation (or umlaut) occurred prior to surviving written English texts, probably in the sixth century A.D. Under front mutation, [i] or [j] in a following syllable changed the preceding vowel as follows.

[æ] > [e], for example, *sættjan > OE settan
[a] + nasal > [e]
[ā] > [ǣ]
[ŏ] > [ĕ]
[ŭ] > [ў̆]
[e] > [i]
[ĕa] > [ў̆]
[ĕo] > [ў̆]

Under front mutation, only the quality of the vowel was affected, not the quantity. Long vowels remained long, and short vowels remained short.

1. For the following OE words, give the vowel *before* front mutation took place.

a. drencan 'to drench' < *dr____ncjan

b. gēs 'geese' < *g____si

c. lǣfan 'to leave' < *l____fjan

2. For the following OE words, give the vowel *after* front mutation had taken place.

a. *fūsjan > f____san 'to hasten'

b. *fōdjan > f____dan 'to feed'

c. *ealdira > ____ldra 'older'

d. *weorcjan > w____rcan 'to work'

e. *steliþ > st____lþ '(he) steals'

f. *hēahista > h____hst 'highest'

g. *brādjan > br____dan 'to extend'

h. *slægi > sl____ge 'blow'

i. *langiþu > l____ngþu 'length'

j. *morgin > m____rgen 'in the morning'

k. *þurstjan > þ____rstan 'to thirst'

l. *cēosiþ > c____st 'she chooses'

3. Because the vowels of all words in the language, regardless of their origin, underwent front mutation under the conditions specified earlier, the presence or absence of mutation can help in dating the entrance of loanwords into English. That is, if a loanword shows mutation in its English form, it must have entered the language *before* mutation took place. If it does not show mutation, it probably was borrowed *after* front mutation had stopped operating. For the following OE words originally borrowed from Latin, indicate which

1 modig mað<u>ðum</u>sigla   fealo | gold glitinian
brave precious jewels many   gold to glitter

2 grunde   getenge | wundur   on wealle <u>ond</u>
(on) ground resting,   wonderful things in barrow, and

3 þæs   wyrmes denn | ealdes uht flogan
(of) the serpent's den,   (of) old dusk-flyer

4 orcas stondan | fyrn manna   fatu   feor
cups to stand, (of) men-of-old vessels pol-

5 mend lease | hyrs<u>tum</u>   behrorene þær wæs
isher-less   ornaments deprived of. There was

6 helm   monig | eald <u>ond</u> omig earmbeaga fela |
helmet many a, old and rusty, bracelets   many

7 searwu<u>m</u>   gesæled sinc   eaðe mæg | gold on grund
(with) skill twisted—treasure easily can,   gold in ground

8 gu<u>m</u> cynnes gehwone | ofer higian hyde   seðe
man   any   overpower, (let) hide he who

9 _____ | _____ _____ _____ _____ _____ eall
wishes.   Likewise,   he   to lie   saw   banner   all

10 _____ | _____ _____ _____ _____ wundra
gilded,   high over treasury, (of) hand-(crafted) wonders

11 _____ | _____ _____ of ð<u>am</u> leoman
greatest,   linked (by) hand-skills. From it   light

12 _____ | þæt   ____ ____ _____ _____ _____ meahte
stood   so that he   the   ground -surface perceive could

13 _____ _____ _____ _____ _____ _____ þær |
ornaments look over, Not was (of) the serpent there

14 _____ _____ _____ _____ _____ | ða   ic on
sight   any,   but him (sword)-edge (had) destroyed.   Then I in

15 _____ _____ _____ _____ | _____ enta
barrow learned treasury to plunder,   old   (of) giants

16 _____ _____ _____ | _____ ____ _____ hlodon
work   a certain   man,   him in   arms to load

17 _____ ____ _____ | _____ _____ _____ eac genom
cups and dishes (at) his own discretion. Standard also (he) took

18 _____ _____ _____ ____ _____ | ____ wæs iren
(of) banners brightest. Sword earlier (had) injured— edge was iron

19 ____ _____ | _____ _____ _____ mundbora
(of) old-lord,   one who (of) the treasures guardian

20 ____ | _____ _____ _____ _____ | ____ for
was (for) long while. Fire-terror (he) waged hot for

21 horde,   _____ _____ | _____ nihtum
treasury, hostilely welling   in middle (of) night

Holt, Rinehart and Winston, Inc.

1. What does a line over a vowel indicate? _____

    _____

2. What is the abbreviation for *and*? _____

3. The letter *s* has three distinctly different forms. What are they? _____

Holt, Rinehart and Winston, Inc.

5.7   Graphics: The OE Runic Alphabet (Futhorc)

As your text explains, the OE runic alphabet (futhorc) was apparently used primarily for inscriptions and only rarely for longer texts. Yet, because medieval English scribes frequently inserted runes into texts written in the Latin alphabet, we know that the futhorc was familiar to the English long after it had been replaced by the Latin alphabet. One version of the futhorc is reproduced here, followed by a brief text adapted from the OE translation of Bede's story of the poet Cædmon, who was miraculously given the power to compose religious poetry in the alliterative style.

Transliterate the runic text back into the Latin alphabet. Then translate the text into modern English. Some words have been translated for you; you should be able to guess the rest of them because of their resemblance to modern English.

Rune	Equivalent	Probable Value	Rune	Equivalent	Probable Value
ᚠ	f	[f]	ᛋ	s	[s]
ᚢ	u	[u]	ᛏ	t	[t]
ᚦ	th	[θ]	ᛒ	b	[b]
ᚩ	o	[o]	ᛖ	e	[e]
ᚱ	r	[r]	ᛗ	m	[m]
ᚳ	c	[k]	ᛚ	l	[l]
ᚷ	g	[g]	ᛝ	ng	[ŋ]
ᚹ	w	[w]	ᛟ	œ	[œ]
ᚻ	h	[h]	ᛞ	d	[d]
ᚾ	n	[n]	ᚪ	a	[ɑ]
ᛁ	i	[i]	ᚫ	æ	[æ]
ᛄ	y	[j]	ᚣ	y	[y]
ᛉ	ēo	[eə]?	ᛡ	io	[io]?[iɑ]?
ᛈ	p	[p]	ᛠ	ea	[æə]
ᛣ	h	[x]			

Holt, Rinehart and Winston, Inc.

Name _____

ᛋᚢᛗ ᛗᛟᚾ ᚻᛁᚾᛖ ᚾᚪᚳᛖᛏᛏᛖ ᛗᚾᚻ ᚷᚱᛖᛏᛏᛖ ᚻᚾᚻ

sum   mon   hine _____
      man   him   saluted   and

ᚾᛁᛏᛖᛒᛖ ᚾᛁᛋ ᛏᛟᛗᚪᚾ ᛏᛖᚻᚻᛖ : "ᚻᚪᛖᛗᚪᚾ, ᛋᛁᚷ ᛗᛖ

    by   name   named: "Cædmon,

ᚾᚠᛏᚾᚠᚢᚷᚢ." ᚦᚱ ᛟᚾᚻᛋᚠᚱᛗᚻᛗ ᚾᛖ ᛗᚾᚻ ᚻᚠᚱᚦ :

  something."   Then   said:

ᛏᛖ ᚻᛟᚷ ᛁᚻ ᛏᛟᛋᛏ ᛋᛁᚸᚷᚱᛏ." ᛗᚠᛏ ᚻᛖ ᚻᚠᚱᚦ :

                I   *nothing*   *Again*

ᚾᚠᚠᚱᛗ ᚦᚢ ᛗᛖ ᚻᛁᛏᛏ ᛋᛁᚸᚷᚱᛏ." ᚦᚱ ᚻᚠᚱᚦ ᚻᛖ:

Nevertheless   *thou*   *canst*

"ᚾᚠᛏ ᛋᚻᛏᛋ ᛁᚻ ᛋᛁᚸᚷᚱᛏ ?"

_____

_____

Holt, Rinehart and Winston, Inc.

Name _____

5.8   ﹍ology: Cases

In C﹍ ﹍most important functions of the nominative, genitive, dative, and accusative
ca﹍ ﹍ as follows:

﹍ *﹍ve*

﹍ject   1, 3, _____

﹍omplement after verbs like "to be"   _____

Direct address (vocative)   _____

Genitive

1. Possessive, including most constructions in which PDE would
   use an "of" possessive   _____

2. Expressions of measure or of larger numbers   3, _____

3. Direct object of some verbs, especially those expressing
   deprivation   _____

4. In certain adverbial phrases   _____

5. In special meanings after some prepositions   _____

Dative

1. Object of most prepositions   _____

2. Indirect object of verbs   _____

3. Direct object of some verbs   5, _____

4. With some adjectives, especially those which would be
   followed by "to" in PDE (e.g., "dear to me")   _____

5. With some possessives, especially involving parts of the body _____

6. Some time expressions (earlier instrumental case, and may
   appear with an instrumental demonstrative)   _____

Accusative

1. Direct object of verbs   _____

2. Object of prepositions expressing movement in time or space   7, _____

3. Some adverbial expressions of time or space   _____

Identify the functions of the cases in the following sentences by putting the number of the
sentence in the appropriate blank above. The cases are identified by letters following the
word or phrase, which is underlined: (N) = nominative, (G) = genitive, (D) = dative, (A)
= accusative. *Note:* Do not confuse the gloss with the original text. For example, the OE
expression *dæges ond nihtes* might be glossed "by day and by night," but this would *not*
be an example of the use of the genitive as object of a preposition in OE because the OE
has no preposition. Instead, it would be an example of the use of the genitive in certain
adverbial phrases.

1. Seo boc (N) com to us binnan feowum gearum (D).
   That book   came to us within few   years.

Holt, Rinehart and Winston, Inc.

2. He wearþ <u>cristnum</u>   monnum (D) swiðe <u>hold</u> (N).
   He was   to Christian men   very   loyal.

3. <u>Eadgar cyning</u> (N) þone <u>cristendom</u> (A) gefyðrode and fela
   Edgar king   the   Christendom   advanced and many

   <u>munuclifa</u> (G) aræde.
   monasteries   established.

4. La! <u>leof hlaford</u> (N), <u>þone</u> (A) þe <u>þu</u> (N) lufast ys nu geuntrumod.
   Oh! dear lord,   the one   whom you love is now become sick.

5. Ne mæg <u>nan man</u> (N) <u>twam</u> <u>hlafordum</u> (D) þeowian.
   Not can no man   two   lords   serve.

6. Gif mon <u>him</u> (D) oftihþ   ðara þenunga (G) and <u>ðæs anwealdes</u> (G)
   If one them   takes away the attendants   and the authority

7. <u>froxas</u> (N) comon geond   eall   <u>Egypta</u> (G) <u>land</u> (A).
   frogs   came through all (of) Egyptians' land.

8. <u>we</u> (N) secgað to soðan þæt <u>se tima</u> (N) wæs <u>gesælig</u> (N) and <u>wynsum</u> (N)
   we   say   in truth that that time   was happy   and joyful

   on <u>Angelcynne</u> (D).
   in England.

9. Windas and sæ <u>him</u> (D) hyrsumiaþ.
   Winds and sea him   obey.

10. Wende <u>he</u> (N) hine   west wiþ   <u>Exanceastres</u> (G).
    Turned he   himself west toward Exeter.

11. Gangaþ inn þurh   ðæt <u>nearwe geat</u> (A).
    Go   in through the narrow gate.

12. <u>We cildra</u> (N) biddaþ þe, eala <u>lareow</u> (N), þæt þu tæce <u>us</u> (D) sprecan
    We children ask you, O teacher,   that you teach us   to speak

13. Næfde se here,   <u>godes þonces</u> (G), <u>Angelcyn</u> (A)
    Not had the army, thanks to God,   England

    <u>ealles</u> (G) forswiðe gebrocod.
    completely utterly   crushed.

14. <u>Israhela folc</u> (N)   on <u>hæftnede</u> (D) <u>Babilonisam cyninge</u> (D) þeowde.
    (Of) Israel people in bondage   Babylonian king   served.

15. <u>þæs halgan Oswoldes</u> (G) <u>ban</u> (N) wurdon eft   bebroht . . .
    of the holy Oswald   bones were   again brought

    to <u>Myrcena</u> (G) lande
    to Mercians'   land

16. þa   sæton <u>hie</u> (N) <u>þone winter</u> (A) æt <u>Cwatbrycge</u> (D)
    then stayed they   that winter   at Bridgnorth

17. <u>him</u> (D) on bearme læg
    his   on lap   lay

Holt, Rinehart and Winston, Inc.

18. nolde   Alexander þæs (G) getygþian.
    not wanted Alexander that   to grant.

19. Ðær   wæron twa hund   and eahta and feowertig wera (G)
    There were   two hundred and eight and forty   men

20. Lætaþ us faran and offrian   urum Gode (D)
    Let   us go   and sacrifice (to) our God

21. þy   ilcan geare (D) sende Ælfred cyning (N) sciphere (A) on   East-Engle.
    that same year   sent Alfred king   fleet   into East Anglia.

Name _____

5.9   Functions of the OE Cases

Identify the case (nominative, genitive, dative, accusative) and function of the underlined words in the following phrases and sentences. If you have trouble identifying them, consult the noun, adjective, and pronoun paradigms in *A Biography of the English Language* for the endings of the cases.

1. and he wearð fornumen æfter <u>feawum dagum</u>
   and he was consumed   after few days

   <u>dative; object of preposition</u> _____

2. Eala, <u>oxanhyrde,</u> hwæt wyrst þu?
   O,   oxherd,   what do   you (do)?

   _____

3. God sende ða sona   <u>sumne encgel</u> him to
   God sent   then at once a certain angel him to

   _____

4. mon   towearp þone weal niþer oþ <u>þone grund</u>
   someone broke   the   wall down to the ground

   _____

5. Nis þæt   nan <u>wundor</u>
   Not is that no   wonder

   _____

6. Se wudu is hundtwelftiges <u>mila</u> lang
   The forest is 120   miles long

   _____

7. Sum   sutere   siwode <u>þæs halgan weres</u> sceos
   A certain shoemaker sewed the holy man's   shoes

   _____

8. ðu ofsloge <u>him</u> fætt   cealf
   you killed   him (a) fat calf

   _____

9. Wrætlice is þes <u>wealstan</u>
   Wondrous is this building stone

   _____

10. he <u>ðæm huse</u> genealæhte
    he the house approached

    _____

Name _____

5.10 Morphology: Gender

OE had grammatical rather than biological gender. In most instances, neither the ending of the word alone nor its meaning was a reliable guide to its gender. Thus gender usually can be identified with certainty only through the form of an accompanying adjective or, especially, an accompanying demonstrative. Even with these, the gender of plural nouns may be ambiguous. By consulting paradigms of OE nouns, adjectives, and demonstratives in *A Biography of the English Language*, identify the gender of the following nouns as masculine (M), feminine (F), or neuter (N), and state what allowed you to make the identification. If it is impossible to ascertain the gender from the form given, write (U) in the blank and state how it is ambiguous.

0. seo *byrne* 'the coat of mail' _F—demonstrative seo is feminine_

1. þone *grund* 'the ground' _____

2. freolic *wif* 'noble woman' _____

3. on þisse *meoduhealle* 'in this mead-hall' _____

4. heoru *stow* 'pleasant place' _____

5. modiges *mannes* 'of the brave man' _____

6. þinum *broþrum* 'to your brothers' _____

7. þa *word* 'those words' _____

8. windige *weallas* 'windy walls' _____

9. æt þære *beorþege* 'at the beer-party' _____

10. þæt *anginn* 'the beginning' _____

Holt, Rinehart and Winston, Inc.

Name _____

5.11   Morphology: Noun Classes and Inflections

A.   Because so many inflectional endings in OE are identical, one cannot always identify the class and gender of a noun from its ending alone. However, a number of endings are unique, and the class, gender, number, and case can be determined by the ending, along with the information provided by the context. For each of the following underlined nouns, give its gender, case, and number, and state whether it is an (A) *a*-stem strong noun, (B) *o*-stem strong noun, (C) *-an* weak noun, or (D) mutated-plural noun. The nominative singular form of the noun is provided in parentheses after each excerpt. If you cannot make a positive identification, explain why.

0. gesihð him   beforan . . . baþian brimfuglas,   brædan <u>feþra</u> (nom. sg. <u>feþer</u>)
    (he) sees him before (to) bathe   sea-birds, (to) spread wings

    feminine o-stem strong noun, accusative plural
    _____

1. And riht is   þæt ealle <u>preostas</u> . . . anræde beon   (nom. sg. <u>preost</u>)
    and proper is that all priests   persevering be

    _____

2. he geseah þa <u>hearpan</u> him nealecan (nom. sg. <u>hearpe</u>—fem.)
    he saw the   harp   him approach

    _____

3. ac hi fæstlice   wið ða <u>fynd</u> weredon   (nom. sg. <u>feond</u>—masc.)
    but they resolutely against the enemies defended

    _____

4. þa <u>flotan</u>   stodon gearowe (nom. sg. <u>flota</u>)
    the seamen stood ready

    _____

5. þeah þe <u>græf</u>   wille golde stregan   (nom. sg. <u>græf</u>)
    although (the) grave (he) may (with) gold strew

    _____

6. of þæm we begietaþ us selfum . . . fodor   urum <u>horsum</u>   (nom. sg. <u>hors</u>—neut.)
    from whom we get   (for) ourselves fodder (for) our horses

    _____

7. Wod under   wolcum to þæs þe he winreced, goldsele <u>gumena</u>,
    (he) walked under clouds   until   he winehall, goldhall (of) men,

    gearwost wisse   (nom. sg. <u>guma</u>—masc.)
    most readily recognized

    _____

8. he . . . his <u>leomu</u> on reste gesette ond onslepte
   he   his limbs at rest   put and fell asleep

   (nom. sg. <u>lim</u>; ignore the vowel change in the root)

   _____

9. Gyf mæsseprest his agen <u>lif</u> rihtlice fadie . . . (nom. sg. <u>lif</u>)
   If mass-priest   his own life properly arranges

   _____

B.   Using the paradigms in your text and the information provided by the glosses, write
the correct form of the noun in the blank. The nominative singular form of the noun and
all other necessary information are given in the parentheses following each excerpt. (The
a-stem and *o*-stem nouns are ''strong'' nouns, and *-an* nouns are ''weak'' nouns.)

0. he nolde fleogan fotmæl ___landes___   (<u>land</u>: neuter *a*-stem gen. sg.)
   he wouldn't flee (a) foot's space (of) land

1. Ne acwele þu þaet _____ (<u>cild</u>: neuter *a*-stem acc.)
   Not kill   you that child

2. bæd þaet _____   gehwylc Byrhtnoð wræce
   (he) ordered that (of the) men each   Byrhtnoð avenge

   (<u>beorn</u>: masc. *a*-stem gen. pl.)

3. þonne he forð scile of _____ læded   weorðan
   when he forth must from body   brought be

   (<u>lichama</u>: masc. *-an* dat. sg.)

4. ond bi oðrum   monegum spellum þæs halgan _____
   and about other many stories   (of) the holy writ

   (<u>gewrit</u>: neuter *a*-stem gen. sg.)

5. on þinum sæde beoð ealle _____ gebletsode (<u>þeod</u>: fem. *o*-stem nom.)
   in your offspring will be all peoples   blessed

6. ðara godena wiotena ðe . . . _____ ealla be fullan geliornod hæfdon
   (of) the good wise men who books   all completely learned had

   (<u>boc</u>: fem. mutated pl.)

7. þa ceare seofdun hat ymb _____ (<u>heorte</u>: fem. *-an* acc.)
   the cares sighed hot around (my) heart

8. þæt Læden and þæt Englisc nabbað na ane wisan
   the Latin   and the English not have at all one manner

   on þære _____ fadunge (<u>spræc</u>: fem. *o*-stem gen.)
   in the language   arrangement

9. Nu her þara _____ byre nathwylces . . . on flet gæð
   now here (of) killers   son some   onto floor walks

   (<u>bana</u>: masc. *-an* gen.)

Holt, Rinehart and Winston, Inc.

Name _____

5.12 Morphology: Pronouns and Demonstratives

In the following OE sentences, identify the person, gender, case, and number of the underlined personal pronouns. (First- and second-person pronouns had no gender distinction, so ignore gender for these.) For demonstrative pronouns, identify the gender, case, and number. Ignore gender in the plural for both personal and demonstrative pronouns. For interrogative pronouns, identify the case and gender. When the form is ambiguous, additional information is provided for you as necessary for a positive identification.

0. þa geseah <u>ic</u> beforan <u>unc</u> onginnan ðeostrian ða stowe.
   Then saw I before us   begin   to darken that place.

   ic: <u>1st person nom. sg.</u>   unc: <u>(dative) 1st pers. dual</u>

1. Her is <u>seo</u> bot, hu <u>ðu</u> meaht <u>þine</u> æceras betan gif <u>hie</u>
   Here is the remedy, how you can your fields restore if they

   nellaþ wel weaxan.
   will not well grow.

   seo: _____   ðu: _____

   þine: _____   hie: _____

2. cweþe ðonne nigon siþon <u>þas</u> word:
   say   then   nine times these words

   þas: _____

3. ond <u>þæs</u> oþres <u>þone</u> mæstan dæl <u>hie</u> geridon ond <u>him</u> to
   and of the rest the greatest part they seized and (to) them

   gecirdon buton <u>þæm</u> cyninge Ælfrede.
   submitted except the king   Alfred.

   þaes: <u>(neuter)</u>   þone: _____

   hie: _____   him: _____

   þæm: <u>(masc.)</u>

4. Her for <u>se</u> here to Cirenceastre of Cippanhamme. Ond <u>þy</u>
   Here went the army to Cirencester from Chippenham. And in that

   geare gegadrode an hloþ wicenga
   year assembled a troop (of) Vikings

   se: _____   þy: <u>(neuter)</u>

5. Ic ahsige <u>eow</u>, forhwi swa geornlice leorni <u>ge</u>?
   I ask you,   why   so   eagerly study you?

   eow: <u>(dative)</u>   ge: _____

6. <u>Hwæt</u> sægst <u>þu</u>, fugelere?
   What say you, bird-hunter?

   hwæt: _____   þu: _____

7. Ic ne dear yppan þe digla ure.
   I not dare reveal (to) you secrets our.

   Ic: _____   þe: _____

   ure: _____

8. Hwa awecþ þe to uhtsancge?
   Who awakens you for matins?

   Hwa: _____   þe: _(accusative)_____

9. ðær næs to lafe   nanðing þe   hiere   wæs
   there was not remaining nothing which hers was

   hiere: _____

10. ða cristenan hine gecuron to bisceope
    the Christians him chose   as   bishop

    ða: _____   hine: _____

11. Wiþ lungenadle   genim þas wyrte erifion;   gecnucude þæm
    Against lung disease take these herbs "goat's rue"; pound them

    gelice þe þu clyþan wyrce, lege to þæm sare; heo hit
    as if you poultice were making; lay on the sore; it it

    gehæleþ. Nim þonne þæt wos þisse sylfan wyrte, syle
    will heal. Take then the juice (of) this same herb, give

    drincan, þu wundrast þæs mægenes þisse wyrte.
    to drink, you will marvel (at) the power (of) this herb.

    þas: _____   þæm: _____

    þæm: _(neut.)_____   heo: _____

    hit: _____   þæt: _____

    þisse: _____   þæs: _(neut.)_____

12. he sende flod and besencte hie ealle
    he sent flood and drowned them all

    he: _____   hie: _____

13. on hwæs naman adræfon   eowre suna þonne?
    in whose name (do you) drive out your sons then?

    hwæs: _____   eowre: _____

Holt, Rinehart and Winston, Inc.

Name _____

5.13   Morphology: PDE Descendants of OE Personal Pronouns

From which OE forms did the following PDE pronouns or pronominal adjectives develop?
If the PDE form does not descend from an OE form, put a dash in the blank. You will
probably need to consult the chart of OE personal pronouns in your text.

Nom. *I* _OE nom. ic_____   Nom. *he* _____

Obj. *me* _____   Obj. *him* _____

Pron. Adj. *my* _____   Pron. Adj. *his* _____

Gen. *mine* _____   Gen. *his* _____

Nom. *we* _____   Nom. *she* _____

Obj. *us* _____   Obj. *her* _____

Pron. Adj. *our* _____   Pron. Adj. *her* _____

Gen. *ours* _____   Gen. *hers* _____

Nom. *you* _____   Nom. *it* _____

Obj. *you* _OE acc. or dat. ēow___   Obj. *it* _____

Pron. Adj. *your* _____   Pron. Adj. *its* _____

Gen. *yours* _____   Gen. *its* _____

Sg. *that* _____   Nom. *they* _____

Pl. *those* _____   Obj. *them* _—— _____

Sg. *this* _____   Pron. Adj. *their* _____

Pl. *these* _____   Gen. *theirs* _____

Name _____

5.14   Morphology: Strong and Weak Adjectives

Identify the underlined adjectives in the following sentences as strong (indefinite) or weak (definite), and state why each is strong or weak. Refer to page 99 of *A Biography of the English Language* as necessary.

0. þæt is æt þæm hehstan goode   <u>Weak; preceded by demonstrative</u>
    that is at the highest good

1. þu woldest nu brucan <u>ungemetlicre</u> wrænnesse? _____
    you would now enjoy immoderate luxury?

2. heo cende   hyre <u>frumcennedan</u> sunu _____
    she gave birth to her first-born son

3. on <u>midne</u> winter _____
    in mid winter

4. þa beoð swyðe <u>dyre</u> mid Finnum   _____
    they are very precious among the Finns

5. Eadmund se <u>eadiga</u> East-Engla cynincg wæs snotor _____
    Edmund the blessed of E. Angles king was wise

6. of þam <u>diglum</u> stowum _____
    from those secret places

Name _____

5.15 Morphology: Strong Verbs

A. OE had seven classes of strong verbs (see Figure 5–12 in *A Biography of the English Language*). There were some irregularities in all the classes, but the most typical vowels of the principal parts of each class are listed in the accompanying chart. The second- and third-person singular present indicative underwent umlaut when applicable and thus had a different vowel from the infinitive in several of the classes. Listed are the principal parts and the third-person singular present indicative for the Class 1 verb *blīcan* 'shine' and the infinitive and vowels for the remaining principal parts of a verb for each of the other six classes. Complete the chart by writing out the principal parts of the verbs of Classes 2 through 7. An asterisk marks verbs that had umlaut in the third-person singular present indicative. If the form is not totally predictable, it is provided for you.

	Infinitive	3d sg. pres.	3d sg. pret.	Pret. pl.	Past part.
Class 1 i a i i	blīcan 'to shine'	blīcþ '(it) shines'	blāc '(it) shone'	blicon '(they) shone'	blicen '(it has) shone'
Class 2 ēo ēa u o	drēopan 'to drip'	drȳpþ* '(it) drips'	_____ '(it) dripped'	_____ '(they) dripped'	_____ '(it has) dripped'
Class 3 i a u u	slincan 'to slink'	_____ '(it) slinks'	_____ '(it) slunk'	_____ '(they) slunk'	_____ '(it has) slunk'
Class 4 e æ ǣ o	cwelan 'to die'	_____* '(it) dies'	_____ '(it) died'	_____ '(they) died'	_____ '(it has) died'
Class 5 e æ ǣ e	swefan 'to sleep'	_____* '(it) sleeps'	_____ '(it) slept'	_____ '(they) slept'	_____ '(it has) slept'
Class 6 a ō ō a	wascan 'to wash'	_____* '(it) washes'	_____ '(it) washed'	_____ '(they) washed'	_____ '(it has) washed'
Class 7 V_1 ēo ēo V_1	feallan 'to fall'	fȳlþ* '(it) falls'	_____ '(it) fell'	_____ '(they) fell'	_____ '(it has) fallen'
Class 8 V_1 ē ē V_1	blandan 'to blend'	blent* '(it) blends'	_____ '(it) blended'	_____ '(they) blended'	_____ '(it has) blended'

B. Many of the vowels that appear in strong verbs are unique to their class. Hence, if you know the form of the verb (infinitive, third-person present, etc.), you can identify the class to which the verb belongs. Identify the class of each of the following strong verbs by placing the appropriate number in the blank to the left. (No infinitive or past participle of Class 7 verbs is included.)

1. _____ drēag '(it) endured'

2. _____ flagen '(it has) flayed'

Holt, Rinehart and Winston, Inc.

3. ____ gælþ '(it) sings'

4. ____ gnagan 'to gnaw'

5. _4_ hæl '(it) hid'; holen '(it has) hidden'

6. ____ hēt '(it was) called'

7. ____ hrēop '(it) shouted'

8. ____ hrēowan 'to distress'

9. ____ hrinon '(they) touched'

10. ____ lēcon '(they) leapt'

11. ____ lesan 'to collect'; lesen '(it has) collected'

12. ____ nuton '(they) used'; noten '(it has) used'

13. ____ slōgon '(they) slew'

14. ____ sniden '(it has) cut'

15. ____ spunnen '(it has) spun'

16. ____ stīgþ '(it) ascends'

17. ____ swīcan 'to fight'

18. ____ swincan 'to labor'

19. ____ wæg '(it) carried'; wegen '(it has) carried'

20. ____ wann '(it) struggled'

21. ____ wōd '(it) waded'

22. ____ wrāþ '(it) writhed'

23. ____ þweran 'to stir'; þworen '(it has) stirred'

C. The OE seven classes of strong verbs have not survived intact in PDE because of sound changes, the tendency of strong verbs to become weak, and analogical changes. In addition, PDE has only three principal parts (infinitive, past tense, and past participle), having lost the distinction between singular and plural in the past tense. Nevertheless, a few strong verbs still reflect their earlier class membership. For each of the PDE descendants of OE strong verbs, list at least one other verb with the same vowel alternation in the principal parts.

OE Class 1: PDE ride, rode, ridden [ai o ɪ] _drive_____

OE Class 3: PDE bind, bound, bound [ai au au] _____

　　　　　　　PDE drink, drank, drunk [ɪ æ ə] _____

OE Class 4: PDE bear, bore, borne [ɛ ɔ ɔ] _____

OE Class 5: PDE speak, spoke, spoken [i o o] _____

OE Class 6: PDE shake, shook, shaken [e ʊ e] _____

OE Class 7: PDE blow, blew, blown [o u o] _____

Name _____

5.16   Morphology: Derivative Prefixes

As in PDE, suffixes in OE tended to change the part-of-speech category while prefixes tended to change the meaning of the base word in some way. Examine the glosses of the following nonprefixed and prefixed pairs, and determine the probable meaning of the prefix.

0. *for-*   bærnan 'burn'   forbærnan 'burn up'
               hogian 'think about'   forhogian 'despise'
               hætan 'heat'   forhætan 'overheat'
               sendan 'send'   forsendan 'banish'
               giefan 'give'   forgiefan 'give, forgive'

   Meaning of prefix   *"very much"; intensifier* _____

1. *ymb(e)-*   sittan 'sit'   ymbsittan 'besiege'
               hycgan 'think'   ymbhycgan 'consider'
               hweorfan 'move, turn'   ymbhweorfan 'revolve'
               sniþan 'cut'   ymbsniþan 'circumcise'
               faran 'go'   ymbfaran 'surround'

   Meaning of prefix _____

2. *el-*   land 'land, country'   elland 'foreign country'
               reord 'speech'   elreord 'barbarous'
               þeod 'people'   elþeod 'strange people'
               (ge)hygd 'mind, thought' elhygd 'distraction'

   Meaning of prefix _____

3. *wan-*   hal 'healthy'   wanhal 'sick'
               hygdig 'thoughtful'   wanhygdig 'careless'
               sped 'prosperity'   wansped 'poverty'
               fot 'foot'   wanfota 'pelican'
               fah 'dyed, shining'   wanfah 'dark-hued'

   Meaning of prefix _____

4. *to-*   weorpan 'throw'   toweorpan 'destroy'
               licgan 'lie'   tolicgan 'separate'
               lucan 'close, lock'   tolucan 'wrench apart'
               fleotan 'swim, sail'   tofleotan 'carry off by flood'
               hælan 'heal'   tohælan 'weaken'

   Meaning of prefix _____

5. *sam-*   grene 'green'   samgrene 'immature'
               hal 'healthy'   samhal 'weakly'
               wis 'wise'   samwis 'stupid'
               (ge)boren 'born'   samboren 'premature'
               bærned 'burnt'   sambærned 'half-burnt'

   Meaning of prefix _____

Name _____

5.17 Morphology: Derivative Suffixes

The following are examples of several common OE derivative suffixes. By examining the patterns of the first two items in each group, you can supply the missing items. Note that umlaut (mutation) is involved in some of the sets.

I. Nouns from Adjectives, Verbs, and Other Nouns

Suffix	Adjective		Noun
-nes	æðel 'noble'		æðelnes 'nobility'
	swet 'sweet'		swetnes 'sweetness'
	<u>halig</u> _____ 'holy'		halignes 'holiness'
	mildheort 'merciful'		_____
	_____ 'bright'		beorhtnes _____
-þu	hean 'lowly'		hynþu 'humiliation'
	fah 'hostile'		fæhþu 'hostility'
	heah _____		hyhþu 'height'
	_____ 'long'		lengþu _____
	earm 'wretched'		_____ 'misery'

Suffix	Verb		Noun
-ung	bletsian 'to bless'		bletsung 'blessing'
	earnian 'to earn'		earnung 'merit'
	heofian _____		heofung 'lamentation'
	_____ 'to lie'		leasung 'falsehood'
	weorðian _____		_____ 'honor'

Suffix	Noun		Noun
-had	preost 'priest'		preosthad 'priesthood'
	geoguþ 'youth'		geoguþhad 'time of youth'
	woruld _____		_____ 'secular life'
	_____ 'child'		cildhad _____
	mægþ 'maiden'		_____ 'virginity'

II. Adjectives from Nouns or Adjectives

Suffix	Noun or Adjective		Adjective
-sum	wynn 'pleasant'		wynsum 'pleasant'
	lang 'long'		langsum 'enduring'
	friþ _____		_____ 'peaceful'
	_____ 'abundance'		genyhtsum _____

Holt, Rinehart and Winston, Inc.

Noun		*Adjective*
-lic	woruld 'world'	woruldlic 'worldly'
	torht 'brightness'	torhtlic 'bright'
	deofol 'devil'	
		_____ 'diabolical'
	_____ 'joy'	hyhtlic 'joyful'
	_____ 'power'	þryþlic 'strong'
-ig	blod 'blood'	blodig 'bloody'
	mod 'courage'	modig 'bold'
	dust _____	_____ 'dusty'
	_____ 'skill'	cræftig _____
	wlite 'beauty'	wlitig _____
-en	ator 'poison'	ætren 'poisonous'
	seolfor 'silver'	sylfren 'made of silver'
	Crist _____	cristen 'Christian'
	wulf 'wolf'	wylfen _____
	stān _____	_____ 'made of stone'

III. Verbs from Adjectives or Nouns

Suffix	*Adjective or Noun*	*Verb*
-sian	yrre 'angry'	yrsian 'to be angry'
	mære 'famous'	mærsian 'to become famous'
	clæne 'clean'	_____ 'to cleanse'
	ege 'fear'	_____ 'to frighten'
	_____ 'powerful'	ricsian _____
	Adjective	*Verb*
-an	wod 'mad'	wedan 'to be mad'
	cuþ 'known, familiar'	cyþan 'to make known'
	brad _____	brædan 'to extend'
	eald 'old'	_____ 'to delay'
	_____ 'full'	fyllan _____

Holt, Rinehart and Winston, Inc.

Name _____

5.18   Syntax

Among the differences between OE syntax and that of PDE are that, in OE,

A. in clauses or sentences preceded by an adverbial, the verb frequently preceded the subject.
B. in subordinate clauses, the finite verb was often at the end.
C. pronoun objects often preceded the verb, especially in subordinate clauses.
D. impersonal verbs (with no expressed nominative subject) were common.
E. if a noun had two modifiers, one often preceded and the other followed the noun.
F. titles used with proper names often followed the name.
G. prepositions sometimes followed their objects.

For the following excerpts, decide which of the above rules applies and enter the appropriate letter(s) in the blank to the left. (In several instances, more than one rule applies.) Then rewrite the excerpt in acceptable PDE.

_A, E_   0. þa comon on sumne sæl ungesælige þeofas eahta on anre
      then came at certain time unfortunate thieves eight on one

   nihte to þam arwurþan halgan . . .
   night to the venerable   saint

   ___Then, at a certain time, eight unfortunate thieves___

   ___came to the venerable saint on one night.___

_____   1. se wæs Ælfredes cyninges godsunu . . .
      he was Alfred's king('s) godson

   _____

   _____

_____   2. Nis eac nan wundor, þeah us mislimpe, forðam we witan
      Not is also no wonder,   if us goes wrong because we know

   ful georne þæt . . .
   very well that

   _____

   _____

_____   3. Ond þa salde se here him foregislas ond micle aþas . . .
      And then gave the army him hostages and great oaths

   _____

   _____

_____   4. Mid þy þe se cyngc þæt geseah, he bewænde hine . . .
      When   the king that saw,   he turned himself

   _____

   _____

————— 5. Se cyng . . . aræde hi up and hire to cwæð: "Leofe dohtor . . ."
The king lifted her up   and her to said: "Beloved daughter"

_____

_____

————— 6. And sona þeræfter com Tostig eorl . . . mid swa miclum liðe,
And at once thereafter came Tostig earl   with as big   fleet

swa he begitan mihte.
as   he   get   could

_____

_____

————— 7. Gif man gewundud sy,   genim wegbrædan sæd, gnid to
If someone wounded is   take   waybread seed, grind to

duste & scead on þa wunde . . .
powder & sprinkle on the wound

_____

_____

————— 8. þa gefengon hie þara þreora scipa tu æt ðæm muðan
Then seized they (of) the 3   ships   2 at the mouth

uteweardum . . .
outside

_____

_____

————— 9. And utan . . . sume getrywða habban us betweonan butan
And let us   some fidelity   keep us between   without

uncræftan
deceit

_____

_____

————— 10. ond hu him ða speow ægðer ge mid wige ge mid
and how them then succeeded both with battle and with

wisdome . . .
wisdom

_____

_____

————— 11. þa gemette hie Æþelwulf aldorman on Engla-felda, ond him
Then met they Athelwulf alderman at Englefield,   and him

þær wiþ gefeaht . . .
there against fought

_____

_____

Holt, Rinehart and Winston, Inc.

Name _____

5.19 Lexicon: Fossilized Survivals

Although much of the OE vocabulary has been lost, a number of items survive as parts of compounds. For each of the following words, use a dictionary to identify the OE etymon and meaning of the italicized portion.

0. ear*wig* _OE wicga "insect"_

1. a*jar* _____

2. black*mail* _____

3. cow*slip* _____

4. after*math* _____

5. *gar*lic _____

6. neigh*bor* _____

7. *cod*piece _____

8. god*send* _____

9. *hench*man _____

10. mid*riff* _____

11. *mid*wife _____

12. *war*lock _____

13. *sti*rrup _____

14. *cob*web _____

Name _____

5.22   Semantics: Semantic Change

Listed below are a number of English words that have undergone semantic change over the centuries. For each word, state whether the change has been (a) generalization, (b) narrowing, (c) amelioration, (d) pejoration, (e) strengthening, (f) weakening, (g) shift in stylistic level, or (h) shift in denotation. For some items, you may feel that more than one of these types of changes has occurred. If so, indicate this.

0. OE lāst 'track, sole of foot, footprint' (PDE last [noun])   b
    Hie ðæs laðan last sceawedon 'They inspected the track of the foe'

1. OE nēah 'near(ly)' (PDE nigh)   _____
    feor oððe neah 'far or near'

2. OE bana 'killer, murderer' (PDE bane)   _____
    Hie næfre his banan folgian noldan 'they would never follow his murderer'

3. OE sellan 'give, supply' (PDE sell)   _____
    Hie him sealdon attor drincan 'They gave him poison to drink'

4. OE fēond 'enemy, devil, the Devil, fiend' (PDE fiend)   _____
    Eowre fynd feallaþ beforan eow 'Your enemies fall before you'

5. OE mōdig 'bold, brave, proud' (PDE moody)   _____
    Ðæt wæs modig secg 'That was (a) brave man'

6. OE drēorig 'bloody, gory, grievous, sorrowing' (PDE dreary)   _____
    Wæter stod dreorig and gedrefed 'Water stood gory and roiled up'

7. OE botm 'ground, physically lowest part' (PDE bottom)   _____
    Heo to ðæs fennes botme com 'She came to the bottom of the fen'

8. OE godsibb 'godparent or godchild' (PDE gossip)   _____
    Nan man on his godsibbe ne wifige 'No man should marry his godchild'

9. OE cwellan 'kill, murder' (PDE quell)   _____
    Ða cwelleras ne woldan hine cwellan 'The executioners did not want to kill him.'

10. OE ādela 'filth, urine, dirt' (PDE addled)   _____
    Ðæt her yfle adelan stinceþ 'That here it stinks of filth'

11. OE smeortan 'to smart' (PDE smart [verb and adjective])   _____
    Ðenne wile his heorte aken and smerten 'Then his heart will ache and smart'

12. OE mægden 'maiden, virgin, girl' (PDE maiden)   _____
    He nam ðæs mædenes modor 'He took the girl's mother'

13. OE morðor 'violent deed, crime, homicide, punishment, manslaughter'   _____
    (PDE murder)
    Seo sawl sceal mid deoflum drohtnoþ habban in morþre and on mane 'The soul shall have company with devils in great sin and in crime'

Holt, Rinehart and Winston, Inc.

5.23   Semantics: Kinship Terms

Listed below are some of the kinship terms in OE.

brōðor 'brother'   mōdor 'mother'
brōðorsunu 'nephew'   mōdorcynn 'maternal descent'
brōðorwīf 'sister-in-law'   mōdrige 'maternal aunt'
dohtor 'daughter'   spinelhealf 'female line of descent'
ēam 'maternal uncle'   suhterga 'brother's son; uncle's son'
fæder 'father'   sunu 'son'
fædera 'paternal uncle'   sweostor 'sister'
fæderencnōsl 'father's kin'   sweostorbearn 'nephew, niece'
faðe 'paternal aunt'   þridde fæder 'great-grandfather'
geswigra 'sister's son'   þridde mōdor 'great-grandmother'
mæg 'male parent, son, brother, cousin'   wæpnedhand 'male line'
māge 'female relative'   wīfhand 'female line'
mago 'son, male descendant'

1. What cultural similarities and differences between the Anglo-Saxon kinship system and

that of contemporary American culture does this list suggest? _____

_____

_____

_____

2. Where did English get the terms *uncle, aunt, niece,* and *cousin*? _____

_____

Why might English have borrowed all these terms, yet none of the terms for members of

the nuclear family? _____

_____

_____

5.24 OE Illustrative Texts

I. The OE Heptateuch

The OE Heptateuch (first seven books of the Old Testament) is a collection of Biblical translations by the Old English scholar, cleric, and writer Ælfric. The translations are in lucid prose that still manages to follow the Latin original fairly closely. The selection here is from Joshua 6:1–4, 12–19, 21–25, 27.

[1]Hiericho seo burh wæs mid weallum ymbtrymed & fæste belocen
Jericho   the city was with walls surrounded and firmly locked

for ðes folces tocyme, & hi ne dorston ut faran ne in faran
against the people's arrival, & they not dared out go nor in go

for him.   [2]Drihten cwæð ða to Iosue: Ic do ðas buruh
because of them. The Lord said then to Joshua: I put this city

Hiericho on ðinum gewealde & ðone cyning samod & ða strengstan
Jericho into your power   & the king together & the strongest

weras ðe wuniað on hyre. [3]Farað nu six dagas symble ymb ða
men who dwell in   it. Go now six days continually around the

burh, ælce dæg æne & ealle suwigende; [4]& seofon sacerdas blawan
city,   each day once & all keeping silent; & seven priests   blow

mid byman eow ætforan. [12]Iosue ða swa dyde, & sacerdas bæron
with trumpets before you. Joshua then thus did, & priests bore

ðæt Godes scrin ymbe ða burh, ælce dæge æne. [13]& oðre seofon
the God's ark around the city, each day once.   & another seven

blewon mid sylfrenum byman. [14]& hi ealle to fyrdwicon ferdon
blew with silver trumpets.   & they all to (the) camp went

æfter ðam. [15]On ðam seofoðan dæge hi ferdon seofon siðon ymb
after them. On the seventh day   they went seven times around

ða burh. [16]& on ðam seofoðan ymbfærelde, ða ða sacerdas blewon,
the city. & on the seventh circuit,   when the priests blew,

& ðæt folc eall hrymde, swa swa Iosue him rædde, ða burston
& the people all cried out, as   Joshua them advised, then burst

ða weallas, ðe ða burh behæfdon, endemes to grunde, & hi
the walls, which the city surrounded, completely to ground, & they

ða in eodon, ælc man swa he stod on ðam ymbgange. [17]Iosue
then in went, each man as he stood at the circumference. Joshua

ða clypode, & cwæð to ðam folce: Sy ðeos burh amansumod & eall
then spoke, & said to the people: Let this city be cursed   & all

ðæt bið on hyre, buton Raab ana libbe & ða ðe lociað to hyre,
that are in it, except Rahab alone live & those who belong to her,

for ðan ðe heo urum ærendracum arfæstnysse cydde. [18]& ge
because she (to) our messengers mercy showed.   & you

Holt, Rinehart and Winston, Inc.

nan ðingc ne hreppon on reafe ne on feo,   ðæt ge ne beon scyldige
nothing not touch   as plunder nor as property, lest you be guilty

sceamlicre forgægednysse,   & Israhela fyrdwic for synne beo gedrefed.
of disgraceful transgression, & Israelite camp for sin be afflicted.

[19]Swa hwæt swa her goldes byð, ðæt beo Gode gehalgod, & on
Whatever here (of) gold is,   that be to God consecrated, & in

seolfre oððe on are, eall in to his hordum. [21]Hi ofslogon ða sona
silver or in brass, all into his treasuries.   They slew then at once

mid swurdes ecge weras & wifmen & ða wepende cild, hryðera &
with sword's edge men & women & the weeping children, oxen &

scep, assan & ealle ðingc. [22]Iosue cwæð ða syððan to ðam foresædum
sheep, asses & all things.   Joshua said then later to the foresaid

ærendracum: Gað nu to ðam huse, ðær ge behydde wæron, &
messengers: Go now to the house where you hidden were, &

lædað ut ðæt wif, ðe eowrum life geheolp, & ða ðe
lead out the woman who your life supported, & that which

hyre to lociað, lædað of ðisre byrig. [23]Hy dydon ða swa swa him
belongs to her, take from this town. They did then as them

gedihte Iosue, & læddon hi of ðære byrig mid eallum hyre magum,
ordered Joshua, & led her from the town with all her kinsmen,

& hi syððan leofodon mid sibbe betwux him. [24]Hi forbærndon ða
& they afterward lived with peace among them. They burned then

ða burh & ðæt ðe binnan hyre wæs. [25]& Iosue bæd ðus: Beo
the city and what within it was.   & Joshua ordered thus: Be

se awyrged, ðe æfre eft geedstaðelie ðas buruh Hiericho. [27]God wæs
he cursed, who ever again reestablishes this city Jericho. God was

ða mid Iosue on eallum his weorcum, & his nama wearð
then with Joshua in all his works,   & his name became

gewidmærsod wide geond ðæt land.
celebrated widely throughout the land.

II. The OE Herbarium
Several medical texts in OE have survived, among them an *herbarium*, or a collection of descriptions of plants useful for medical purposes. This selection, a description of the medicinal uses of rue, is from MS. V. London, British Library, Cotton Vitellius CIII.

Ðeos wyrt þe man rutam montanam & oþrum naman þam gelice
This herb which one Ruta montana *& another name to it similar*

rudan nemneþ byþ cenned on dunum & on unbeganum stowum.
rude *calls   is produced on hills   & in uncultivated places.*

   1. Wið eagena dymnysse & wið yfele dolh   genim þysse wyrte
    Against eyes' dimness & against bad wound take this herb

leaf þe we rutam montanam nendun on ealdum wine gesodene, do
leaf that we Ruta montana *named in old   wine boiled, put (it)*

þonne on an glæsen fæt, smyre syþþan þærmid.
then in a glass vessel,   rub   then   with (it).

    2. Wiþ ðæra breosta   sare genim þas ylcan wyrte rutam
       Against of the breasts pain take this same herb Ruta

siluaticam, cnuca on trywenan fæte, nim þonne swa micel swa ðu
silvatica,   pound in wooden vessel,   take then as   much as you

mid ðrim fingron gegripan mæge, do on an fæt & þærto anne scenc
with three fingers grasp   can,   put in a vessel and to it a cup

wines & twegen wæteres, syle drincan, gereste hyne þonne sume
of wine & two of water, give to drink, let him rest then for a

hwile, sona he byð hal.
while, at once he will be healthy.

    3. Wið lifersare   genim þysse ylcan wyrte anne gripan & oþerne
       Against liver-pain take (of) this same herb   a handful & another

healfne sester wæteres & ealswa mycel huniges, wyll tosomne,
half measure of water & also a lot of honey,   boil together,

syle drincan þry dagas, ma gyf him þearf sy, þu hine miht
give to drink   3 days, more give him if need be, you him can

gehælan.
cure.

III. Riddles Nos. 24 and 47

The Exeter Book, a manuscript preserving numerous OE poems, contains ninety-five metrical riddles varying greatly in length, subject matter, elegance, and decency. Some of them are based on Latin riddles; others are apparently original compositions. The answers to the two reproduced here, Nos. 24 and 47, are "magpie" and "bookworm," respectively. Riddle No. 24 contains six runic characters, which, rearranged, spell out *higoræ*, the OE word for jay or magpie.

Riddle No. 24

    Ic eom wunderlicu wiht,   wræsne mine stefne,
    I am wonderful creature,   modulate my voice,

hwilum beorce swa hund,   hwilum blæte swa gat,
sometimes bark like dog,   sometimes bleat like goat,

hwilum græde swa gos,   hwilum gielle swa hafoc,
sometimes cry out like goose, sometimes shriek like hawk,

hwilum ic onhyrge   þone haswan earn,
sometimes I imitate   the gray   eagle,

guðfugles hleoþor, hwilum   glidan   reorde
bird of war's song, sometimes (like) vulture speak

muþe gemæne,   hwilum mæwes song,
(with) mouth universal, sometimes sea-gull's song,

þær ic glado sitte. ᛜ mec nemnað,
where I joyful sit. G   me names,

swylce . ᚠ. ond · R · ᛝ . fullesteð,
also   Æ   and R   O   supports,

· ᚻ · ond · / ·   Nu ic haten eom
H   and I   Now I called am

swa þa siex stafas   sweotule becnaþ.
as the six characters   clearly signify.

Riddle No. 47

Moððe word fræt.   Me þæt þuhte
(A) moth words ate. (To) me it seemed

wrætlicu wyrd, þa ic þæt wundor gefrægn,
curious event,   when I the marvel heard of,

þæt se wyrm forswealg wera gied sumes,
that the worm devoured the song of certain men

þeof in þystro, þrymfæstne cwide
thief in dark,   illustrious utterance

ond þæs strangan staþol. Stælgiest   ne wæs
and of the strong position. Thievish stranger not was

wihte þy gleawra, þe he þam wordum swealg.
a bit the wiser,   though he the words swallowed.

IV. The Peterborough Chronicle

One of the most interesting surviving prose works of OE is the *Anglo-Saxon Chronicle*, the umbrella title given to several different but related chronicles. King Alfred probably initiated the writing of the Chronicle toward the end of the ninth century, and some of the regional chronicles were kept up to date until well after the Norman Conquest. The following passage is the entry for 1085 in the Peterborough Chronicle, telling about the instituting of the Domesday Book. Note the indignation of the scribe at this point—the people suspected the king was up to no good with his census; they rightly feared new taxes.

On þisum geare menn cwydodon & to soðan sædan þet Cnut
In this   year men   declared & in truth   said that Canute

cyng of Denmearcan, Swægnes sune cynges, fundade hiderward
king of Denmark,   King Swegn's son,   set out toward this place

& wolde gewinnan þis land mid Rodbeardes eorles fultume of
& wanted to conquer this land with Earl Rotbert's help of

Flandran, forðan þe Cnut heafde Rodbeardes dohter. Ða Willelm
Flanders, because   Canute had Rotbert's daughter. When William

Englalandes cyng, þe þa wæs sittende on Normandige forðig he
England's king,   who   was dwelling in Normandy because he

ahte ægðer ge Englaland ge Normandige, þis geaxode, he ferde into
held both   England and Normandy, this learned, he went into

Englalande mid swa mycclan here ridendra manna & gangendra
England with so great (an) army (of) horsemen & foot soldiers

of Francrice and of Brytlande swa næfre ær þis land ne gesohte,
from France and from Wales   as never before this land approached,

Holt, Rinehart and Winston, Inc.

swa þet menn wundredon he þis land mihte eall þone here afedan;
so that men marveled how this land could all the army support;

ac se cyng let toscyfton   þone here geond eall þis land to
but the king ordered to distribute the army through all this land to

his mannon, & hi fæddon þone here, ælc be his
his men,   and they fed the army, each according to his

landefne.   & Men heafdon mycel geswinc þæs geares. & Se
proportion of land. & men had great hardship this year.   And the

cyng lett   awestan þet land abutan þa sæ, þet gif his
king ordered to lay waste the land around the sea, so that if his

feond comen upp þet hi næfdon   na on hwam   hi
enemies came up that they would have nothing on which they

fengon swa rædlice.   Ac þa se cyng geaxode to soðan þet his
could seize so quickly. But when the king learned in truth that his

feond gelætte wæron & ne mihten na   geforðian heora fare,
enemies departed were & not could at all carry out their attack,

þa lett he sum þone here faren to heora agene lande, & sum he
then had he part of the army go to their own land, & part he

heold on þisum lande ofer winter. Ða to þam Midewintre wæs
held in   this land over winter.   Then at Midwinter was

se cyng on Gleaweceastre mid his witan & heold þær his hired
the king at Gloucester with his councillors & kept there his retinue

v dagas. & Syððan þe arcebiscop & gehadode men hæfden sinoð
5 days.   & afterward the archbishop & ordained men had (a) synod

þreo dagas. Ðær wæs Mauricius gecoren to biscope on Lundene &
three days. There was Mauricius chosen as bishop of London and

Willelm to Norðfolce, & Rodbeard to Ceasterscire: hi wæron ealle
William of Norfolk, and Rotbert of Cheshire: they were all

þæs cynges clerecas. Æfter þisum hæfde se cyng mycel geþeaht
the king's clerks.   After this had the king great counsel

& swiðe deope spæce wið his witan   ymbe þis land, hu hit
& very serious speech with his councillors about this land, how it

wære gesett oððe mid hwylcon mannon. Sende þa ofer eall
was settled or   by which people.   (He) sent then over all

Englaland into ælcere scire his men & lett agan ut hu fela
England into   each shire his men & had find out how many

hundred hyda wæron innon þære scire, oððe hwet se cyng himsylf
hundred hides were within the shire, or what the king himself

hæfde landes & orfes innan þam lande, oððe hwilce gerihtæ he
had of land and livestock in the land, or which privileges he

ahte to habbanne to xii monþum of ðære scire. Eac he lett
ought to have for   12 months from the shire. Also he ordered to

gewritan hu mycel landes his arcebiscopas hæfdon & his
write   how much land his archbishops   had and his

Holt, Rinehart and Winston, Inc.

leodbiscopas & his abbodas & his eorlas, &, þeah ic hit lengre telle,
provincials & his abbots & his earls, &, though I it longer tell,

hwæt oðð e hu mycel ælc mann hæfde þe landsittende wæs innan
what or how much each man had who occupying land was inside

Englalande, on lande oðð e on orfe, & hu mycel feos hit wære
England, in land or in livestock, and how much money it was

wurð. Swa swyðe nearwelice he hit lett ut aspyrian þet næs
worth. So very strictly he it ordered to investigate that not was

an ælpig hide ne an gyrde landes, ne furð on—hit is sceame
one single hide nor one quarter hide of land, nor even—it is shame

to tellanne, ac hit ne þuhte him nan sceame to donne—an oxe ne
to tell, but it not seemed to him no shame to do—one ox nor

an cu ne an swin næs belyfon þet næs gesæt on
one cow nor one swine not was spared that was not set down in

his gewrite. & Ealle þa gewrita wæron gebroht to him syðð an.
his document. & all the documents were brought to him afterwards.

V. *Alexander's Letter to Aristotle*
The *Beowulf* manuscript (MS. Cotton Vitellius A XV) also contains the prose *Alexander's Letter to Aristotle*, a fictional work ultimately based on an early Greek original. It is particularly interesting because it reveals a knowledge of and taste for Eastern romances in Anglo-Saxon England.

Swelce eac laforas þær cwoman unmætlicre micelnisse & monig
Moreover leopards there came (of) enormous size & many

oþer wildeor & eac tigris us on þære nihte þær abisgodon.
other wild animals & also tigers us in the night there kept busy.

Swelce þær eac cwoman hreaþemys. þa wæron in culefrena gelic-
Further there also came bats which were in pigeons' like-

nesse swa micle. & þa on ure ondwlitan sperdon & us pulledon.
ness so big, & they in our faces struck & us pecked.

hæfdon hie eac þa hreaþemys teð in monna gelicnisse. & hie
Had they also the bats' teeth in men's shape. And they

mid þæm þa men wundodon & tæron. Eac ðæm oþrum bisgum
with them then men wounded & tore. Also (to) the other afflictions

& geswencnissum þe us on becwom. þa cwom semninga swiðe micel
& troubles that (to) us happened, then came suddenly very big

deor sum mare þonne þara oðra ænig hæfde þæt deor þrie hornas
animal greater than (of) the others any. Had that animal 3 horns

on foran heafde & mid þæm hornas wæs egeslice gewæpnod. þæt
on front (of) head & with the horns was dreadfully armed. That

deor indeos hataðdentes tyrannum. hæfde þæt deor horse heafod.
animal Indians call "tyrant teeth." Had that animal horse head,

& wæs blæces heowes. Ðis deor mid þy ð e hit þæs wætres ondronc
& was dark in color. This animal, while it (of) the water drank,

Holt, Rinehart and Winston, Inc.

þa beheold hit þa ure wicstowe. & þa semninga on us & on ure
then saw it there our camp, & then suddenly on us & on our

wicstowe ræsde. Ne hit for þæm bryne wandode þæs hatan leges
camp rushed. Not it because of the fire flinched of the hot flame

& fyres þe him wæs ongean ac hit ofer eall wod & eode. Mid þy
& fire which it was facing, but it over all walked & went. Thereupon

ic þa getrymede þæt mægen greca heriges, & we us wið him
I then exhorted the troop (of) Greek army & we us against it

scyldan woldon þa hit ofsloh   sona   minra þegna
to defend wanted, then it struck down at once (of) my warriors

•xxvi• ane ræse   & •lii• hit oftræd. & hie to loman gerenode,
26 (in) one attack & 52 it trampled & them to earth drove down,

þæt hie mec   nænigre note nytte beon meahton. & we hit þa
so that they to me not any use beneficial be could.   & we it then

unsofte   mid strælum & eac mid longsceaftum sperum of
with difficulty with arrows & also with long-shafted spears from

scotadon & hit ofslogon & acwealdon. þa hit wæs foran to uhtes.
shot   and it slew and destroyed.   Then it was early toward dawn.

þa æteowde þær wolberende lyft hwites hiowes. & eac missenlices
Then appeared there pestilential air (of) white color, & also diversely

wæs heo on hringwisan fag. & monige men for heora þæm
was it in rings variegated.   & many men because of the

wolberendan stence swulton mid þære wolberendan lyfte   þe
pestilential stench perished with the pernicious atmosphere which

þær swelc æteowde þa   ðær cwoman eac indisce mys in þa
there such appeared then; there came also Indian mice into the

fyrd in foxa gelicnisse . . .
camp in foxes' likeness . . .

VI. *Deor*

This 42-line poem is typically OE in its somewhat gloomy emphasis on misfortune and depression, but unusual in its stanzaic form with a refrain. Deor was a *scop*, or poet, who formerly had served his lord for many years, but then was supplanted by another *scop*, Heorrenda. The six examples of misfortunes that were overcome or outlived refer to various stories from Germanic history and legend.

Welund him be wurman   wræces cunnade,
Weland from the Vermars exile experienced,

anhydig eorl   earfoþa dreag,
resolute warrior torments suffered,

hæfde him to gesiþþe   sorge ond longaþ
had as his companions sorrow and longing,

wintercealde wræce;   wean oft onfond,
wintry cold exile;   misery (he) often suffered,

siþþan hine Niðhad on   nede legde,
after Niðhad on him   fetters laid,

Holt, Rinehart and Winston, Inc.

swoncre seonobende   on syllan monn.
supple sinew-bonds   on (a) better man.

þæs ofereode,   þisses swa mæg!
That passed away, so may this!

Beadohilde ne wæs   hyre broþra deaþ
(To) Beadohild not was her brothers' death

on sefan swa sar   swa hyre sylfre þing,
in heart so painful as her own state,

þæt heo gearolice   ongieten hæfde
when she clearly   perceived had

þæt heo eacen wæs;   æfre ne meahte
that she pregnant was; (she) never could

þriste geþencan,   hu ymb þæt sceolde.
without shame think; (of) how it must (end).

þæs ofereode,   þisses swa mæg!
That passed away, so may this!

We þæt Mæðhilde   monge gefrugnon
We (for) Mæðhild   many (of us have) heard

wurdon grundlease   Geates frige,
(that was) bottomless Geat's love,

þæt hi seo sorglufu   slæp ealle binom.
That him the sad love sleep all deprived.

þæs ofereode,   þisses swa mæg!
That passed away, so may this!

Ðeodric ahte   þritig wintra
Ðeodric ruled thirty years

Mæringa burg;   þæt wæs monegum cuþ.
Merovingians' stronghold; that was to many known.

þæs ofereode,   þisses swa mæg!
That passed away, so may this!

We geascodan   Eormanrices
We have heard of Eormanric's

wylfenne geþoht;   ahte wide folc
wolf-like mind;   (he) ruled widely (the) people

Gotena rices.   þæt wæs grim cyning.
Goths' kingdom. He was (a) savage king.

Sæt secg monig   sorgum gebunden,
Sat many a man   (by) sorrows bound,

wean on wenan,   wyscte geheahhe
despair in mind,   (he) wished often

þæt þæs cynerices   ofercumen wære.
that this kingdom   overthrown would be.

Holt, Rinehart and Winston, Inc.

þæs ofereode,   þisses swa mæg!
That passed away, so may this!

Siteð sorgcearig,   sælum bidæled,
Sits sad-faced (one) of joys deprived,

on sefan sweorceð,   sylfum þinceð
in heart grieves,   (to) him (it) seems

þæt sy endeleas   earfoða dæl.
that is endless   of sufferings (his) share.

Mæg þonne geþencan,   þæt geond þas woruld
(He) can then think,   that throughout this world

witig dryhten   wendeþ geneahhe,
wise Lord   changes often

eorle monegum are gesceawað,
(to) many a man favor shows,

wislicne blæd,   sumum weana dæl.
wise spirit,   (to) some (a) portion of woes.

þæt ic me sylfum secgan wille,
This I about myself want to say,

þæt ic hwile wæs   Heodeninga scop,
that I once was   (of) Heodenings (the) bard,

dryhtne dyre.   Me wæs Deor noma.
(to a) lord dear. My name was Deor ['wild animal'].

Ahte ic fela wintra   folgað tilne,
Had I many years   employment good,

holdne hlaford,   oþþæt Heorrenda nu,
gracious lord,   until Heorrenda now,

leoðcræftig monn   londryht geþah,
skilled-in-song man land-rights took,

þæt me eorla hleo   ær gesealde.
that (to) me warriors' protector earlier had given.

þæt ofereode,   þisses swa mæg!
That passed away, so may this!

VII. A Ninth-Century Charter

A number of legal documents in OE have survived, among them a Kentish charter that specifies one Abba's division of his inheritance. An abridged version of this charter is reproduced here.

ic abba geroefa cyðe   & writan hate hu min will is
I Abba officer make known & order to write how my will is

þæt mon ymb min ærfe   gedoe æfter minum dæge.
that people about my property should do after my day.

ærest ymb min lond þe ic hæbbe, & me   god lah, & ic
First about my land that I have, & (to) me God granted, & I

æt minum hlafordum begæt, is min willa, gif me god bearnes unnan
from my   lords   obtained, is my will,   if (to) me God child grant

Holt, Rinehart and Winston, Inc.

wille, ðæt hit foe to   londe æfter me & his bruce mid minum
will, that it take to (the) land after me & it use   with my

gemeccan, & sioððan swæ forð min cynn ða hwile þe god wille
wife,   & afterward thus forth my family as long as God may will

ðæt ðeara ænig   sie þe londes weorðe sie & land gehaldan cunne.
that (of) them any   be who (of) land worthy be & land hold can.

gif me ðonne gifeðe sie ðæt ic bearn begeotan ne mege, þonne is min
If (to) me then granted be that I child beget not can, then is my

willa þæt hit hæbbe min wiif ða hwile ðe hia hit mid clennisse
will that it have my wife   as long as she it with chastity

gehaldan wile, & min broðar alchher hire fultume & ðæt lond hire
wants to keep, & my brother Alchhere her help & the land (to) her

nytt gedoe. & him man selle   an half swulung
use put.   & (to) him people should give a half sulung *[land mea-*

      ciollan dene to habbanne & to brucanne, wið ðan ðe he ðy
sure] in Cioll *valley to have   & to use, provided that he the*

geornliocar hire ðearfa bega   & bewiotige. & mon selle
more willingly her needs attend to & care for. & people should give

him to ðem lond IIII oxan, & II cy, & L scepa, & ænne horn. gif min
him for the land 4 oxen, & 2 cows, & 50 sheep, & one horn. If my

wiif ðonne hia nylle mid clennisse swæ gehaldan, & hire liofre
wife then she not wants chastity thus to keep, & her more agreeable

sie oðer hemed to niomanne, ðonne foen mine megas to ðem londe,
be another marriage to take, then let take my kinsmen the land,

& hire agefen hire agen. gif hire ðonne liofre sie
& (to) her return her own. If (to) her then more agreeable be to a

. . . nster to ganganne oðða suð to faranne, ðonne agefen hie twægen
nunnery to go   or south to go,   then yield (to) her two

mine megas, alchher & æðel . . . hire twa ðusenda & fon him to
my kinsmen, Alchhere & Æðel . . . her two thousand & take them

ðem londe. & agefe mon   to liminge L cawa & V cy fore hie,
the land. & people should deliver to Liming 50 ewes & 5 cows for it.

& mon selle to folcanstane in mid minum lice X oxan, & X cy, &
& one should give to Folkstone with my body 10 oxen, & 10 cows, &

C eawa, & C swina,   & higum an sundran D pend'   wið ðan
100 ewes, & 100 swine, & to monks separately 500 pennies provided

ðe min wiif þær benuge innganges swæ mid minum lice swæ
that my wife there have entry whether with my body or

sioððan yferran dogre, swæ hwæder swæ hire liofre sie.
after at a later date,   whichever (to) her preferable may be.

gif higan ðonne oððe hlaford þæt nylle hire mynsterlifes
If monks then or lord that not want (to) her monastic life

Holt, Rinehart and Winston, Inc.

geunnan, oðða hia siolf nylle,   & hire oðer ðing
to allow, or she herself not wants, & (to) her another thing

liofre sie,   þonne agefe mon   ten hund pend' inn
preferable be, then one should bestow 10 hundred pennies inside

mid minum lice me wið   legerstowe & higum an sundran
with my body in return for burial place & to monks separately

fif hund pend' fore mine sawle.
five hundred pennies for my soul.

    & ic bidde & bebeode swælc monn se ðæt min lond hebbe
    & I ask & command such man as   my land may have

ðæt he ælce gere agefe ðem higum æt folcanstane L ambra maltes,
that he each year give the monks at Folkstone 50 pails of malt.

of VI ambra gruta, & III wega   spices & ceses, & CCCC hlafa, &
& 6 pails of groats, & 3 measures of bacon & cheese, & 400 loaves, &

an hriðr, & VI scep. & swælc monn se ðe to minum ærfe foe,
one cow, & 6 sheep. & such man   as to my property takes,

ðonne gedele   he ælcum messepreoste binnan cent mancus
then should distribute he to each mass-priest inside 100 mancus

goldes, & ælcum   godes ðiowe   pend', & to sancte petre min
of gold, & (to) each of God's servants (a) penny, & to St. Peter my

wærgeld twa ðusenda. . . . & gif þæt gesele þæt min cynn to ðan
wergeld (of) two thousand. . . . & if it happens that my family after-

    clane   gewite ðæt   ðer ðeara nan ne sie ðe
ward completely depart so that there (of) them none be who (of)

londes weorðe sie, þonne foe se hlaford to & ða higan æt kristes
land worthy be, then take (it) the lord & monks at Christ's

cirican, & hit minum gaste nytt gedoen. . . .
church, & it (to) my soul's use put. . . .

    ic ciolnoð mid godes gefe ærcebiscop ðis write & ðeafie, &
    I Ciolnoð by God's grace archbishop this write & approve, &

mid cristes redetacne hit festniæ. ic beagmund pr' ðis ðeafie
with Christ's sign of cross it confirm. I Beagmund priest this confirm

& write. ic wærhard pr' ðis ðeafie & write.   ic abba geroefa ðis
& write. I Wærhard priest this approve & write. I Abba officer this

write & festnie mid Kristes rodetacne.   ic æðelhun pr' ðis
write & confirm with Christ's sign of cross. I Æðelhun priest this

ðeafie & write. ic abba pr' ðis þeafie & write. . . .
confirm & write. I Abba priest this confirm & write. . . .

    heregyð hafað ðas wisan binemned ofer hire deg & ofer abban.
    Heregyð has this director named over her day & over Abba's.

ðæm higum et cristes cirican of londe et cealflocan: ðæt is ðonne
(To) the monks at Christ's church from land at Cealfloc: it is then

ðritig ombra alað, ðreo hund   hlafa, ðeara bið   fiftig
thirty pails of ale, & three hundred loaves, of which will be fifty

Holt, Rinehart and Winston, Inc.

hwitehlafa, an weg   spices & ceses, an ald hriðr, feower
white loaves, 1 measure (of) bacon & cheese, one old ox, four

weðras, an suin oððe weðras,   sex gosfuglas, ten hennfuglas,
wethers, one swine or six wethers, six geese,   ten hens,

ðritig teapera, gif hit wintres deg sie, sester fulne huniges,
thirty tapers, if it winter's day be, measure full (of) honey,

sester fulne butran,   sester fulne saltes.   & heregyð bibeadeð
measure full (of) butter, measure full (of) salt. & Heregyð instructs

ðem mannum ðe efter hire to londe foen on godes noman ðæt hie
the people who after her to land take in God's name that they

fulgere witen   ðæt hie ðiss gelesten   ðe on ðissem gewrite
very well take care that they this carry out which in this document

binemned is ðem higum to cristes cirican . . .
named is (to) the monks at Christ's church . . .

VIII. Ælfric's Lives of the Saints: St. Cecilia

The prolific Ælfric was also the author of thirty-seven homilies detailing the suffering, martyrdom, and miracles of saints. These saints' lives are written in an alliterative prose that so resembles alliterative verse that early editors often printed them as verse. The selection here is the closing lines of his life of St. Cecilia.

Almachius hire andwyrde, "Awurp þine dyrstignysse and geoffra
Almachius her answered, "Cast aside your insolence and offer

þam godum arwurðlice onsægednysse." Cecilia him cwæð to, "Cunna
to the gods honorable sacrifice."   Cecilia to him said, "Test

mid grapunge hwæðer hi stanas synd and stænene anlicnysse, þa
by touching whether they stones are and stone idols,   those

þe þu godas gecigst, begotene mid leade, and þu miht swa witan
which you gods call, covered with lead, and you can thus find out

gewislice mid grapunge gif ðu geseon ne miht þæt hi synd stanas.
for sure by touching   if you see not can that they are stones.

Hi mihton wel   to lime gif man hi lede on ad. Nu
They would completely (turn) to lime if one them put in fire. Now

hi ne fremiað him sylfum, ne, soðlice, mannum, and hi mihton
they not help themselves, nor, truly, men, and they would

     to lime gif hi man lede on fyr."
(turn) to lime if them one put in fire."

     þa   wearð se arleasa dema deoflice   gram and het
     Then became the wicked judge diabolically angry and ordered

hi lædan sona and seoðan on wætere on hire agenum huse for þæs
her led at once and boiled in water in her own house for the

hælendes naman. þa dydon þa hæþenan swa swa hi het
Savior's name. Then did the heathens just as them ordered

almachius; and heo læg on þam bæðe bufan byrnendum fyre
Almachius; and she lay in that bath over (a) burning fire

Holt, Rinehart and Winston, Inc.

ofer dæg and niht   ungederodum lichaman, swa swa on cealdum
throughout day & night (with) uninjured body, as if   in cold

wætere, þæt heo ne swætte furðon. Hi cyddon þa almachie hu
water, so that she not sweat even. They told then Almachius how

þæt mæden þurh-wunode on þam hatum baðe mid halum
the maiden persevered   in the hot bath   with healthy

lichaman, and furþon butan swate. þa sende he ænne cwellere
body,   and even without sweat. Then sent he an executioner

to   and het hi beheafdian on þam hatan wætere. Se cwellere
to (her) & ordered to behead her in the hot water. The executioner

hi sloh þa mid his swurde, æne eft, and þryddan siðe, ac hire swura
her struck with his sword, once again, & third time, but her neck

næs forod.   and he forlet hi sona   swa samcuce
not was cut through. And he left her immediately as half-alive

licgan forþam-þe witan cwædon þæt nan cwellere ne sceolde feower
to lie because counselors said that no executioner not should four

siðan slean to þonne man sloge scyldigne. Heo leofode þa þry dagas,
times strike   when one struck (a) criminal. She lived then 3 days,

and þa geleaffullan tihte and hire mædena betæhte   þam maran
and the faithful (she) taught & her maids entrusted (to) the splendid

papan and hire hus wearð gehalgod to haligre cyrcan. þær wurdon
pope and her house was sanctified as holy church. There were,

þurh god wundra gelome   and urbanus se papa bebyrigde hi
through God, miracles often (done), and Urban the pope buried her

arwurðlice to wuldre   þam ælmihtigan þe on ecnysse rixað.
honorably to (the) glory (of) the Almighty who in eternity reigns.

Holt, Rinehart and Winston, Inc.

CHAPTER 6

MIDDLE ENGLISH

6.1 Important Terms and Names

1. analytic language
2. Anglo-French
3. anomalous verb
4. back formation
5. Black Death
6. blend (portmanteau word)
7. Carolingian minuscule
8. causative verb
9. Central French
10. clipping
11. closed syllable
12. compounding
13. cumulative sentence
14. Danelaw
15. digraph
16. double possessive
17. East Midland dialect
18. epenthetic vowel
19. folk etymology
20. group possessive
21. Hundred Years' War
22. impersonal verb
23. Insular hand
24. isogloss
25. London dialect
26. Middle English dialects
27. modal auxiliary
28. Norman Conquest
29. Norman French
30. noun adjunct
31. Old Norse
32. open syllable
33. perfect infinitive
34. periodic sentence
35. periphrastic construction
36. progressive tense
37. quasi-modal
38. Scandinavian loans
39. synthetic language
40. voiced fricative
41. William the Conqueror

Holt, Rinehart and Winston, Inc.

6.2   Questions for Review and Discussion

1. Summarize the effects of the Norman Conquest on the English language.
2. What happened to the use of French in England over the course of the ME period?
3. Norman French, and later Anglo-French, differed from Central (Parisian) French. What were the implications of this fact for the English language?
4. What influence did the Hundred Years' War have on the history of English?
5. How did the Black Death affect the English language?
6. What were the effects of the Danelaw settlement on the English language?
7. When and where did a ''standard'' English begin to arise?
8. On what dialect was the rising new standard based?
9. We have few texts that show a linguistic continuity between OE and ME. Explain.
10. How did the consonant phonemes of English change during the ME period?
11. What happened to the OE diphthongs during ME?
12. Explain the influence of open and closed syllables on ME vowels.
13. How was English word stress influenced by the thousands of French loanwords introduced during ME?
14. Summarize the changes in the English alphabet during ME.
15. What influence did the French have on English spelling?
16. What change in handwriting styles took place during ME?
17. What are some of the probable reasons for the nearly total loss of English inflections during ME?
18. What happened to OE strong and weak adjectives in ME?
19. Where did the PDE forms of the third-person plural pronouns come from?
20. Where did the PDE form *she* come from?
21. What happened to the OE demonstrative adjectives/pronouns during ME?
22. Describe the development of OE strong verbs during ME.
23. Did the number of English prepositions increase or decrease during ME?
24. Where did the indefinite article *a/an* come from?
25. List a few PDE syntactic features that originated during ME.
26. How did the use of the negative in ME differ from its use in PDE?
27. What are the probable origins of the PDE progressive tense?
28. What happened to impersonal verbs during ME?
29. How did the word order of sentences with pronoun objects in ME differ from that of PDE?
30. What were the major sources of loanwords during ME?
31. How did Scandinavian loanwords differ from French loans?
32. Which foreign influence provided new place-name elements in ME?
33. What were some of the minor ways of forming new words during ME?
34. Was the majority of the OE vocabulary retained in ME?
35. Suggest reasons why narrowing was the commonest type of semantic change from OE to ME.
36. What are the traditional five major dialectal areas of ME? Why is this division unsatisfactory?
37. What major change in English poetics occurred during ME?

gossamer _goose_

holiday _____

kindred _____

Lammas _____

lit _____

nostril _____

sheriff _____

southern _____

stealth _____

throttle _____

utter (extreme) _____

width _____

Holt, Rinehart and Winston, Inc.

6.5   Phonology: Sporadic Sound Changes

In addition to systematic changes in consonants and vowels, ME experienced numerous sporadic sound changes that involved only a limited number of words. Among the types of sporadic sound changes were the following:

A. Addition of unetymological consonants, as when PDE *drowned* is pronounced [drɑʊndɪd]

B. Loss of consonants, as when PDE *husband* is pronounced [həzbən]

C. Dissimilation, when one of the two similar or identical sounds in a word is changed, as when Latin *turtur* became English *turtle*

D. False division, when the boundary between two words that frequently appear together is shifted, as when PDE *ice cream* is pronounced as if it were *I scream*

E. Metathesis, or the inversion of the order of two sounds in a word, as when PDE *nuclear* is pronounced [nukələr]

Each of the following words underwent one of the listed changes (A–E) during ME. Use a college dictionary to determine the earlier form of the word and put it in the blank to the right. Identify the type of change in the blank to the left. Some words may show more than one type of change.

0. __E__ dirt _ME drit < ON drit_

1. ____ pomander _____

2. ____ sister _____

3. ____ spindle _____

4. ____ nonce _____

5. ____ slumber _____

6. ____ lawn (grass) _____

7. ____ hasp _____

8. ____ messenger _____

9. ____ marble _____

10. ____ passenger _____

11. ____ adder (snake) _____

12. ____ curl _____

13. ____ scrimmage _____

14. ____ newt _____

15. ____ mulberry _____

16. ____ tine _____

17. ____ eyas _____

18. ____ thrill _____

Name _____

6.6 Graphics: Changes in the Spelling of Consonants

A. Listed below are a number of OE words with digraphs (two letters representing a single sound, as in PDE ⟨ch⟩ = [č]), along with typical spellings of these same words in ME. By examining the list, decide how the OE digraphs were changed in ME. Note that some of them were spelled in more than one way in ME.

OE ecg 'edge'; ME egge, edge
OE fisc 'fish'; ME fishsh, fischche, etc.
OE hricg 'ridge'; ME rigge, ridge
OE hwæl 'whale'; ME whale
OE hwæte 'wheat'; ME whete
OE hweol 'wheel'; ME wheele
OE hwit 'white'; ME white
OE mycg 'midge'; ME migge, mydge
OE nahwær 'nowhere'; ME nowher
OE scal 'shall'; ME schal, ssel, shal, xal, etc.
OE scearp 'sharp'; ME scharp, sharp, ssarp, etc.
OE scield 'shield'; ME shild, schilde, etc.
OE scort 'short'; ME short, schort, etc.
OE wecg 'wedge'; ME wegge
OE wyscan 'wish'; ME wisshen, wisse, whysshe, etc.

OE *cg* → ME _____

OE *sc* → ME _____

OE *hw* → ME _____

B. Listed below are a number of words in their OE and ME spellings. By examining the list, you should be able to describe the graphic (spelling) environments that determined the change in spelling of OE *c* during ME.

OE candel 'candle'; ME candel
OE castel 'castle'; ME castel
OE cese 'cheese'; ME chese
OE cest 'chest'; ME chest
OE ciele 'chill'; ME chile
OE cild 'child'; ME child
OE clæg 'clay'; ME clay
OE cleofan 'cleave'; ME cleven
OE cnif 'knife'; ME knif
OE cniht 'knight'; ME kniht
OE corn 'corn'; ME corn
OE crypel 'cripple'; ME crepel
OE cuppe 'cup'; ME cup

OE cwalm 'qualm'; ME qualm

Holt, Rinehart and Winston, Inc.

OE cwellan 'quell'; ME quell
OE (a)cwencan 'quench'; ME quenchen
OE cweorn 'quern'; ME quern
OE cycene 'kitchen'; ME kichene
OE kynd 'kind'; ME kind
OE cyrnel 'kernel'; ME kernell

OE *c* → ME *c*   before ⟨a⟩, _____

OE *c* → ME *ch* _____

OE *c* → ME *k* _____

OE *c* → ME *q* _____

C.   The graphemes *g* and *h* each represented more than one sound in OE, though the distinction was not made in writing. In ME, these sounds came to be spelled differently, although not necessarily consistently. Examine the following lists and determine the written environments under which the ME spellings of OE *g* and *h* appeared.

OE behindan 'behind'; ME behinde(n)
OE beorht 'bright'; ME brycht, briȝt, brigth, etc.
OE feohtan 'to fight'; ME fiȝten, fyghte, fecht, fyþt, etc.
OE frogge 'frog'; ME frog(e), frogge, etc.
OE gærs 'grass'; ME grasse, grase, etc.
OE gamen 'game'; ME game(n)
OE gearn 'yarn'; ME ȝern, yarn, etc.
OE geolu 'yellow'; ME ȝelwa, ȝealwe, yelow, etc.
OE gielpan 'yelp'; ME yelpe, ȝelpen, etc.
OE giet 'yet'; ME ȝit, ȝet, yet, etc.
OE gif 'if'; ME ȝif, yef, etc.
OE glæs 'glass'; ME gles, glas(e), etc.
OE gnæt 'gnat'; ME gnatte, gnet, etc.
OE gold 'gold'; ME gold(e)
OE grædig 'greedy'; ME gredie, gredy, gredi, etc.
OE gylt 'guilt'; ME gult(e), gelte, guilt(e), etc.
OE heah 'high'; ME hegh, heeȝ, hye, heich, heigh, etc.
OE hefig 'heavy'; ME heui, heuy, hevye, etc.
OE hlid 'lid'; ME lede, lid(e)
OE hliehhan 'laugh'; ME leuhwen, lahȝhhen, lauch, lawhe, etc.
OE hnecca 'neck'; ME nekke, necke
OE hogg 'hog'; ME hogge, hog
OE hring 'ring'; ME ring(e), reynge, ryng, etc.
OE hulu 'hull'; ME hul, hull
OE mæg 'may'; ME mai, may
OE oferherian 'overhear'; ME ouerhere(n)
OE pægel 'pail'; ME payle, paille, payelle, etc.
OE ruh 'rough'; ME rowgh, roch, rowhe, rough, etc.
OE sarig 'sorry'; ME sary, sori, etc.
OE segl 'sail'; ME sail(le)
OE sihþ 'sight'; ME sihthe, syhte, sycht, siȝhte, siȝt, etc.
OE singan 'to sing'; ME singe(n)
OE unhalig 'unholy'; ME unholi, vnholy, vnhooli, etc.

OE *g* → ME *g* _____

OE *g* → ME *ȝ, i, y* _____

OE *h* → ME *h* _____

OE *h* → ME *ch, gt, ȝh, ȝ, wh*, etc. _____

OE *h* → ME ∅ _ when OE ⟨h⟩ preceded ⟨r, n, l⟩ at beginning of syllable _____

6.7   Graphics: ME Handwriting

The text reproduced here is the top part of a page from the Bodley Rawlinson D.99 manuscript of *Mandeville's Travels*, a popular medieval narrative (see p. 218, *A Biography of the English Language*). The manuscript was written in the first half of the fifteenth century. The handwriting is exceptionally clear and legible for this late date.

The first five lines of the passage have been transliterated for you, and a word-for-word gloss of the entire text is provided. Complete the transliteration of the passage.

Holt, Rinehart and Winston, Inc.

Name _____

ȝE shal vnderstonde þat this Babilonye þat I speke of where þe
Ye shall understand that this Babylon   that I speak of where the

Sawdoun dwelleþ is a gret   Cite and fair enhabited. but it is noȝt
Sultan   dwells   is a great city and fair inhabited   but it is not

the Babilonye where the confusioũn and dyuersite of tungis   was made
the Babylon   where the confusion   and diversity of tongues was made

whanne the Tour   of Babilonye was in makinge the wiche is in deserte
when   the Tower of Babylon   was in making   the which is in desert

of Arabie. ffor it is long tyme sithenes þat any man durst   þider goen
of Arabia. For it is long time since   that any man dared there go

__ ____ ____ ____ __ _____ ___ __ __ ___ __ _____ ___ ___
to visit that same wretched place For it is full of vermin and dragons

__ ____ ___ ____ _____ ____ __ __ _____ ____ ___ ___
and adders and many other venom(ous) beasts for the vengeance that God

____ __ ___ _____ __ ___ ____ __ ___ __ ____ ____ ____ ___
took at the beginning of that tower (so) that no man dares come there. ¶And

_____ __ ___ ____ ___ ___ _____ __ ___ ___ ___ ____ ___
the circle of that tower with the compass of the city of Babylon that there

_____ ___ _____ ____ _____ ___ ____ ____ ___ __ __
was   once   contains   25   miles   around.   But   nevertheless   if   it   be

____ __ ____ ___ ___ ___ ___ __ ___ ___ ___ ___ ___
called   a   tower,   yet   there   was   once   in   that   circle   many   fair   edi-

____ ___ ___ __ ____ ___ ___ ___ __ _____ ___ ___ ___ ___
fices that now is destroyed and become all wilderness and that same tower

__ _____ _____ __ ___ __   _____Nembrok __ ___ __ __
of Babylon founded the king that (is) called Nimrod that was king of that

___ ___ _____ __ ___ ___ ___ ____ ___ ___ __ __ ___
land and thereof he was the first king that ever was on earth. ¶And that

_____ ____ ____ ___ __ _ __ ____ ____ ____ ___Ryuere
same Babylon was once set on a fair plain field upon the River

1. What major differences in graphics do you find here from the OE facsimile in the
preceding chapter? _____

_____

_____

_____

2. Are any OE letters missing? _____

If so, what has replaced them? _____

Are there any new letters? _____

Holt, Rinehart and Winston, Inc.

3. Do *y* and *i* have different sound values? _____

How do you know? _____

_____

4. What evidence for a lack of fixed spelling do you find? _____

_____

5. The letter *s* has three different physical forms in this passage. What are they? _____

Is their distribution arbitrary? Explain. _____

_____

6. The letter *z* appears only once. To what other letter is it very similar? _____

7. What is unusual about the formation of the sequences *da*, *de*, and *do*? _____

_____

8. What does a wavy line over a vowel mean? _____

_____

9. What is the abbreviation for *er* (lines 3, 6, 9, 10, 14)? _____

_____

Holt, Rinehart and Winston, Inc.

Name _____

6.8   Morphology: Adjective Inflections

During ME, all the OE adjectival inflections were lost except for a trace of the earlier strong versus weak declensions. Even here, the distinction was retained only for monosyllabic adjectives ending in a consonant. For these, a strong singular adjective had no ending; strong plural adjectives and both singular and plural weak adjectives ended in *-e.*

	Strong	*Weak*
Sg.	blind	blinde
Pl.	blinde	blinde

Adjectives were weak if they appeared

  a. after a definite article, a demonstrative adjective, a possessive pronoun, or a possessive noun
  b. in direct address

Adjectives were strong if they appeared

  a. without a preceding definite article, demonstrative, or possessive
  b. in predicate adjective position

This remaining inflectional distinction was breaking down during ME, and texts frequently show incorrect forms (although sometimes a seemingly incorrect form can also be interpreted as a remnant of an OE dative).

For the following sentences or phrases, state whether the italicized adjective is *strong* or *weak*, and identify the reason as (a) or (b) as outlined above. If the distinction does not apply because the adjective is polysyllabic or ends in a vowel, write *not applicable* in the blank. Finally, note whether the usage is correct or incorrect according to the rules described above. The base form of the adjective is provided for you.

  0. Alss *wise* men haue writen the wordes before. (Base form: *wis*)
     As

  Strong, (a), correct plural
  _____

  1. Bothe failet hym the fode and the *fyne* clothes (Base: *fyn*)
        he lacked   food

  _____

  2. Ethiope is departed in two *princypall* parties (Base: *princypall*)
              divided   parts

  _____

  3. God . . . chargiþ not siche song, but . . . *goode* werkis (Base: *good*)
        orders   such singing   works

  _____

  4. Goth henne swiþe, *fule* þeues! (Base: *ful*)
     Go   away quickly, foul thieves

  _____

  5. Of *green* jaspe and *rede* corale (Bases: *gren, red*)
        green jasper   red coral

  Both are Strong-(a)-Incorrect, but could be remnants of a dative ending
  _____

Holt, Rinehart and Winston, Inc.

6. Rideȝ þurȝ   þe *roȝe* bonk ryȝt to þe dele (Base: *roȝ*)
    Rides through the rough slope   valley

---

7. þai counted no course of the *cold* stormys (Base: *cold*)
    took no account

---

8. þat him was so *hard* grace yȝarked (Base: *hard*)
    to him   (a) fate ordained

---

9. þat welle ys . . . noȝt *deop* bote to þe kneo (Base: *deop*)
    not deep just   knee

---

10. þat with the Grekys was *gret*, and of Grice comyn (Base: *gret*)
    that (one)   great   from Greece come

---

11. þe Franche men er *fers* and *fell* (Bases: *fers*, *fell*)
    fierce   cruel

---

12. þe *swifte* barge was Duk Henri (Base: *swyft*)
    Duke Henry's

---

13. þes foolis schullen lerne what is *actif* lif and *contemplatif*
    (Bases: *actif*, *contemplatif*)

---

14. þis *goode* schip I may remene (Base: *good*)
    interpret

---

15. This Yris, fro the *hihe* stage (Base: *hih*)
    Iris, from   high

---

16. Vnder a *fair* ympe-tre (Base: *fair*)
    sapling

---

17. when þe weder was *clere* and *briȝt* (Bases: *clere*, *briȝt*)
    weather

Name _____

6.10   Morphology: Strong and Weak Verbs

A.   During ME, many verbs that had been strong in OE became weak, though the period still had many more strong verbs than does PDE. In a very few instances, previously weak verbs became strong. The following sentences are from ME texts from the thirteenth through the fifteenth centuries. An (S) after the underlined verb means that it was strong in OE; a (W) means that it was weak. (OF) means that it was a French loan into ME, and (ON) means that it was a Norse loan. Indicate by an (S) or a (W) whether the verb is strong or weak in the ME excerpt, and then indicate whether it is strong or weak in PDE.

1. And feendes . . . <u>stode</u> (S) _S,S_ on iche halfe on hym and <u>shewed</u> (W) ____
   And fiends   stood   on each side of him and showed

   vnto hym all is liff . . . and <u>weyden</u> (S) ____ þem in a balaunce.
   to him all his life   and weighed   them in a balance.

2. Suilk als þei <u>brued</u> (S) ____ now ha þai <u>dronken</u> (S) ____.
   Such as they brewed   now have they drunk.

3. Gnattes gretely me <u>greuede</u> (OF) ____ and <u>gnewen</u> (S) ____ myn eghne.
   Gnats greatly me grieved   and gnawed   my eyes.

4. þo <u>wex</u> (S) ____ her hertes niþful and bold, /
   Then waxed   their hearts envious and bold

   Quanne he hem adde is dremes <u>told</u> (W) ____.
   when he them had his dreams told.

5. Scho <u>wippe</u> (S) ____ and hir hondis <u>wronge</u> (S) ____.
   She wept   and her hands wrung.

6. He had <u>lepte</u> (S) ____ in to the ryver and <u>drowned</u> (ON) ____
   He had leapt   into the river and drowned

   hym-self . . . Thei did his comaundement and <u>lepe</u>
   himself . . . They did his commandment and leapt

   (S) ____ to horse.
   to horse.

7. And whan þis creatur was þus gracyowsly <u>comen</u> (S) ____
   And when this creature was thus graciously come

   ageyn to hir mende, sche <u>thowt</u> (W) ____ she was <u>bowndyn</u>
   again to her mind, she thought   she was bound

   (S) ____ to god.
   to God.

8. hir yonge sone Iulo, / And eke Ascanius also, / <u>Fledden</u> (S) ____.
   her young son Iulus, And also Ascanius also, Fled.

9. Lewed men <u>leued</u> (W) ____ hym wel and <u>lyked</u> (W) ____
   Laymen believed   him well and liked

   his wordes, <u>Comen</u> (S) ____ vp knelyng to kissen his bulles.
   his words, came   up kneeling to kiss his documents.

10. The ladye <u>lough</u> (S) _____ a loud laughter, / As shee <u>sate</u> (S) _____ by the king.
    The lady laughed   a loud laughter   As she sat   by the king.

11. I have <u>yelded</u> (S) _____ you agen that ye <u>lended</u> (W) _____ me right now.
    I have yielded (repaid) you back what you lent   me right now.

12. þey <u>founde</u> (S) _____ a mannis hede in þat place while þey digged (OF) _____.
    They found   a man's head in that place while they dug.

13. Y <u>dwelled</u> (W) _____ yn þe pryorye fyftene ȝere yn cumpanye.
    I dwelt   in the priory fifteen years in company.

14. He seynge the citee, <u>wepte</u> (S) _____ on it.
    He seeing the city,   wept   about it.

15. and so long he <u>knawed</u> (S) _____ it that the lace <u>brake</u> (S) _____.
    and so long he gnawed   it that the lace broke.

16. He set ane sege thar-to stoutly, / And <u>lay</u> (S) _____
    He set a siege thereto stoutly,   And lay

    thair quhill it <u>ȝolden</u> (S) _____ was.
    there until it yielded   was.

17. þenne þe burde byhynde þe dor for busmar <u>laȝed</u> (S) _____.
    Then the girl behind   the door for scorn laughed.

18. þi best cote . . . Hath many moles and spottes; it most be <u>ywasshe</u> (S) _____.
    Your best coat has many stains and spots;   it must be washed.

B.   A number of verbs in PDE are strong when intransitive (e.g., *shine/shone/shone*) but weak when transitive (*shine/shined/shined*). Other verbs have variant strong forms (e.g., *it shrank* or *it shrunk*) or variant weak forms (e.g., *I dreamt* or *I dreamed*). A few verbs have, in at least one of their principal parts, alternative strong and weak forms. One example is *show*, with variant past participles *showed* and *shown*. List a few more PDE verbs

of this last type. _____

_____

Holt, Rinehart and Winston, Inc.

6.11　Syntax

Reproduced here are two English translations of the gospel of St. John, 3:1–17, the first from OE and the second from ME. The OE text is from the Anglo-Saxon Gospels, c. 1000, and the ME text is from the Wycliffite version, 1389. Punctuation is modern. A complete gloss of the OE text is provided, along with a partial gloss of the ME text.

John 3:1–17, Old English

[1]Soþlice sum Phariseisc man wæs, genemned Nichodemus, se wæs
Truly a certain Pharisee man was, named　Nicodemus, who was

Iudea ealdor.　[2]Ðes　　com to him on niht, and cwæþ to him,
(of) Jews leader. This (one) came to him at night, and said to him,

Rabbi, ðæt is lareow, we witon, ðæt ðu come fram Gode; ne mæg
Rabbi, that is teacher, we know that you come from God; not can

nan man ðas tacn wyrcan ðe ðu wyrcest, buton God beo mid him.
no man these tokens work that you work　unless God be with him.

[3]Se Hælend him andswarode, and cwæþ, Soþ, ic ðe secge, buton
The Savior him answered　and said,　True, I (to) you say, unless

hwa beo edniwan gecenned, ne mæg he geseon Godes rice. [4]Ða
someone be anew born,　　not can he see God's kingdom. Then

cwæþ Nichodemus to him, Hu mæg man beon eft acenned, ðonne he biþ
said Nicodemus to him,　How can one be again born,　when he is

eald? Cwyst ðu mæg he eft cuman on his moder innoþ, and beon
old? Say you can he again come　in his mother's womb, and be

eft acenned? [5]Se Hælend him andswarode and cwæþ, Soþ, ic ðe
again born? The Savior him answered and said,　True, I (to) you

secge, buton hwa beo ge-edcenned of wætere, and of Haligum Gaste,
say, unless one be re-created　　by water, and by Holy Ghost,

ne mæg he in-faran on Godes rice.　[6]Ðæt ðe acenned is of flæsce,
not can he go in into God's kingdom. That which born is of flesh,

ðæt ys flæsc; and ðæt ðe of gaste　is acenned, ðæt is gast. [7]Ne
that is flesh; and that which of spirit is born, that is spirit. Not

wundra ðu, forðam ðe ic sæde ðe,　Eow gebyraþ ðæt ge beon
marvel you, because I said (to) you, (To) you befits that you be

acennede edniwan. [8]Gast oreðaþ ðar he wile,　　and ðu gehyrst his
born　again.　Spirit breathes where it wishes, and you hear its

stefne, and ðu nast,　　hwanon　he cymþ, ne hwyder he gæþ;
voice, and you do not know, from where it comes, nor where it goes;

swa is ælc ðe acenned is of gaste. [9]Ða andswarode Nichodemus, and
thus is each who born is of spirit. Then answered Nicodemus and

cwæþ, Hu magon ðas þing ðus geweorðan? [10]Se Hælend andswarode,
said, How can these things thus happen?　The Savior answered

Holt, Rinehart and Winston, Inc.

and cwæþ to him, Ðu eart lareow Israhela folce,   and ðu
and said to him, You are teacher (of) Israel people, and you

nast ðas þing?   [11]Soþ, ic ðe secge, ðæt we sprecaþ, ðæt
not know these things? True, I (to) you say, what we speak, that

we witon, and we cyðaþ, ðæt we gesawon, and ge ne underfoþ ure
we know, and we proclaim what we saw,   and you not receive our

cyðnesse. [12]Gif ic eow eorþlice þing sæde, and ge ne gelyfaþ,
testimony. If I (to) you earthly things said, and you not believe,

humeta gelyfe ge, gif ic eow heofenlice þing secge? [13]And nan man
how believe you, if I (to) you heavenly things say? And no man

ne astihþ to heofenum, buton se ðe   nyðer com of heofenum,
not ascends to heaven, except he who down came from heaven,

mannes sunu se ðe com of heofenum. [14]And swa swa Moyses ða
man's son   who came from heaven.   And just as Moses the

næddran up-ahof on ðam westene, swa gebyraþ ðæt mannes sunu
serpent up-raised in the desert,   so befits that man's son

beo up-ahofen, [15]Ðæt nan ðara ne forweorðe, ðe on hyne belyfþ,
be up-raised,   That none of those not perish, who in him believe,

ac hæbbe ðæt ece lif.   [16]God lufode middan-eard swa, ðæt he sealde
but have the eternal life. God loved world   so, that he gave

his an-cennedan sunu, ðæt nan ne forweorðe ðe on hine belyfþ, ac
his only-born son,   that none not perish   who in him believes, but

hæbbe ðæt ece lif.   [17]Ne sende God his sunu on middan-eard, ðæt
have the eternal life. Not sent God his son into   world   that

he demde middan-earde, ac ðæt middan-eard sy gehæled þurh hine.
he judge world,   but that world   be saved through him.

John 3:1–17, Middle English

[1]Forsothe ther was a man of Pharisees, Nicodeme bi name, a prince
Truly   by

of Jewis. [2]He cam to Jhesu in the nyȝte, and seide to him, Raby,
                    Jesus   night   Rabbi

We witen, for of God thou hast come a maister; sothli no man may
       know because from   teacher; truly   can

do thes signes that thou dost, no but God were with him. [3]Jhesu
                                    unless

answeride, and seyde to him, Treuli, treuli, I seye to thee, no but
                              Truly, truly,   unless

a man schal be born aȝen, he may not se the kyngdom of God.
              again,   can   see

[4]Nycodeme seide to him, How may a man be born, whanne he is
                              can   when

olde? wher he may entre aȝen in to his modris wombe, and be
     whether can   again   mother's

born aȝein? [5]Jhesus answeride, Treuli, treuli, I seie to thee, no but
   again?   *say*   *unless*

a man schal be born aȝen of watir, and of the Hooly Gost, he may
             again by   *by*   *can*

not entre in to the kyngdom of God. [6]That that is born of fleisch, is
                                  which

fleisch; and that that is born of spirit, is spirit. [7]Wondre thou not,
                                Do not marvel,

for I seye to thee, It behoueth ȝou for to be born aȝein. [8]The spirit
          behooves   *again.*

brethith wher it wole, and thou heerist his vois, but thou wost not,
breathes   *wishes,*   *hear its voice*   *know*

fro whennis he cometh, or whidir he goth; so is ech man that is
  where it   *where it goes*   *is (for) each*

borun of the spirit. [9]Nycodeme answeride, and seide to him, Hou
born

mown thes thingis be don? [10]Jhesu answeride, and seyde to him,
can these

Art thou a maister in Israel, and knowist not thes thingis? [11]Treuli,
      teacher

treuli, I seye to thee, for that that we witen, we speken, and that
                    know   *speak*

that we han seyn, we witnessen, and ȝe taken not our witnessing.
  have seen   *testify*   *you accept*

[12]If I haue seid to ȝou ertheli thingis, and ȝe bileuen not, how if I
    said   *you*   *believe*

schal seie to ȝou heuenli thingis, schulen ȝe bileue? [13]And no man
      heavenly   *shall you believe?*

styeth to heuene, no but he that cam doun fro heauene, mannis sone
ascends   *except*   *from*   *man's son*

that is in heuene. [14]And as Moyses reride vp a serpent in desert, so
           just as   *raised up*

it bihoueth mannus sone for to be areysid vp, [15]That ech man that
behooves man's son   *raised*   *each*

bileueth in to him, perische not, but haue euerelastinge lyf.
believes in

[16]Forsothe God so louede the world, that he ȝaf his oon bigetun
Truly   *loved*   *gave* *one begotten*

sone that ech man that bileueth in to him perische not, but haue
son so that

euere lasting lyf. [17]Sothli God sente not his sone in to the world,
          Truly

that he iuge the world, but that the world be sauyd by hym.
  judge   *saved*

Holt, Rinehart and Winston, Inc.

Name _____

For each of the categories listed below, note what changes in English syntax have occurred between the OE and the ME translations. (See *A Biography of the English Language*, Chapter 6, for general remarks about ME syntax.) Be sure to base your answers on the syntax of the original text, not on that of the gloss.

A.   The Syntax of Phrases

1. Position of noun modifiers _____

_____

2. Use of definite and indefinite articles _____

_____

3. Position of adverbial modifiers _____

_____

4. Negation of verbs _____

_____

5. Prepositional phrases (frequency; number of different prepositions used) _____

_____

6. Verb phrases

   a. Use of perfect tense (*have* + past participle) _____

   _____

   b. Formation and use of passive _____

   _____

   c. Formation and use of future _____

   _____

   d. Use of modal auxiliaries _____

   _____

   e. Expression of passive infinitive _____

   _____

B.   The Syntax of Clauses

1. Word order in independent clauses _____

_____

2. Word order in subordinate clauses _____

_____

3. Word order of questions _____

_____

4. Word order of imperatives _____

_____

5. Impersonal verbs and "dummy" subjects (*there*; *it*) _____

_____

_____

C. Reproduced here is the text of the same passage from the Revised Standard Version of the Bible of 1952.

[1]Now there was a man of the Pharisees, named Nicodemus, a ruler of the Jews. [2]This man came to Jesus by night and said to him, "Rabbi, we know that you are a teacher come from God; for no one can do these signs that you do, unless God is with him." [3]Jesus answered him, "Truly, truly, I say to you, unless one is born anew, he cannot see the kingdom of God." [4]Nicodemus said to him, "How can a man be born when he is old? Can he enter a second time into his mother's womb and be born?" [5]Jesus answered, "Truly, truly, I say to you, unless one is born of water and the Spirit, he cannot enter the kingdom of God. [6]That which is born of the flesh is flesh, and that which is born of the Spirit is spirit. [7]Do not marvel that I said to you, 'You must be born anew.' [8]The wind blows where it wills, and you hear the sound of it, but you do not know whence it comes or whither it goes; so it is with every one who is born of the Spirit." [9]Nicodemus said to him, "How can this be?" [10]Jesus answered him, "Are you a teacher of Israel, and yet you do not understand this? [11]Truly, truly, I say to you, we speak of what we know, and bear witness to what we have seen; but you do not receive our testimony. [12]If I have told you earthly things and you do not believe, how can you believe if I tell you heavenly things? [13]No one has ascended into heaven but he who descended from heaven, the Son of man. [14]And as Moses lifted up the serpent in the wilderness, so must the Son of man be lifted up, [15]that whoever believes in him may have eternal life." [16]For God so loved the world that he gave his only Son, that whoever believes in him should not perish but have eternal life. [17]For God sent the Son into the world, not to condemn the world, but that the world might be saved through him.

Compare the syntax of the ME text with that of the PDE text. Is the syntax of the ME text more similar to that of the OE or to that of the PDE text? Give specific examples.

_____

_____

_____

_____

_____

_____

Holt, Rinehart and Winston, Inc.

Name _____

6.12   Lexicon: Loanwords and Native Words

The Norman Conquest changed the entire fabric of the English vocabulary, partly through the thousands of French loanwords that resulted directly from the Conquest and partly because English thereafter became permanently receptive to loanwords from virtually any source. Today it is difficult to write even a paragraph without using at least a few loanwords. Still, it can be done.

On a separate piece of paper, rewrite the following paragraph using only native English words. In your dictionary, these will have *O.E.* or *A-S* (and perhaps also *Germanic*) listed as their ultimate source. To save time in looking up etymologies, treat all personal pronouns; the conjunctions *and*, *but*, and *or*; all parts of the verbs *to be* and *to have*; and all prepositions of four or fewer letters as native words (even this is not quite accurate because *they*, *them*, and *their* are from Old Norse). If a word is affixed, look up the base; for example, for the word *unsuccessfully*, look up *success*. Leave all proper nouns as they are in the passage. Whenever your dictionary lists the direct source of one of the words in the passage as a language other than English, look the word up in the *OED*, note the date of its first recorded appearance in English, and enter the word and the date on the appropriate line.

By the eleventh century, the English and the Norse had achieved an uneasy peace, and the Norse settlers were becoming assimilated into English society. But in 1066, another invasion occurred that was to have a great effect on the history of English. Taking advantage of a somewhat dubious claim to the throne of England, William of Normandy (William the Conqueror) successfully invaded and then took over England. William and most of his followers were racially Germanic, but their ancestors had abandoned their original language for French when they settled in Normandy during the ninth and tenth centuries A.D. Hence the language brought to England by William was French. French became the official language of the court, of law, and of administration for the next 300 to 350 years. However, there were many more English people than French people in England, and the conquered English continued to speak their native language. Many natives surely learned to speak French, but the French also had to learn at least some English in order to be able to speak to their English servants. The English spoken and written from about 1100 (that is, shortly after the Conquest) until about 1500 is called Middle English.

French Loanwords

_____   _____   _____

_____   _____   _____

_____   _____   _____

_____   _____   _____

_____   _____   _____

_____   _____   _____

_____   _____   _____

Latin Loanwords

_____ _____ _____
_____ _____ _____
_____ _____ _____

Old Norse Loanwords

_____ _____ _____
_____ _____ _____

1. Which words did you find it most difficult to replace with native equivalents? _____

_____

2. How does your "translation" differ from the original passage? _____

_____

_____

3. Comment on the date of entry into English of the words from French, Latin, and Old Norse. _____

_____

_____

4. How do the Norse loans differ from the French and Latin loans? Suggest reasons for this difference. _____

_____

_____

Holt, Rinehart and Winston, Inc.

Name _____

6.13   Lexicon: Minor Processes of Word Formation

I. Among the minor processes of word formation in ME were
   A. **Clipping**, in which the latter part of a word (as in PDE *recap* from *recapitulation*) or the first part (as in PDE *mum* from *chrysanthemum*) is dropped, creating a new, shorter word.
   B. **Back-formation**, in which a new word is formed by mistakenly interpreting an existing word as having been derived from it, as in PDE *peeve* from *peevish*.
   C. New words from **proper nouns**, as in PDE *limerick* from Limerick, Ireland, or *farad* from (Michael) Faraday.
   D. **Folk etymology**, in which an unfamiliar word is altered to make it seem more familiar or to fit English patterns more closely, as in PDE *alewife* (fish) from earlier *allowes*.

Using a college dictionary, check the etymologies of the following words that first appeared in ME. (In some instances, the process took place prior to the word's being borrowed into English.) Write the original form in the space to the right. Indicate which process is involved by writing the appropriate letter (A–D) in the space to the left.

a. ____ mace (spice) _____   g. ____ peal (ring) _____

b. ____ lapwing _____   h. ____ polecat _____

c. ____ pheasant _____   i. ____ sample _____

d. ____ noisome _____   j. ____ magnet _____

e. ____ chat _____   k. ____ patter (talk) _____

f. ____ gun _____   l. ____ wall-eyed _____

II. The following new words in ME, some native and some borrowed, are all derived from either phrases or other parts of speech. Find the origin of each in a dictionary and write it in the space to the right.

a. placebo _____   d. debonair _____

b. bastard _____   e. memento _____

c. constable _____   f. ado _____

III. All of the following words borrowed during ME ultimately derive from animal names. Identify the animals.

a. arctic _____   f. chameleon _____

b. cockney _____   g. chivalry _____

c. pedigree _____   h. dauphin _____

d. musket _____   i. marshal _____

e. spermaceti _____

6.14   Lexicon: Lost Vocabulary

Biblical translations tend to be highly conservative in their language, partly because of the religious nature of the texts and partly because of translators' awareness of previous translations. For example, the language of the King James Bible was old-fashioned by the time it first appeared in 1611; the same is true of much of the language of the Revised Standard Version of 1952. Consequently, when we find lexical replacements from one translation to a later one, we can at least suspect that the words used in the earlier translation were no longer suitable (though, of course, words are also sometimes replaced because of the stylistic preferences of the translators). The following excerpts are from a late OE and a ME translation of Matthew 13:44–46.

Anglo-Saxon Gospels, c. 1000

[44]Heofona rice is gelic   gehyddum gold-horde on ðam æcere,
Heaven's kingdom is like hidden treasure   in the field,

ðone behyt se man   ðe hine fint; and for his blysse gæþ, and
which hides the man who it finds; and because of his joy goes, and

sylþ eall ðæt he ah,   and gebigþ ðone æcer. [45]Eft is heofena
sells all that he owns, and buys that field.   Again is heaven's

rice gelic ðam mangere,   ðe sohte ðæt gode meregrot; [46]Ða he
kingdom like the monger,   who sought the good pearl;   When he

funde ðæt an deorwyrðe meregrot, ða eode he, and sealde eall ðæt
found the one precious   pearl,   then went he, and sold all that

he ahte,   and bohte ðæt meregrot.
he owned, and bought that pearl.

Wycliffite Gospels, 1389

[44]The kyngdame of heuenes is lijk to tresour   hid in a feeld,
The kingdom of heaven   is like to treasure hidden in a field,

the whiche a man that fyndith, hidith; and for ioye of it he goth,
the which a man   that finds, hides;   and for joy of it he goes,

and sellith alle thingis that hath,   and bieth the ilk feeld. [45]Eftsones
and sells   all things that (he) has, and buys the same field. Again

the kyngdam of heuenes is lic to a man marchaunt,   seekyng good
the kingdom of heaven is like to a man merchant,   seeking good

margarytis; [46]Sothely oo preciouse margarite founden, he wente,
pearls;   Truly one precious   pearl found,   he went,

and solde alle thingis that he hadde, and bouȝte it.
and sold all   things that he had,   and bought it.

Holt, Rinehart and Winston, Inc.

Name _____

1. The following words from the Anglo-Saxon version have been replaced in the Wycliffite version. Look each of them up in the *OED* and write the date of the *latest* citation given there for each in the meaning intended in the OE text.

rice _____

gold-horde (*gold-hoard*) _____

æcere (*acre*) _1635 in nonpoetic context; 1844 in poetry_____

blysse (*bliss*) _____

ah (*owe*) _____

mangere (*monger*) _____

deorwyrðe (*dearworth*) _____

eode (look under *go*) _____

2. The following words from the Wycliffite version replace the words listed in item 1. Check the origin and first citation in English of each in the *OED*. If the word was used in its meaning here in OE, simply write OE.

kyngdame _____

tresour _____

feeld _____

ioye _____

hath _____

marchaunt _____

preciouse _____

wente _____

3. What is the first citation in the *OED* for *acre* in the meaning of a definite measure of land? _____ How might this have affected the decision of the translators of the Wycliffite version to use the word *field* instead? _____

_____

4. Which of the replaced words from the Anglo-Saxon passage are totally lost (in all meanings) today? _____

_____

5. What are the sources of the newly appearing words in the Wycliffite passage? _____

_____

6. What type of semantic shift in the meaning of *mangere* (monger) was already taking place by the time of the Wycliffite text? _____

_____

7. Both the King James Bible (1611) and the Revised Standard Version (1952) use the word *joy* in Matthew 13:44. What type of semantic shift has *bliss* undergone that makes it unsuitable in this context today? _____

_____

Holt, Rinehart and Winston, Inc.

Name _____

6.15   Semantic Change

Many of the words borrowed during the ME period had already undergone significant semantic change from their etymons in Latin or Greek. Using a good dictionary, find the *ultimate* root of the following loanwords in ME.

1. comet _____

2. coward _____

3. faucet _____

4. noise _____

5. pupil (of the eye) _____

6. story (floor) _____

7. tercel _____

8. chapel _____

9. calculate _____

10. sinister _____

6.16　ME Dialects

As your text explains, the dialectal picture during the ME period was very complex. After the Norman Conquest, dialectal differences proliferated, partly because, with French as the official language, English was written down less frequently than before, and there was no standard for English to serve as a brake on linguistic change. The different regions of England developed their own scribal habits and traditions to some extent, but how closely these reflected differences in speech is uncertain.

Despite all the complexities, one can usually, with a little experience, identify the general area in which a text was written, although more specific location of texts requires specialized knowledge and practice beyond the scope of the novice.

Reproduced here are four texts, all written within approximately a 25-year period and all reasonably pure representatives of their regions of origin, which we can call North, South, East Midlands, and West Midlands. Following the texts is a chart outlining some of the typical characteristics of each region. You will not find all of the features in any one text and you will encounter anomalies. Nonetheless, you should be able to identify the general geographical area in which each of the four texts originated.

Text No. 1 (c. 1365)

Hunger in haste þo hent Wastour bi þe mawe,
　　　　　　then seized　　　　　stomach

And wronge hym so bi þe wombe þat bothe his eyen wattered;
　　　　　　　　　　belly　　　　　　eyes

He buffeted þe Britoner aboute þe chekes,

þat he loked like a lanterne al his lyf after.
so that

He bette hem so bothe he barste nere here guttes;　　　　　　　　　　5
　beat them　　　　　　nearly their

Ne hadde Pieres with a pese-lof preyed Hunger to cesse,
If Piers had not　　　loaf of peas-bread

They hadde ben doluen bothe, no deme þow non other
　　would have been buried　　think you (= no 2 ways about it)

'Suffre hem lyue,' he seyde, 'and lete hem ete with hogges,
Let them

Or elles benes and bren ybaken togideres,
　　　beans　　bran

Or elles melke and mene ale': þus preyed Pieres for hem . . .　　　　　　*10*
　　milk　　inferior

　　þanne hadde Peres pite and preyed Hunger to wende
　　　　　　　　　　　　　go

Home into his owne erde and holden hym þere—
　　　　　　　land　　keep himself

Holt, Rinehart and Winston, Inc.

'For I am wel awroke now of wastoures, þorw þi myȝte.
    avenged   *through power*

Ac I preye þe, ar   þow passe,' quod Pieres to Hunger,
        before   *go*

'Of beggeres and of bidderes, what best be to done?   15
        beggars   *is*   *do*

For I wote wel, be þow went, þei wil worche ful ille:
       if thou goest   *work very badly*

For myschief it maketh þei beth so meke nouthe,
    trouble   *they are*   *now*

And for defaute of her fode þis folke is at my wille.
      lack   *their*

þei are my blody brethren,' quod Pieres, 'for God bouȝte vs alle;
      blood

Treuthe tauȝte me ones to louye hem vchone,   20
        once   *love them each one*

And to helpen hem of alle þinge ay as   hem nedeth.
               always is necessary for them

And now wolde I witen of þe what were þe best,
    want I to know from you what would be

And how I myȝte amaistrien hem and make hem to worche.'
    govern

Text No. 2 (c. 1375)

Ant heere þe freris wiþ þer fautours seyne þat it is heresye to
    friars   *supporters say*

write þus goddis lawe in english, & make it knowun to lewid men.
    thus God's   *lay*

& fourty signes þat þey bringen for to shewe an heretik ben not
                       in order to show

worþy to reherse, for nouȝt groundiþ hem but nygromansye.
    repeat   *nothing supports them*   *conjuring*

It semyþ first þat þe wit of goddis lawe shulde be tauȝt   5
      meaning

in þat tunge þat is more knowun, for þis wit is goddis word.
                 meaning

whanne crist seiþ in þe gospel þat boþe heuene & erþe shulen passe
    says

but his wordis shulen not passe, he vndirstondith bi his woordis his
                        means

wit. . . . Sum men seyn þat freris trauelen & þer fautours in þis
  meaning   *say*   *work*   *supporters*

cause for þre chesouns, þat y wole not aferne, but god woot   10
    three reasons   *affirm*   *God knows*

wher þey ben soþe. First þey wolden be seun so nedeful to þe
whether are true   *seen*

engliȝschmen of oure reume þat singulerly in her wit layȝ
      kingdom   *their knowledge lies*

þe wit of goddis lawe, to telle þe puple goddis lawe on what maner
meaning   *people*

euere þey wolden. & þe secound cause herof is seyd to stonde in þis

sentense: freris wolden lede þe puple in techinge hem goddis   *15*

lawe, & þus þei wolden teche sum, & sum hide, & docke sum. For
      curtail

þanne defautis in þer lif shulden be lesse knowun to þe puple, &
      faults

goddis lawe shulde be vntreweliere knowun boþe bi clerkis & bi
      less truly

comyns.   þe þridde cause þat men aspien stondiþ in þis, as þey
common men   *see*

seyn: alle þes newe ordris dreden hem þat þer synne shulde   *20*
      orders of friars fear

be knowun, & hou þei ben not groundid in god to come into þe

chirche; & þus þey wolden not for drede þat goddis lawe were

knowun in engliȝsch, but þey myȝten putte heresye on men ȝif
      in

engliȝsch toolde not what þey seyden.

Text No. 3 (c. 1340)

The bee has thre kyndis. Ane es þat scho es neuer ydill, and
      qualities.   *she*   *idle*

scho es noghte with thaym þat will noghte wyrke, bot castys thaym
(= has nothing to do with)

owte and puttes thaym awaye. Anothire es þat when scho flyes

scho takes erthe in hyr fette, þat scho be noghte lyghtly
      feet   *easily*

ouerheghede in the ayere of wynde. The thyrde es þat scho   *5*
raised too high   *air by*

kepes clene and bryghte hire wyngeȝ. Thus ryghtwyse men þat
      righteous

lufes God are neuer in ydyllnes; for owthyre þay ere in trauayle,
love   *either*   *are*   *toil*

prayand, or thynkande, or redande, or othere gude doande, or
praying   *reading*   *doing*

withtakand ydill mene and schewand thaym worthy to be put fra
scolding   *men*   *showing*   *from*

Holt, Rinehart and Winston, Inc.

þe ryste of heuene, for þay will noghte trauayle here.   *10*
    rest   heaven   work

    þay take erthe, þat es, þay halde þamselfe vile and erthely,
                                    themselves

that thay be noghte blawene with þe wynde of vanyte and of
                blown by

pryde. Thay kepe thaire wynges clene, that es, þe twa commande-

mentes of charyte þay fulfill in gud concyens, and thay hafe othyre

vertus, vnblendyde with þe fylthe of syne and vnclene luste.   *15*
        unmingled

    Arestotill sais þat þe bees are feghtande agaynes hym þat will
        says   fighting against

drawe þaire hony fra thaym. Swa sulde we do agaynes deuells þat
                Thus should

afforces thame to reue fra us þe hony of poure lyfe and of grace.
endeavor   rob   poor

For many are þat neuer kane halde þe ordyre of lufe ynence þaire
                                    love toward

frendys, sybbe or fremmede; bot outhire þay lufe þaym ouer   *20*
    related   unrelated   either

mekill, settand thaire thoghte vnryghtwysely on thaym, or þay luf
much

thayme ouer lyttill, yf þay doo noghte all as þey wolde till þame.
                                    toward

Swylke kane noghte fyghte for thaire hony, forthy þe deuelle turnes
Such   because

it to wormode, and makes þeire saules oftesythes full bitter in
    wormwood   often   very

angwys and tene and besynes of vayne thoghtes and oþer   *25*
anguish   pain   busy-ness

wrechidnes. For thay are so heuy in erthely frenchype þat þay
                                friendship

may noghte flee intill þe lufe of Iesu Criste, in þe wylke þay moghte
                into   which   might

wele forgaa þe lufe of all creaturs lyfande in erthe.
    forgo   living on

Text No. 4 (c. 1340)

Sleȝþe zayþ, "Hyt lykeþ þet   þou zayst. Ac uor of echen of þe holy
Prudence says It is pleasing what   say   But because each

ordres wondres þou hest yzed, we byddeþ þet þou zigge ous huet is
            hast said   say (to) us what

Holt, Rinehart and Winston, Inc.

hare dede ine mennesse and huet is þe conversacion of uelaȝrede;
their deed in common   (holy) life   fellowship

zay ous!'' þe Wylyngge of þe Lyue wyþoute end zayþ, ''Vor zoþe ich
      Desire   Life   says   Forsooth I

wylle zygge. þe dede of alle ine mennesse ys zeueuald: hy   5
      say   sevenfold they

lybbeþ, hy smackeþ, he louyeþ, hy byeþ glede, he heryþ, he byeþ
live   experience they love   are glad   praise   are

zuyfte, hy byeþ zikere.'' Sleȝþe zayþ, ''þaȝ ich somdel þis onder-
swift   secure Prudence   though I somewhat

stonde, uor ham þet lhesteþ of echen zay.''
      for them   listen about each tell

      Wylnynge of þe lyue wyþoute ende zayþ, ''zuo by hyt. Hy
      Desire   life   so be it.   They

lybbeþ be lyue wyþoute ende, wyþoute enye tyene, wyþoute   10
live according to life   pain

enye lessinge, wyþoute enye wyþstondynge. Hyre lyf is þe zȝyþe
      decrease   adversity   Their   sight

and þe knaulechynge of þe holy trinyte, ase zayþ oure lhord iesus.
      knowledge   as says   lord

þis is þet lyf wyþoute ende, þet hy knawe þe zoþe god and huam þe
                                    true   him that

zentest, iesu crist. And þeruore ylyche hy byeþ, uor hy yxyeþ ase
sent   alike they are   see (Him)

he is. Hy smackeþ þe redes and þe domes of god. Hy   15
      they know   counsels   judgments

smackeþ be kendes and the causes and þe begynnynges of alle
      by natures

þynges. Hy louyeþ god wyþoute enye comparisoun, uor þet hy
            beyond   because they

wyteþ huerto god his heþ ybroȝt uorþ. Hy louyeþ ech oþren ase
know wherefore   has brought forth

ham zelue. Hy byeþ glede of god   onzyginde; hy byeþ glede of zuo
themselves   are glad because of God unstintingly   so

moche of hare oȝene holynesse; and uor þet ech loueþ oþren   20
      their own   because

ase him zelue, ase moche blisse heþ ech of oþres guode ase of his
as   has each because of other's good

oȝene. . . . Yef þanne on onneaþe nymþe al his blisse, hou ssel he
      If then one scarcely (can) receive   shall

nyme zuo uele and zuo manye blyssen? And þeruore hit is yzed,
receive numerous   said

'guo into þe blysse of þyne lhorde' . . .
      thy

FEATURES OF ME DIALECTS

	North	South	East Midlands	West Midlands
a. 3d sg. pres. ind.	-(e)s[1]	-(e)þ[2]	-(e)þ[2]	-(e)þ[2]
b. 3d pl. pres. ind.	-(e)s, -e	-(e)þ	-(e)n	-(e)þ, -n, -e
c. Pres. part.[3]	-and(e)	-ind(e), *later* -ing(e)	-end(e), *later* -ing(e)	-end(e), *later* -ing(e)
d. 3d pl. pronouns[4]	they, them, their	hi, hem, hire	they, hem, hire	they, hem, hire
e. 'she'[5]	scho, sco	heo, he	sche	scho, he, ho, ha
f. Pres. pl. 'to be'	er, are, es	be(n)	be(n), are(n)	be(n), beþ
g. Past pl. 'to be'	ware	weren	weren	weren
h. Noun pls.	-(e)s(s)	-(e)n, -(e)s	-(e)n, -(e)s	-(e)n, -(e)s
i. Prep. with infin.	at, to, ∅	to, ∅	to, ∅	to, ∅
j. Infin. ending	∅	∅	-(e)n	-(e)n
k. Strong past part.	-(e)n	∅	-(e)n, ∅	-(e)n, ∅
l. Weak past part.	-it, -d	-(e)d	-(e)d	-(e)t, -(e)d
m. Past part. prefix	∅	i-, y-	i-, y-, ∅	y-, i-, ∅
n. OE [ā]	ā[6]	ō	ō	ō
o. OE [k]	[k] ⟨c, k⟩	[č] ⟨ch⟩	[č] ⟨ch⟩	[č] ⟨ch⟩
p. OE [ă] + [m, n][7]	a	a	a	o
q. OE [ў][8]	⟨i, y⟩ [ɪ, i]	⟨u⟩ [y] ⟨e⟩ [e] (Kent)	⟨i, y⟩ [ɪ, i]	⟨u⟩ [y]
r. OE initial ⟨f, s⟩	⟨f, s⟩	⟨v, z⟩	⟨f, s⟩	⟨f, s⟩
s. OE ⟨hw⟩	⟨qu, quh⟩	⟨hu⟩, *later* ⟨w⟩	⟨w, wh⟩	⟨hw⟩, *later* ⟨wh⟩
t. OE [š] in 'shall, should'	⟨s⟩	⟨ss⟩	⟨s, sh, sch⟩	⟨sh⟩

[1]Parentheses mean the sound or letter may or may not appear. Note that square brackets indicate sound values and angled brackets indicate spelling values.

[2]⟨t⟩ or ⟨th⟩ may appear instead of ⟨þ⟩.

[3]By later ME, all dialects had *-ing*.

[4]The spelling of everything after the initial consonant may vary.

[5]Only a few of the many different forms in each dialect area are listed here.

[6]If the word has an ⟨a⟩ where PDE has ⟨o⟩, it is probably an example of this.

[7]If the word has ⟨om⟩ or ⟨on⟩ where PDE has ⟨am⟩ or ⟨an⟩, it is probably an example of this.

[8]The PDE words would normally be pronounced with [ɪ] or [i]. A ⟨u⟩ spelling indicates that the vowel is still rounded in these dialects.

Name _____

WORKSHEET FOR ME DIALECTS

	No. 1	*No. 2*	*No. 3*	*No. 4*
a. 3d sg. pres. ind.				
b. 3d pl. pres. ind.				
c. Pres. part.				
d. 3d pl. pronouns				
e. 'she'				
f. Pres. pl. 'to be'				
g. Past pl. 'to be'				
h. Noun pls.				
i. Prep. with infin.				
j. Infin. ending				
k. Strong past part.				
l. Weak past part.				
m. Past part. prefix				
n. OE [ā]				
o. OE [k]				
p. OE [ǎ] + [m, n]				
q. OE [ў̆]				
r. OE initial ⟨f, s⟩				
s. OE ⟨hw⟩				
t. OE [š] in 'shall, should'				

Holt, Rinehart and Winston, Inc.

Name _____

1. Fill in the blank chart with examples of the specific features from each text. (You will not find examples of every feature in every text.)

2. Identify the probable dialect area from which each text comes by writing "North," "South," "East Midlands," or "West Midlands" at the top of the appropriate column.

3. Did you find any anomalies or evidence of dialect mixture? _____

_____

_____

4. Which passage(s) do you find it easiest to read in the original? _____

_____

The hardest? _____

Can you offer any explanations for your answers here? _____

_____

5. One of these texts is a translation from French; the other three are original English

compositions. Which one do you think is the translation and why? _____

_____

6. Which text seems to have the highest proportion of loanwords from French?

_____ The lowest proportion? _____ Since all of the texts were written at

roughly the same time, what might account for the difference in the proportions?

_____

_____

6.17   ME Illustrative Texts

I. The Peterborough Chronicle
The Peterborough Chronicle was continued for almost a century after the Norman Conquest, well into the ME period. The following is the final entry, that for the year 1154. Though at first glance the text may look like OE, many changes in the language have taken place since even the entry for 1085. Note in particular the undeclined definite article and such French loanwords as *court* and *procession*.

On þis gær wærd þe king Stephne ded & bebyried þer his
In this year was the king Stephen   dead & buried where his

wif & his sune wæron bebyried æt Fauresfeld;   þaet ministre hi
wife & his son were buried at Faversham;   that minster they

makeden. þa þe king was ded,   þa was þe eorl beionde sæ;
founded. When the king was dead, then was the earl overseas;

& ne durste nan man don oþer bute god for þe micel eie of him.
& not dared no man do other but good for the great fear of him.

þa he to Engleland com,   þa was he underfangen mid micel
When he to England came, then was he received with great

wurtscipe, & to king bletcæd in Lundene on þe Sunnendæi beforen
honor,   & as king ordained in London on the Sunday before

Midwintre Dæi, & held þære micel curt. þat ilce dæi þat
Midwinter Day, & held there great court. That same day that

Martin abbot of Burch   sculde þider faren, þa sæclede he,
Martin abbot of Peterborough was to go there,   then took sick he,

& ward ded iiii Nonarum Ianuarii. & Te munekes innen dæis cusen
& was dead 4 the nones January. & the monks within a day chose

oþer of heomsælf,   Willelm de Walteruile is gehaten,
another from themselves, William of Walterville is called,

god clerc & god man   & wæl luued of þe king & of alle gode men;
good cleric & good man & well loved by the king & by all good men;

& on morgen byrieden þabbot hehlice. & Sone þe cosan abbot
& in morning buried   the abbot nobly. & at once the elected abbot

ferde, & te muneces mid him, to Oxenforde to þe king; & he iaf
went, & the monks   with him, to Oxford   to the king; & he gave

him þat abbotrice. & He ferde him   sone to Lincol, & wæs
him the abbacy.   & he took himself at once to Lincoln, & was

þær bletcæd to abbot   ær he ham come;   & sithen was
there ordained as abbot before he home came; & afterward was

underfangen mid micel wurtscipe at Burch   mid micel
received   with great honor at Peterborough with great

processiun; & sau he was alsua at Ramsæie, & at Torneie, & at
procession; & thus he was also at Ramsey,   & at Thorney, & at

Holt, Rinehart and Winston, Inc.

Cruland & Spallding,   & at S. Albanes & F. . . . & Nu is abbot &
Crowland & Spalding,   & at St. Albans & F. . . . & now is abbot &

fair haued begunnon: Xrist him unne þus enden!
fair had begun: Christ him grant thus (to) end!

II. *Hali Meidenhad*

Hali Meidenhad, or "Holy Virginity," is a prose homily in praise of virginity. It is one member of a five-text group (the others are *Seinte Marharete, Seinte Iuliene, Seinte Katerine,* and *Sawles Warde*) collectively termed The Katherine Group. All date from the late twelfth or early thirteenth century and are written in a West Midlands dialect.

Ga we nu forthre   ant loki we hwuch   wunne ariseth threfter
Go we now further and look what sort of delight arises thereafter

i burtherne of bearne   hwen thet streon   in the awakeneth ant
in pregnancy of (a) child when that offspring in you quickens and

waxeth ant hu monie earmthen anan awakeneth therwith, the
grows and how many miseries immediately spring up with it, that

wurcheth the wa inoh,   fehteth o thi seolve flesch ant weorrith with
occupy you woe enough, fight in your own flesh   and struggle with

feole weanan o thin ahne cunde. Thi rudie neb schal leanin   ant
many woes in your own flesh.   Your rosy face will grow lean and

ase gres grenin,   thine ehnen schule doskin ant underneothe
as grass turn green, your eyes will become dim and underneath

wonnin,   ant of thi breines turnunge thin heaved aken sare;
become dark, and of your brain's activity your head ache sorely;

inwith i thi wombe   swelle thi butte   the bereth the forth
inside in your womb swells your belly, which sticks out in front of

as a weater-bulge;   thine thearmes thralunge, ant stiches i
you like a water-barrel; of your guts pain,   and stitches in

thi lonke, ant i thi lendene sar eche rive,   hevinesse in
your side, and in your loins painful ache prevalent, heaviness in

euch lim; thine breostes burtherne o thine two pappes ant te milc-
every limb; your breasts' weight   in your two nipples and the milk-

strunden the the of striketh.   Al is with a weolewunge thi wlite
streams which you from flow. All is with a nausea   your face

overwarpen. Thi muth is bitter   ant walh al thet tu cheowest,
downcast.   Your mouth is bitter and insipid all that you chew,

ant hwetse thi mahe   hokerliche underveth, thet is with
and whatever your stomach nauseatedly receives, it is with

unlust, warpeth hit eft ut.   Inwith   al thi weole ant ti
distaste, throws it back out. In the midst of all your joy and your

weres wunne forwurthest.   A wrecche! The cares
husband's pleasure, [you are] perishing. Ah, wretch! The anxieties

ayein thi pinunge thrahen bineometh the nahtes slepes. Hwen hit
about your pain spasms deprive   you of night's sleep. When it

thenne therto kimeth, thet sore sorhfule angoise,   thet stronge ant
then thereto comes,   that painful sorrowful agony, that strong and

stikinde stiche, thet unroles uvel,   thet pine   over pine,
piercing spasm, that restless misery, that torment after torment,

thet wondrinde yeomerunge, hwil thu swenchest terwith i thine
that amazing lamentation,   while you labor therewith in your

deathes dute scheome teke   thet sar with the alde wifes
death's fear shame (in addition to) that pain with the old women's

scheome creft, the cunnen of   thet wa-sith, hwas help the
shame skill, who are familiar with that woe-time, whose help to you

bihoveth ne beo hit neaver se uncumelich; ant nede most hit tholien
is necessary not be it never so unseemly;   and needs must it endure

thet te   therin itimeth.   Ne thunche the nan uvel of, for we ne
what to you therein happens. Not seem to you no evil of, for we not

edwiteth nawt wifes hare   weanen thet ure alre modres drehden
reproach not women their woes which all our mothers suffered

on us seolven,   ah we schawith ham forth forte warni meidnes
through ourselves, but we reveal them forth to   warn maidens

thet ha beon the leasse efterwart swuch thing ant witen herthurh
that they be the less afterward such things   and know thereby

the betere hwet ham beo to donne.
the better what to them is to do.

Efter al this kimeth of thet bearn   ibore thus wanunge ant
After all this comes from that child born thus lamentation and

wepunge, the schal abute midniht   makie the to wakien other theo
weeping, that will around midnight make you to wake or those

the hire stude halt the thu most forcarien.   Ant hwet
who her place holds that you must worry about. And what about

the cader-fulthen ant bearmes: unbestunde to feskin ant to
the baby-filth and (your) breasts: at times to swaddle and to

fostrin hit se moni earmhwile?   Ant his waxunge se let ant
nurse it so many wretched times? And its growth so late and

se slaw his thriftre, ant eaver habbe   sar care ant lokin efter
so slow its growth, and always having vexing care and looking after

al this hwenne hit forwurthe ant bringe on his moder sorhe. Thah
all this when it dies   and brings on its mother grief. Though

thu riche beo ant nurrice habbe, thu most as moder carien for al
you rich be and (a) nurse have, you must as mother care for all

thet hire limpeth to donne. Theose ant othre earmthen the of
that she ought to do.   These and other miseries which from

wedlac awakenith Seinte Pawel biluketh in ane lut wordes,
wedlock arise   St. Paul   expresses in a few words,

Holt, Rinehart and Winston, Inc.

Tribulaciones carnis, et cetera. Thet is on Englisch 'Theo thet
Tribulation in the flesh, etc.   That is in English, 'Those that

thulliche beoth schulen derf drehen.' Hwase thencheth on al this
such be must cruel suffer.'   Whoever thinks about all this

ant o mare thet ter is ant nule   withbuhe thet thing thet
and of more that there is and not wants to avoid that thing that

hit al of awakeneth, ha is heardre iheortet then adamantines stan
it all springs from,   she is harder hearted than adamantine stone

ant mare amead, yef ha mai,   than is meadschipe seolf, hire ahne
and more mad, if she can (be), than is insanity itself, her own

fa ant hire feont,   heateth hire seolfen.
foe and her enemy, hates herself.

III. Lyrics
The lyric as we know it today makes its first appearance in English during the ME period. The subject matter may be religious or secular; of the four reproduced here, only the second is secular in theme. Their dates range from the twelfth to the fifteenth century. Note that all of these lyrics use end rhyme to tie the lines together instead of the OE alliteration.

St. Mary Virgin

Sainte Marye Virgine,
St.   Mary Virgin

Moder Jesu Christes Nazarene,
Mother of Jesus Christ the Nazarene

Onfo, schild, help thin Godric,
Receive, defend, help your Godric,

Onfang, bring heyilich with thee in Godes Riche.
Take, bring on high   with you into God's kingdom.

Sainte Marye, Christes bur,
St. Mary, Christ's chamber,

Maidenes clenhad, moderes flur,
Virgins' purity, motherhood's flower,

Dilie min sinne, rix in min mod,
Wipe out my sin, rule in my heart,

Bring me to winne with the self God.
Bring me to joy with that same God.

Merry It Is

Mirie it is, while sumer ilast,
Merry it is, while summer lasts,

With fugheles song.
With birds' song.

Oc nu necheth windes blast,
But now approaches wind's blast,

And weder strong.
And weather strong.

Holt, Rinehart and Winston, Inc.

Ey! ey! what this night is long!
Alas! Alas! how long this night is!

And ich, with well michel wrong,
And I, because of very great wrong,

Soregh and murne and fast.
Sorrow and mourn and fast.

When I See on the Rood

Whanne ic se on Rode
When I see on (the) cross

Jesu, my lemman,
Jesus, my lover,

And besiden him stonden
And beside him stand

Marye and Johan,
Mary and John,

And his rig iswongen,
And his back scourged,

And his side istungen,
And his side pierced,

For the luve of man;
For the love of man;

Well ou ic to wepen,
Well ought I to weep,

And sinnes for to leten,
And sins to abandon,

Yif ic of luve can,
If I of love know,

Yif ic of luve can,
If I of love know,

Yif ic of luve can.
If I of love know.

Adam Lay Bound

Adam lay ibounden,
Adam lay bound,

Bounden in a bond:
Bound in a bond:

Foure thousand winter
Four thousand years

Thought he not too long.
Thought he not too long.

And all was for an apple,
And all was because of an apple,

Holt, Rinehart and Winston, Inc.

An apple that he tok,
An apple that he took,

As clerkes finden
As clerics find

Wreten in here book.
Written in their book.

Ne hadde the apple take ben,
(If) not had the apple taken been,

The apple taken ben,
The apple taken been,

Ne hadde never our Lady
(Then) not had never our Lady

A ben Hevene Quen.
Have been heaven's queen.

Blissed be the time
Blessed be the time

That apple take was!
That apple taken was!

Therfore we moun singen,
Therefore we may sing,

'Deo gracias!'
'Thanks be to God!'

IV. Proclamation of Henry III

Though the official language of England was French after the Conquest, English continued to be the language of the great majority of the people. In recognition of this fact, some official documents were written in both French and English, as was the case of this 1258 proclamation of King Henry III.

Henri, þurȝ godes fultume king on Engleneloande, lhoauerd on
Henry, through God's help, king in England,   lord in

Yrloande, duk on Normandie, on Aquitaine, and eorl on Aniow send
Ireland, duke in Normandy, in Aquitaine,   and earl in Anjou, sends

igretinge to alle hise holde, ilærde and ileawede, on Huntendoneschire.
greeting to all his faithful, clerical and lay,   in Huntingtonshire.

þæt witen ȝe wel alle,   þæt we willen and vnnen þæt þæt vre
That know you well all,   that we wish and grant that, that our

rædesmen alle, oþer þe moare dæl of heom, þæt beoþ ichosen þurȝ
counselors all, or the greater part of them,   that are chosen by

us and þurȝ þæt loandes folk on vre kuneriche, habbeþ idon and
us and by the land's people in our   kingdom, have done and

schullen don in þe worþnesse of gode and on vre treowþe for þe
shall do in the   honor of God and in our faith   for the

freme of þe loande, þurȝ þe besiȝte of þan to-foren inseide redesmen,
profit of the land,   through the provision of the aforesaid counselors,

Holt, Rinehart and Winston, Inc.

beo stedefæst and ilestinde in alle þinge a buten ænde.
be steadfast and stable   in all things always without end.

And we hoaten alle vre treowe   in þe treowþe þæt heo vs
And we command all our faithful in the fidelity that they us

oȝen, þæt heo stedefæstliche healden and swerian to healden and
owe, that they steadfastly   hold   and swear to hold and

to werien þo isetnesses þæt beon imakede and beon to makien þurȝ
to defend those statutes that are made   and are to (be) made by

þan to-foren iseide rædesmen, oþer þurȝ þe moare dæl of heom,
the aforesaid   counselors, or by   the greater part of them,

alswo alse hit is biforen iseid; and þæt æhc oþer helpe þæt
also as it is before said; and that each (the) other help that

for to done bi þan ilche oþe aȝenes alle men riȝt for to done and to
to do by the same oath toward all men right   to do and to

foangen; and noan ne nime of loande ne of eȝte,   wherþurȝ
take;   and none not take from land nor from property, by which

þis besiȝte muȝe beon ilet   oþer iwersed on onie wise.
this provision can be hindered or damaged in any way.

And ȝif oni   oþer onie cumen her onȝenes, we willen and
And if any one or ones come here against,   we want and

hoaten þæt   alle vre treowe heom healden deadliche ifoan.
command that all our faithful them consider deadly foes.

And for þæt we willen, þæt þis beo stedefæst and lestinde, we
And because we want that this be steadfast and lasting,   we

senden ȝew þis writ open, iseined wiþ ure seel, to halden a-manges ȝew ine hord.
send   you this writ open, marked with our seal, to keep amongst   you in treasury.

Witnesse vs seluen æt Lundene þane eȝtetenþe day on the
Witness ourselves at London   the eighteenth day in the

monþe of Octobre, in þe two and fowertiȝþe ȝeare of vre cruninge.
month of October, in the two and fortieth   year of our crowning.

And þis wes idon ætforan vre isworene redesmen: Boneface,
And this was done before our sworn counselors: Boniface,

archebischop on Kanterburi; Walter of Cantelow, bischop on
archbishop in Canterbury;   Walter of Cantelow, bishop in

Wirechestre; Simon of Muntfort, eorl on Leirchestre; Richard of
Worcester;   Simon of Montfort, earl in Leicester;   Richard of

Clare, eorl on Glowchestre and on Hurtforde; Rogeṙ Bigod, eorl on
Clare, earl in Gloucester and in Hertford;   Roger Bigod, earl in

Northfolke and marescal on Engleneloande; . . .
Norfolk   and Marshal in England; . . .

And al on þo ilche worden is   isend in-to æurihce oþre schire
And all in those same words is (to be) sent into every other shire

ouer al þære kuneriche on Engleneloande, and ek in-tel Irelonde.
over all the kingdom   of England   and also into Ireland.

Holt, Rinehart and Winston, Inc.

V. *Sir Orfeo*

During the ME period, romances, adventure tales usually in verse, became popular in England. Many of them were translations of French originals. A subdivision of the romance was the Breton lai, usually a short romance emphasizing love and the supernatural. *Sir Orfeo*, one of the most charming of the English Breton lais, retells the classical story of Orpheus and Eurydice—and gives it a happy ending. The manuscript from which this excerpt was taken was written about 1335.

> Orfeo was a king,
> *Orpheus was a king.*

In Inglond an heiȝe lording,
In England a high lord,

A stalworþ man and hardi bo,
A valiant man and hardy both,

Large and curteys he was also.
Generous and well-bred he was also.

His fader was comen of King Pluto,
His father was descended from King Pluto,

And his moder of King Juno,
And his mother from King Juno,

þat sum time were as godes yhold,
That once were as gods considered,

For auentours þat þai ded and told.
For feats that they did and told.

> Orpheo most of ony þing
> *Orpheus most of any thing*

Louede þe gle of harpyng;
Loved the minstrelsy of harping;

Syker was euery gode harpoure
Certain was every good harpist

Of hym to haue moche honoure.
From him to have much honor.

Hymself loued for to harpe,
(He) himself loved to (play the) harp,

And layde þeron his wittes scharpe.
And applied to it his wits sharp.

He lernyd so,   þer noþing was
He learned so (well), there nothing was

A better harper in no plas;
A better harpist in no place;

In þe world was neuer man born
In the world was never man born

þat ones Orpheo sat byforn,
That once Orpheus sat in front of,

And he myȝt of his harpyng here,
If he could of his harping hear,

He schulde þinke þat he were
He would think that he was

In one of þe ioys of Paradys,
In one of the joys of Paradise,

Suche ioy and melody in his harpyng is.
Such joy and melody in his harping is.

    þis king soiournd in Traciens,
    This king lived in Thrace,

þat was a cité of noble defense;
That was a city of good fortification;

For Winchester was cleped þo
For Winchester was called then

Traciens wiþouten no.
Thrace undoubtedly.

þe king hadde a quen of priis,
The king had a queen of excellence

þat was ycleped Dame Herodis,
That was called Dame Eurydice,

þe fairest leuedi, for þe nones,
The fairest lady, to be sure,

þat miȝt gon on bodi and bones,
That could walk in body and bones,

Ful of loue and of godenisse;
Full of love and of goodness;

Ac no man may telle hir fairnise.
But no man can describe her beauty.

    Bifel   so in þe comessing of May,
    (It) happened so in the beginning of May,

When miri and hot is þe day,
When merry and hot is the day,

And oway beþ winter-schours,
And away are winter showers,

And eueri feld is ful of flours,
And every field is full of flowers,

And blosme breme on eueri bouȝ
And blossom glorious on every bough

Oueral wexeþ miri anouȝ,
Everywhere grows merry enough

þis ich quen, Dame Heurodis,
This same queen, Dame Eurydice,

Tok to maidens of priis,
Took two maidens of worth,

And went in an vndrentide
And went in a morning

To play bi an orchard side,
To play by an orchard side,

To se þe floures sprede and spring,
To see the flowers spread and spring,

And to here þe foules sing.
And to hear the birds sing.

þai sett   hem   doun al þre
They set themselves down all three

Vnder a fair ympe-tre,
Under a lovely sapling,

And wel sone þis fair quene
And very soon this fair queen

Fel on slepe opon þe grene.
Fell asleep upon the green.

þe maidens durst hir nouȝt awake,
The maidens dared her not awake,

Bot lete hir ligge and rest take.
But let her lie   and rest take.

So sche slepe til afternone,
So she slept till afternoon,

þat vndertide was al ydone.
That morning was all done.

Ac as sone as sche gan awake,
But as soon as she did awake,

Sche crid and loþli bere gan make,
She cried and horrible outcry did make,

Sche froted hir honden and hir fet,
She rubbed her hands and her feet,

And crached hir visage, it bled wete;
And scratched her face, it bled wet;

Hir riche robe hye al torett,
Her rich robe noble all tore to pieces,

And was reueysed out of hir witt.
And was driven out of her wits.

þe tvo maidens hir biside
The two maidens her beside

No durst wiþ hir no leng abide,
Not dared with her no longer stay,

Holt, Rinehart and Winston, Inc.

Bot ourn to þe palays ful riȝt,
But ran to the palace immediately,

And told boþe squier and kniȝt
And told both squire and knight

þat her quen awede wold,
That their queen go mad would,

And bad hem go and hir athold.
And bade them go and her restrain.

Kniȝtes vrn, and leuedis also,
Knights ran, and ladies also,

Damisels sexti and mo,
Damsels sixty and more,

In þe orchard to þe quen hye come,
In the orchard to the queen they came,

And her vp in her armes nome,
And her up in their arms took,

And brouȝt hir to bed atte last,
And brought her to bed at last,

And held hir þere fine fast;
And held her there very fast;

Ac euer sche held in o cri,
But always she kept up the same cry,

And wold vp and owy.
And wanted up and away.

VI. Barbour's *Bruce*

John Barbour, a Scottish cleric, was the author of *The Bruce*, a long, quasi-historical verse chronicle of the deeds of Robert Bruce, king of Scotland. It was written in the Northern dialect in 1376. The following passage from the early part of the poem tells of the famous battle of Bannockburn.

And fra schir amer with the king
And after Sir Aymer with the king

Wes fled,   wes nane that durst abyde,
Had fled, (there) was none that dared stay,

Bot fled, scalit on ilka syde,
But fled, dispersed on every side.

And thair fais thame presit fast,
And their foes them pressed diligently,

Thai war, to say   suth, all agast,
They were, to tell (the) truth, all terrified,

And fled swa richt effrayitly
And fled in such a frightened way

That of thame a full gret party
That of them a very great party

Fled to the wattir of forth; and thar
Fled to the water of Forth; and there

Holt, Rinehart and Winston, Inc.

The mast part of thame drownit [war].
The most part of them drowned were.

And bannokburn, betuix the braiß,
And Bannockburn, between the banks,

Of horß and men so chargit waß,
Of horses and men so loaded was,

That apon drownit horß and men
That upon drowned horses and men

Men mycht paß dry atour it then
Men could pass dry across it then.

[And] laddis, swanys, and rangall,
And lads, peasants, and camp-followers,

Quhen thai saw vencust the battall,
When they saw vanquished the battalion,

Ran emang thame and swa can sla
Ran among them and so did slay

Thai folk, that no defens mycht ma,
Those people, who no defense could make,

That it war pite for to se.
That it was pity to see.

I herd neuir quhar, in na cuntre,
I heard never where, in no country,

Folk at swa   gret myschef war stad;
People in such great misfortune were beset;

On a syde thai thair fais had,
On one side they their foes had,

That slew thame doune vithout mercy,
That slew them   down without mercy,

And thai had on the tothir party
And they had on the other side

Bannokburne, that sa cummyrsum was
Bannockburn, that so hard to cross was

Of slyk, and depnes for till pas,
With slime, and depth to pass,

That thair mycht nane atour it ryde.
That they could none across it ride.

Thame worthit,   magre thairis,   abyde;
It behooved them, despite themselves, (to) remain;

Swa that sum slayne, sum drownit war;
So that some slain, some drowned were;

Micht nane eschap that euir com thar.
None could escape that ever came there.

Holt, Rinehart and Winston, Inc.

The quhethir mony gat avay,
Nevertheless, many got away,

[That ellis-whar fled], as I herd say.
That elsewhere fled,   as I heard say.

The kyng, with thame he with him had,
The king, with them he with him had,

In a rout till the castell raid,
In a band to the castle rode,

And wald haue beyn tharin, for thai
And wanted to have been therein, for they

Wist nocht quhat gat to get avay.
Knew not what way to get away.

VII. Chaucer's ''Second Nun's Tale''
Chaucer's ''Second Nun's Tale,'' a version of the legend of St. Cecilia, was probably
written in the 1370s. Reproduced here are the closing lines. You might compare this
version with the OE one by Ælfric, written roughly four centuries earlier.

''Do wey thy booldnesse,'' seyde Almachius tho,
''Leave off your boldness,'' said Almachius then,

''And sacrifice to oure goddes er thou go.
And sacrifice to our gods before you go.

I recche nat what wrong that thou me profre,
I care not what wrong that you (to) me present,

For I kan suffre it as a philosophre,
For I can suffer it as a philosopher,

''But thilke wronges may I nat endure
''But those wrongs can I not endure

That thou spekest of oure goddes heere,'' quod he.
That you speak of our gods here,''   said he.

Cecile answerde, ''O nyce creature!
Cecilia answered, ''O foolish creature!

Thou seydest no word syn thou spak to me
You said no word since you spoke to me

That I ne knew therwith thy nycetee;
That I knew not thereby your foolishness;

And that thou were, in every maner wise,
And that you were, in every way,

A lewed officer and a veyn justise.
An ignorant officer and an ineffectual justice.

''Ther lakketh no thyng to thyne outter eyen
''There lacks nothing in your outer eyes

That thou n'art blynd, for thyng that we seen alle
That you aren't blind, with regard to things that we all see

That it is stoon—that men may wel espyen—
That it is stone—that men can easily spot—

Holt, Rinehart and Winston, Inc.

That ilke stoon a god thow wolt it calle.
That same stone a god you will it call.

I rede thee, lat thyn hand upon it falle
I advise you, let your hand upon it fall

And taste it wel and stoon thou shalt it fynde,
And feel it well and stone you shall it find,

Syn that thou seest nat with thyne eyen blynde.
Since that you see not with your eyes blind.

"It is a shame that the peple shal
"It is a shame that the people must

So scorne thee and laughe at thy folye,
So scorn you and laugh at your folly,

For communly men woot it wel overal
For commonly men know it well overall

That myghty God is in his hevenes hye.
That mighty God is in his heavens high.

And thise ymages, wel thou mayst espye
And these images, easily you can spot

To thee ne to hemself ne mowen noght profite,
To you nor to themselves not can nothing profit,

For in effect they been nat worth a myte."
For in effect they are not worth a mite."

Thise wordes and swiche othere seyde she,
These words and such others said she,

And he weex wrooth and bad men sholde hir lede
And he grew angry and ordered men should her lead

Hom til hir hous, and "In hire house," quod he,
Home to her house, and "In her house," said he,

"Brenne hir right in a bath of flambes rede."
"Burn her completely in a bath of flames red."

And as he bad, right so was doon in dede;
And as he ordered, just so was done in deed;

For in a bath they gonne hire faste shetten,
For in a bath they did her firmly shut,

And nyght and day greet fyr they under betten.
And night and day great fire they under fed.

The longe nyght and eek a day also
The long night and moreover a day also

For al the fyr and eek the bathes heete
For all the fire and also the bath's heat

She sat al coold and feelede no wo;
She sat all cold and felt no woe;

It made hire nat a drope for to sweete.
It made her not a drop to sweat.

But in that bath hir lyf she moste lete,
But in that bath her life she had to leave,

For he Almachius, with ful wikke entente,
For he Almachius, with very wicked intent,

To sleen hire in the bath his sonde sente.
To slay her in the bath his messenger sent.

Thre strokes in the nekke he smoot hire tho,
Three strokes in the neck he struck her then,

The tormentour, but for no maner chaunce
The tormenter, but for no manner of chance

He myghte noght smyte al hir nekke atwo.
He could not strike all her neck in two.

And for ther was that tyme an ordinaunce
And because there was that time an ordinance

That no man sholde doon man swich penaunce
That no man should do anyone such punishment

The ferthe strook to smyten, softe or soore,
The fourth stroke to smite, soft or hard,

This tormentour ne dorste do namoore,
This tormenter not dared do no more,

But half deed, with hir nekke ycorven there,
But half dead, with her neck carved there,

He lefte hir lye, and on his wey he went.
He left her lie, and on his way he went.

The Cristen folk which that aboute hire were
The Christian people that around her were

With sheetes han the blood ful faire yhent.
With sheets have the blood very well caught.

Thre dayes lyved she in this torment,
Three days lived she in this torment,

And nevere cessed hem the feith to teche
And never ceased them the faith to teach

That she hadde fostred. Hem she gan to preche,
That she had fostered. Them she began to preach,

And hem she yaf hir moebles and hir thyng,
And them she gave her furniture and her things,

And to the Pope Urban bitook hem tho,
And to Pope Urban entrusted them then,

And seyde, ''I axed this at Hevene Kyng,
And said, "I asked this from Heaven's King,

Holt, Rinehart and Winston, Inc.

To han respit thre dayes and namo,
To have respite three days and no more,

To recomende to yow er that I go
To recommend to you before I go

Thise soules, lo, and that I myghte do werche
These souls, lo, and that I could have made

Heere of myn hous perpetuelly a cherche.''
Here of my house perpetually a church.''

Seint Urban with his deknes prively
St. Urban with his deacons secretly

The body fette and buryed it by nyghte
The body fetched and buried it by night

Among his othere seintes honestly.
Among his other saints honorably.

Hir hous the chirche of Seinte Cecilie highte.
Her house the church of St. Cecilia called.

Seint Urban halwed it as he wel myghte,
St. Urban consecrated it as he well could,

In which into this day in noble wyse
In which up to this day in noble fashion

Men doon to Crist and to his seinte servyse.
Men do to Christ and to his saint service.

VIII. Caxton's Introduction to Chaucer's *Canterbury Tales*
England's first printer, William Caxton, printed about a hundred works, some of which he himself had translated from French into English. Among the books he published was Chaucer's *Canterbury Tales* (1484). Reproduced here is the first part of the introduction he wrote to his edition of the *Canterbury Tales*.

Grete thankes, laude, and honour ought to be gyuen vnto the
Great thanks, praise, and honor ought to be given to the

clerkes, poetes, and historiographs, that haue wreton many noble
clerks, poets, and historians   that have written many noble

bokes of wysedom of the lyues, passions, and myracles of holy
books of wisdom of the lives,   passions, and miracles of holy

sayntes, of hystoryes, of noble and famous actes and faittes, and of
saints, of histories,   of noble and famous acts and deeds, and of

the cronycles sith the begynnyng of the creacion of the world vnto
the chronicles since the beginning of the creation of the world up to

thys present tyme, by whyche we ben dayly enformed and have
this present time, by which   we are daily informed and have

knowleche of many thynges, of whom we shold not haue knowen,
knowledge of many things,   of which we should not have known,

yf they had not left to vs theyr monumentis wreton. Emong whom
if they had not left to us their documents   written. Among whom

and inespecial to-fore alle other   we ought to gyue a synguler laude
and in particular before all others we ought to give a special praise

vnto that noble and grete philosopher Gefferey Chaucer, the whiche
to that noble and great philosopher   Geoffrey Chaucer, who,

for his ornate wrytyng in our tongue may wel haue the name of a
for his ornate writing in our tongue can well have the name of a

laureate poete.
laureate poet.

    For to-fore that he by hys labour enbelysshyd, ornated, and
    For, before   he by his labor embellished, decorated, and

made faire our Englisshe,   in thys royame was had rude speche and
made beautiful our English, in this realm was had rude speech and

incongrue, as yet it appiereth by olde bookes, whyche at thys day
incongruous, as yet it appears in old books,   which in this day

ought not to haue place ne be compared emong ne to hys
ought not to have place nor be compared among nor to his

beauteuous volumes and aournate writynges, of whom he made
beautiful volumes and ornate writings, of which he made

many bokes and treatyces of many a noble historye as wel in metre
many books and treatises of many a noble history in meter as well

as in ryme and prose, and them so craftyly made, that he
as in rhyme and prose, and them so skillfully made, that he

comprehended hys maters in short, quyck, and hye sentences,
comprised his matters in short, vivid, and lofty sentences,

eschewyng prolyxyte, castyng away the chaf of superfluyte, and
eschewing prolixity, casting away the chaff of superfluity, and

shewyng the pyked grayn of sentence, vtteryd by crafty and sugred
showing the refined grain of judgment, uttered by skillful and sweet

eloquence, of whom emonge all other of hys bokes I purpose
eloquence, of which among all other of his books I intend

temprynte by the grace of god the book of the Tales of
to print by the grace of God the books of the tales of

Cauntyrburye, in whiche I fynde many a noble hystorye of euery
Canterbury, in which I find many a noble story of every

astate and degre.   Fyrst rehercyng the condicions and tharraye of
estate and degree. First describing the conditions and the order of

eche of them as properly as possyble is to be sayd, and after
each of them as properly as possible is to be said, and afterward

theyr tales whyche ben of noblesse, wysedom, gentylesse, myrthe,
their tales, which are of nobility, wisdom, gentility, mirth,

and also of veray holynesse and vertue, wherin he fynysshyth thys
and also of true holiness and virtue, with which he finishes this

Holt, Rinehart and Winston, Inc.

sayd booke; whyche book I haue dylygently ouersen and duly
said book;   which book I have diligently looked over and fitly

examyned, to thende that it be made accordyng vnto his owen
examined, to the end that it be made according   to his own

makyng.
making.

For I fynde many of the sayd bookes, whyche wryters haue
For I find many of the said books, which writers have

abrydgyd it and many thynges left out; and in somme place haue
abridged it and many things left out; and in some places have

sette certayn versys, that he neuer made ne sette in hys booke. Of
put certain verses that he never made nor put in his book. Of

whyche bookes so incorrecte was one brought to me ·vj· yere
which books so incorrect was one brought to me six years

passyd, whyche I supposed had ben veray true and correcte. And
past, which I assumed had been completely true and correct. And

accordyng to the same I dyde do enprynte a certayn nombre
accordingly   I had a certain number of them printed,

of them, whyche anon were sold to many and dyuerse gentyl-men,
which at once were sold to many and diverse gentlemen,

of whome one gentylman cam to me, and said, that this book was
of whom one gentleman came to me and said that this book did

not accordyng in many places vnto the book that Gefferey Chaucer
not accord to many places to the book that Geoffrey Chaucer

had made. To whom I answered, that I had made it accordyng to
had made. To whom I answered that I had made it according to

my copye, and by me was nothyng added ne mynusshyd.
my copy, and by me was nothing added nor removed.

Holt, Rinehart and Winston, Inc.

CHAPTER 7

EARLY MODERN ENGLISH

7.1   Important Terms and Names

1. Joseph Aickin
2. assibilation
3. Nathaniel Bailey
4. blend
5. Thomas Blount
6. John Bullokar
7. William Caxton
8. Chancery scribes
9. Chaucerisms
10. Sir John Cheke
11. clipping
12. Henry Cockeram
13. Elisha Coles
14. diacritic
15. double negative
16. doublet
17. ''dummy'' auxiliary
18. Sir Thomas Eliot
19. enclitic
20. folk etymology
21. functional shift
22. Alexander Gil
23. gloss
24. glossary
25. Great Vowel Shift
26. group genitive
27. John Hart
28. impersonal verbs
29. the Industrial Revolution
30. inkhorn terms
31. Samuel Johnson
32. King James Bible
33. Latinate style
34. ''long s''
35. Robert Lowth
36. modal auxiliary
37. Richard Mulcaster
38. oversea language
39. Edward Philipps
40. plain adverb
41. plain style
42. Joseph Priestley
43. proclitic
44. quasi-modal
45. reduplication
46. the Reformation
47. the Renaissance
48. spelling pronunciation
49. two-part verb
50. universal grammar
51. John Wallis
52. Noah Webster
53. Jeremiah Wharton
54. zero derivation (= functional shift)

7.2 Questions for Review and Discussion

1. What were some of the effects of the introduction of printing on the English language?
2. How did the EMnE translations from classical languages affect English?
3. Upon what aspect of English has the King James Bible had the most influence?
4. Explain how the enclosures affected the English language.
5. How did the Industrial Revolution have an effect on English vocabulary?
6. What was the most important scholarly language in England at the beginning of the EMnE period? At the end?
7. Summarize the EMnE dispute over vocabulary.
8. What effect did the EMnE spelling reformers have on the subsequent history of English?
9. Why had there been no English-to-English dictionaries prior to the EMnE period?
10. What is the difference between a gloss and a translation?
11. Who were the most important dictionary makers of EMnE?
12. Why did the English never establish an English Academy?
13. Why did the early grammarians consider existing English grammar to be very corrupt?
14. What language was the most important ''model'' for English grammars during EMnE?
15. Compare and contrast the attitudes toward English grammar of (a) Robert Lowth, (b) Joseph Priestley, and (c) Noah Webster.
16. What changes in the English consonant phonemes took place during EMnE?
17. Give some examples of assibilation.
18. Give some examples of spelling pronunciation.
19. Summarize the operation of the Great Vowel Shift (GVS), including date, details, and order in which the changes took place.
20. Explain apparent exceptions to the GVS such as *threat* [θrɛt] rather than predicted [θrit] or *blood* [bləd] rather than predicted [blud].
21. How has the use of proclitic and enclitic contracted forms changed between EMnE and PDE?
22. By what time were PDE punctuation patterns established?
23. How did possessive constructions in EMnE differ from those in PDE?
24. What changes in the use of relative pronouns occurred between ME and EMnE?
25. How did the formation of the perfect tense in EMnE differ from that in PDE?
26. Compare the nature of the Latin loanwords into English in EMnE with that of French loanwords into English in ME.

Holt, Rinehart and Winston, Inc.

Name _____

7.3 Phonology: Minor Consonant Changes

Numerous minor changes in consonants occurred during EMnE, some of them permanent, some of them to be reversed later in the standard language, some of them to remain in some dialects but not in others. Among these are the following.

1. Assibilation, whereby poststress /sj/, /zj/, /tj/, and /dj/ became /š/, /ž/, /č/, and /ǰ/, respectively. For example, earlier /fɔrtjən/ 'fortune' became /fɔrčən/.
2. Loss of preconsonantal /r/ (especially after back vowels) and of final unstressed /r/. For example, earlier /rɛkərdz/ 'records' became /rɛkədz/. Also, development of nonetymological intrusive /r/, as in /marθər/ 'Martha'.
3. Loss of /t/ and /d/ in consonant clusters and finally after other consonants. For example, earlier /nɛkst/ 'next' became /nɛks/.
4. Loss of /l/ after a low vowel and before a labial or velar consonant. For example, /tɔlk/ 'talk' became /tɔk/.
5. Loss of [ç] and [x] as allophones of /h/ after a vowel. For example, [brɪçt] 'bright' became [braɪt].
6. Continued loss of the phonemic distinction between /hw/ and /w/. For example, earlier /hwɪč/ 'which' became /wɪč/.

Because the standard spelling had become fixed at the beginning of the EMnE period, it is difficult to see these changes in the writings of educated people. However, the misspellings of the semiliterate can be very revealing. That is, if such people frequently write *lan* for *land*, we can be reasonably certain that they did not pronounce a final /d/ in this word. Reverse spellings are also instructive. For example, if writers spell *gallons* as *gallonds*, we can assume they knew that many words ending in /n/ in speech have an additional consonant in spelling; in the case of *gallonds*, they just guessed wrong.

All of the following items are taken from texts by semiliterate EMnE writers. Identify by number which of the minor consonantal changes described above is illustrated by the misspelling.

a. __5__ drigh (dry)

b. ____ suffishent (sufficient)

c. ____ grinstone (grindstone)

d. ____ whome (home)

e. ____ matte (matter)

f. ____ memorander (memoranda)

g. ____ haf (half)

h. ____ wite (white)

i. ____ behing (behind)

j. ____ menchened (mentioned)

k. ____ sighned (signed)

l. ____ Leonad (Leonard)

m. ____ Norwack (Norwalk)

n. ____ eastwart (eastward)

o. ____ wilst (whilst)

p. ____ tweney (twenty)

q. ____ nit (night)

r. ____ trashewer (treasurer)

s. ____ whithin (within)

t. ____ andvell (anvil)

u. ____ Indjans (Indians)

v. ____ imbercillity (imbecility)

w. ____ prudencshall (prudential)

x. ____ assistand (assistant)

Holt, Rinehart and Winston, Inc.

3. In the seventeenth and eighteenth centuries, (a) *entreat, beat, wheat, heat, meat, seat, eat, repeat, threat, yet, sweat, get, great*; (b) *speak, weak, neck, break*. For example,

> Though I must go, enture not *yet* . . .
> Like gold to airy thinness *beat*
> > —John Donne, 1633

> But those do hold or *break*,
> As men are strong or *weak*.
> > —Andrew Marvell, 1681

Probable vowel in all the words _____

4. In the seventeenth and eighteenth centuries, (a) *feature, creature, nature*; (b) *sea, tea, away, obey*. For example,

> Bestow this jewel also on my *creature*, . . .
> And rest in Nature, not the God of *Nature*;
> > —George Herbert, 1633

> To cross this narrow *sea*, . . .
> And fear to launch *away*.
> > —Isaac Watts, 1707

Probable vowel in all the words _____

5. Throughout the EMnE period, *lost, ghost, cost, most, crossed, boast, frost, toast, coast, host*. For example,

> Not all the tresses that fair head can *boast*,
> Shall draw such envy as the Lock you *lost*.
> > —Alexander Pope, 1712

Probable vowel in all the words _____

6. Primarily in the seventeenth and eighteenth centuries, *doom, come, home, Rome, tomb, bloom, room, become*. For example,

> Souls as thy shining self, shall *come*
> And in her first ranks make thee *room*
> > —Richard Crashaw, 1652

> The soul, uneasy and confined from *home*,
> Rests and expatiates in a life to *come*.
> > —Alexander Pope, 1733

Probable vowel in all the words _____

7. Throughout EMnE, *mind, blind, kind, behind, wind* (breeze), *bind, unconfined*. For example,

> She ware no gloves, for neither sun nor *wind*
> Would burn or parch her hands; but to her *mind* . . .
> > —Christopher Marlowe, 1598

Probable vowel in all the words _____

Holt, Rinehart and Winston, Inc.

7.6   Graphics: A Letter to a New England Town Meeting

Reproduced here is the first page of a letter written by the early American settler, scholar, and political leader Roger Williams, in the year 1650–51. The first few lines have been transliterated for you. Read the letter, complete the transliteration, and answer the questions that follow the facsimile of the letter.

Courtesy of the Rhode Island Historical Society.

Name ____ _____

Beginning of Transliteration

1 NAR: 22.11.50 (so calld)
2 Well beloved friends: Lo: [ving] respects to   of
3 you presented with heartie desires of yor
4 present & eternall peace. I am sorrie y^t
5 I am occasioned to trouble you in y^e mi
6 of many yor other Troubles. Yet vpon   ɔe
7 rience of yor wonted Lo: [ving] kindn   Gentle

a. Does Williams distinguish *i* and *j*? ____ _____

b. What is the distribution of *u* and *v*? _   _____

_____   _____

c. What two variants of *e* does Willi   ıse? _____

d. What two variants of *d* does he   _____

e. How does Williams form an   .and? _____

f. What words does Williams   viate? _____

_____   _____

What are his ways of indic   that a form is abbreviated? _____

_____   _____

g. What marks of pun   n does he use? _____

_____   _____

h. How does his c   zation differ from that of PDE? _____

_____   _____

i. Williams wa   ghly educated man, so we may assume that his spelling was "correct"
for his time.   differences from PDE spelling do you find (apart from capitalization

differences)   _____

_____   _____

_____   _____

j. Wi   spells at least one word in two different ways. What is that word? _____

_____   _____

Holt, Rinehart and Winston, Inc.

7.7   Grammar: Noun Inflections

A.   By EMnE, noun inflection was in all essentials identical to that of PDE. Still, a few nouns had variant plurals throughout most of the period.

>"My *howsys* ther be in decay" (1529)
>"The *housen* wherein they dwell" (1557)
>"Two busshels of gray *pees*" (1523)
>"*Peasyn* are muche in the nature of beanes" (1533)

Similar variation is found for the nouns *hose*, *shoe*, and *eye*.

1. What three PDE nouns retain plurals in *-en*? _____

_____

2. If you wanted to make an uncomplimentary reference to two large but stupid people,

you might call them a "couple of dumb ox____ ."

Why did you choose the plural form you did? _____

_____

What does this imply? _____

3. Would you refer to your two male siblings as your "two brethren"? _____

Why or why not? _____

B.   Like PDE, EMnE had a number of nouns that varied between regular plurals in *-s* and zero plurals (that is, the plural form was identical to the singular form). Consider the following examples.

>"command our present *numbers* be muster'd" (c. 1608)
>"and those poor *number* saved with you" (c. 1600)
>"I knew a man of eightie *winters*" (1612)
>"Now I am xix *wynter* olde" (1522)
>"The most usual *Kindes* of Apples" (1652)
>"Such *kind* of Pamphlets work Wonders" (1681)
>"Two miles from an excellent water for *trouts*" (1790)
>"The *trout* . . . there have been over praised" (1789)

1. In PDE, we say, "The number of them *is* uncertain," but "A number of them *are*

uncertain." Comment. _____

_____

2. Is *kind* ever used as a zero plural in PDE? _____

_____

3. If you were describing a fairly tall person, you would say, "He is six _____

tall." If you were describing an even taller person, you would say, "He is six _____ four." What determines the difference between the marked-plural and the zero-plural forms?

_____

4. Complete the following with the appropriate form of *dozen*. (The same rules apply to *hundred*, *thousand*, *million*, etc.)

"We need three _____ folding chairs."

"We need _____ of folding chairs."

What determines the difference between the two forms? _____

_____

C. Consider the following examples of genitive nouns, all from Shakespeare.

for his mercy sake	for duty's sake
for fashion sake	for fame's sake
for god sake	for god's sake
for heaven sake	for wealth's sake
for safety sake	for wisdom's sake
for alliance sake	for your friend's sake

1. Do you think there was a difference in how the genitive ending was pronounced in these two sets of examples? _____

_____

2. Why was the possessive [s] often omitted in this construction? _____

_____

3. In PDE, how is the expletive "for Christ's sake" sometimes spelled in representing dialogue? _____

Why? _____

4. Can you suggest a possible origin for the colloquial expression "for Pete's sake"?

_____

Holt, Rinehart and Winston, Inc.

7.8 Grammar: Relative Pronouns and Relative Adverbs

Usage of relative pronouns and adverbs was in a state of flux during the EMnE period (as, indeed, it still is today to some extent). For each of the following sentences, indicate in the blank to the left whether the construction with the italicized relative would be acceptable (A) or unacceptable (U) today.

1. ____ ''much less then is it lawful for subjects to resist their godly and Christian princes *which* do not abuse their authority'' (1547)

2. ____ ''And soon after he called his high court of Parliament, *in the which* was demanded by King Henry's friends what should be done with King Richard.'' (1569)

3. ____ ''the Bishop of Carlisle, *which* was a man well learned and of a good courage, stood up . . .'' (1569)

4. ____ ''There was a lionesse *which* had whelpes in her den, *the which* den was obserued by a Beare, . . .'' (1607)

5. ____ ''Happy is that city *which* in time of peace thinks of war'' (1621)

6. ____ ''And now, lastly, will be the time to read with them those organic arts *which* enable men to discourse and write perspicuously, elegantly, and according to the fitted style of lofty, mean, or lowly.'' (1644)

7. ____ ''Coriolanus, who could not attain to that as he wanted, should have forsaken *that which* he had received.'' (1650)

8. ____ ''that man, *which* looks too far before him, in the care of future time, hath his heart all the day, gnawed on by fear of death'' (1651)

9. ____ ''I had the loose Earth to carry out; and *which* was of more Importance, I had the Cieling to prop up.'' (1719)

10. ____ ''I entreated him to give order that my cabinet should be brought, *of which* I kept the key in my pocket'' (1726)

11. ____ ''That man *that* thy horse hath eten his corne or grasse wyll be greued at the [= thee].'' (1523)

12. ____ ''I earne *that* I eate: get *that* I weare'' (1600)

13. ____ ''Be *that* thou know'st thou art, and then thou art As great as *that* thou fear'st'' (1601)

14. ____ ''they cease not still to search for *that* they have not and know not'' (1616)

15. ____ ''He *that* hath wife and children hath given hostages to fortune'' (1625)

16. ____ ''Coriolanus, who could not attain to *that as* he wanted, should have forsaken that which he had received.'' (1650)

17. ____ ''A Tree *that* grew near an old Wall'' (1712)

18. ____ ''there presented him selfe a tall clownishe younge man, *who* falling before the Queen of Faeries desired a boone'' (1589)

19. ____ ''*Who* soweth in raine, he shall reape it with teares'' (1573–80)

Holt, Rinehart and Winston, Inc.

20. ____ "Every man gladly would be neighbour to a quiet person, *as who* . . . doth afford all the pleasure of conversation, without any . . . trouble" (c. 1677)

21. ____ "Sir Roger is one of those *who* is not only at Peace within himself, but beloved and esteemed by all about him" (1711)

22. ____ "I counsel . . . all wise . . . men, that they doo not accompany wyth those *whom* they know are not secret." (1557)

23. ____ "Her cursed tongue . . . Appear'd like Aspis sting, that closely kils, Or cruelly does wound *whom so* she wils." (1596)

24. ____ "For *whom* in the world do you think that I was kept so long kicking my heels?" (1780)

25. ____ "A virgin spoused to a man, *whose* name was Ioseph" (1526)

26. ____ "*Whose* house is of glasse, must not throw stones at another." (1633)

27. ____ "Things, *whose* particular Discussion would . . . exceed the Design of this Book" (1730)

28. ____ "The lawyer saith *what* men have determined; the historian *what* men have done" (1595)

29. ____ "To those *as* have no children" (1603)

30. ____ "Life it self . . . is a burden *[no relative pronoun]* cannot be born under the lasting . . . pressure of such an uneasiness." (1690)

31. ____ "There were of [her Majesty's ships] but six in all, *whereof* two but small ships" (1591)

32. ____ "This night I hold an old accustom'd Feast, *Whereto* I have inuited many a Guest." (1592)

33. ____ "He lick'd the ground *whereon* she trod." (1667)

Summarize how the usage of each of the following relatives differed in EMnE from what is considered acceptable in PDE. Base your answers only on the sentences listed here.

which _____

_____

that _____

_____

_____

who _____

_____

whom _____

_____

whose _____

_____

what _____

_____

as _____

_____

whereof, whereon, whereto _____

_____

ø (i.e., no relative pronoun used in a relative construction) _____

_____

Holt, Rinehart and Winston, Inc.

Name _____

7.9   Grammar: Pronouns and Pronominal Adjectives

Although few changes in the inflection of pronouns and pronominal adjectives have taken place since ME, pronominal usage during EMnE still differed in many minor ways from that of PDE. For each of the following excerpts, identify the nature of the difference from PDE and rewrite the phrase as necessary to put the phrase into acceptable modern English. The relevant pronouns or pronominal adjectives are italicized; numbers 2 and 4 have two separate constructions to be considered.

0. ''For some haue gret plenty . . . and *other some* haue scantly so moche as they nede''

(1532) _PDE does not use the two together like this. Rewrite as_

"others," as "some," or as "some others."

1. ''Doth *any of both* these examples prove that . . . ?'' (1540) _____

_____

2. ''I feare *me some* will blushe that readeth this, if he be bitten'' (c. 1581) _____

_____

3. ''sit *thou* by my bedde'' (1597) _____

_____

4. ''*myself* am Naples, / Who with *mine* eyes, . . . beheld / The King my father wrack'd.''

(1611) _____

_____

5. ''[They] are so proud, so censorious, that *it* is no living with them.'' (a. 1617) _____

_____

6. ''Wee . . . owe him [God] obedience according to *euery* his morall commands'' (1626)

_____

7. ''But *whether ever* beginneth, he may be sure the other will follow'' (1632) _____

_____

8. ''How to renew and make good any sort of Gun-powder that hath lost *his* strength''

(1644) _____

_____

9. ''The nature of young tulip roots is to runne down deeper into the ground, every year

more than *other*'' (1660) _____

_____

10. ''Presuming on the Queen *her* private practice'' (1659) _____

_____

Holt, Rinehart and Winston, Inc.

11. ''he whispered *me* in the Ear to take notice of a Tabby Cat that sate in the Chimny-Corner'' (1711–12) _____

_____

12. ''I will relate *somewhat* concerning the Earl of Antrim'' (c. 1715) _____

_____

13. ''*Every* of the said chirurgeons is to have twelvepence a body searched by them'' (1722) _____

_____

14. ''We came in full View of a great Island or Continent (for we knew not *whether*).'' (1726) _____

_____

15. ''We must not let this hour pass, without presenting *us* to him.'' (1729) _____

_____

16. ''Fontenelle and Voltaire were men of unequal merit; yet how different has been the fate of *either*'' (1759) _____

_____

17. ''A retreat for St. Bridget and *other* nine virgins'' (1799) _____

_____

Name _____

7.10   Grammar: Adjectives

A.   In each of the following sentences, the italicized adjectives would be unacceptable in some way in PDE. In the blank following each sentence, rewrite the phrase as it might appear in standard PDE.

0. "For in his books be contained . . . not only the documents *martial* and discipline of arms but also . . ." (1531) _"martial documents"_

1. "all appeals made to Rome were clearly void and of *none* effect" (1548) _____

2. "the Percies, affirming them to be their awn [own] *proper* prisoners and their *peculiar* preys, did utterly deny to deliver them" (1569) _____

3. "Sometimes he was sorry and repented, much grieved for that he had done, after his anger had cooled, by & by *outrageous* again." (1621–51) _____

4. "In this Catalogue, Borage and Bugloss [names of plants] may challenge the *chiefest* place" (1621–51) _____

5. "Round about him those fiends danced a *pretty* while, and then came in three more as ugly as the rest" (1624) _____

6. "notwithstanding *what* imputations *soever* shall be laid" (1662) _____

7. "the *more fuller* statement" (1680) _____

8. "some of [the Country People] will needs have it that Sir Roger has brought down a *Cunning* Man with him, to cure the old Woman" (1711) _____

9. "Many of the laws which were in force during the monarchy being *relative* merely to that form of government, . . . the first assembly which met after the establishment of the commonwealth appointed a committee to revise the whole code" (1784) _____

10. "we consider *academical* institutions as preparatory to a settlement in the world"

(1791) _____

_____

B.   Throughout the entire history of English, past participles of verbs have served as adjectives. In some instances, earlier irregular forms of participles have survived as adjectives although the verb itself has become regular in PDE. One example is *wrought* (from the verb *work*). Add other examples to the types listed below.

1. Participles in *-en* (e.g., "He has *shaved*" vs. "a closely *shaven* man" _____

_____

2. Participles in which the *-ed* of the adjective is pronounced as a separate syllable although it is not as a verb (e.g., "She *dogged* my footsteps" vs. "a *dogged* expression on

her face") _____

_____

Holt, Rinehart and Winston, Inc.

Name _____

7.11   Grammar: Verb Phrases

The grammar of EMnE verb phrases is usually similar enough to that of PDE so that modern readers can understand the general sense even if they often miss the subtleties. Nevertheless, the differences are numerous. For each of the following excerpts, identify the nature of the difference from PDE of the italicized items and rewrite the excerpt as necessary to turn it into acceptable PDE.

0. ''Ye *are come* together, fathers and right wise men, to enter council'' (c. 1530) _____

In PDE, auxiliary for perfect tense is always "have." Rewrite

as "You have come together."

1. ''I *endeavored myself* to prove that, by the order of man's creation, preeminence in degree should be among men according as they *do excel* in the pure influence of understanding'' (1531) _____

_____

2. ''the chief praise of a writer *consisteth* in the enterlacing of pleasure with profit'' (1582) _____

_____

3. ''With that word his voice *brake* so with sobbing that he could *say* no further'' (1590)

_____

_____

4. ''You *never saw* her *since* she was deform'd.'' (c. 1590) _____

_____

5. ''Dangerous it *were* for the feeble brain of man to wade far into the doings of the Most High'' (1594) _____

_____

6. ''Sirrah Jack, thy horse *stands* behind the hedge. When thou need'st him, there thou shalt find him.'' (c. 1596) _____

_____

7. ''The sheeted dead / *Did squeak* and *gibber* in the Roman streets'' (1599) _____

_____

_____

8. ''*Never did* the English nation *behold* so much black worn as there was at her funeral.'' (1624) _____

_____

Holt, Rinehart and Winston, Inc.

9. "*Present not* yourself on the stage . . . until the quaking prologue *hath* (by rubbing) got color into his cheeks" (1609) _____

_____

_____

10. "Wadley in Berkshire is *situate* in a vale" (1621–51) _____

_____

11. "the bell that rings to a sermon *calls not* upon the preacher only" (1623) _____

_____

12. "To make myself believe that our life is something, I *use* in my thoughts *to compare* it to something, if it be like anything that is something." (1624) _____

_____

13. "They *will* on in sinne to their utter ruine" (1647) _____

_____

14. "And he that can tell [count to] ten, if he *recite* them out of order, will lose himself, and not know when he *has done*." (1651) _____

_____

15. "I was formerly a great companion of his, for the which I now *repent me*" (1682)

_____

_____

16. "I *am so used to consider* my self as Creditor and Debtor, that I often state my Accounts after the same manner" (1712) _____

_____

17. "There was but one small objection to complete our happiness; which was no more than—that she *was married* three months before to Mr. Shrimp" (1762) _____

_____

18. "The spoil of the church *was* now *become* the only resource of all their operations in finance" (1790) _____

_____

Name _____

7.12 Grammar: Adverbs

In each of the following excerpts from EMnE, the italicized adverb (or adverbs) differs in some way from what would be acceptable in PDE. Indicate whether the difference is morphological, syntactic, or lexical/semantic. In some instances, there may be more than one type of difference. Then rewrite as much of the excerpt as is necessary to turn the adverbial portion(s) into acceptable PDE.

0. "albeit he was *sore* enamored upon her, yet he forbare her" (1557) _lexical and_
morphological. Rewrite: "extremely enamored" or "very enamored."

1. "he laid heinously to her charge that thing that herself could not deny, that all the world wist was true, and that *natheles* every man laughed at . . ." (1513) _____

2. "He therefore that will be a good scholar . . . must *evermore* set all his diligence to be like his master." (1561) _____

3. "this answer pleased *nothing* the Earl of Worcester, but put him in a great choler" (1569) _____

4. "When the king had well advised upon and considered this matter, he made answer and said that the Earl of March was *not* taken prisoner *neither* for his cause *nor* in his service" (1569) _____

5. "in the company of so many wise and good men together as *hardly* then could have been picked out again out of all England *beside*" (1570) _____

6. "inquire out those taverns . . . whose masters are *oftenest* drunk" (1609) _____

7. "Jack could no sooner get a crown but *straight* he found means to spend it" (1619)

8. "Yet that night *betimes* they got down into the bottom of the bay" (1630) _____

9. "His Godhead is in such sort *eachwhere*, that it filleth both heaven and earth" (1649)

Holt, Rinehart and Winston, Inc.

10. "*What* should I mention beauty; that fading toy?" (1677) _____

_____

11. "I *last night* sat very late in company with this body of friends" (1711) _____

_____

12. "There is *scarce* a single humour in the body of man . . . in which our glasses do not discover myriads of living creatures." (1712) _____

_____

_____

13. "But it is *exceeding* apparent that such ideas have nothing in them which is spiritual and divine" (1746) _____

_____

14. "Accordingly, the next time that Johnson did come, as soon as he was *fairly* engaged with a book, Mr. Barnard stole round to the apartment where the King was, and . . . mentioned that Dr. Johnson was then in the library." (1767) _____

_____

_____

15. "I pressed him to persevere in his resolution to make *this year* the projected visit to the Hebrides" (1791) _____

_____

Name _____

7.13   Grammar: Prepositions

Although prepositions are not added or dropped from the language with the ease of nouns or verbs, new ones do enter English and older ones are lost. Further, the meanings change over time. For each of the italicized prepositions in the following sentences from EMnE, indicate what the PDE equivalent would be. Check the *OED* if you are not sure.

0. ''All the people of the cyte came *ageynste* hym wyth ioye and praysynge'' (a. 1520)

PDE "toward" _____

1. ''They coude not go by it, neither *of* the right honde ner [nor] *of* the left'' (1535) __

_____

2. ''It was forbidden vnto them to marie *without* their owne tribe'' (1558) _____

_____

3. ''to restore their cousin Edmund, Earl of March, *unto* the crown'' (1569) _____

4. ''[John Winchcomb] . . . being so good a companion, he was called *of* old and young Jack of Newbury'' (1619) _____

_____

5. ''*For* the abundance of milk she [the cow] did give, the owner might eate butter'' (1641) _____

6. ''And when the endeavour is *fromward* something, it is generally called AVER-SION.'' (1651) _____

7. ''He was . . . restored *till* his liberty and archbishoprick'' (1655) _____

_____

8. ''The Bears and Foxes, who *sans* question / Than we by odds have warmer Vests on'' (a. 1687) _____

9. ''He . . . spent his time *in* the Solitary Top of a Mountain'' (1701) _____

_____

10. ''His Cunning is the more odious *from* the resemblance it has to Wisdom'' (1710)

_____

11. ''The really good are so far less in number *to* the bad'' (1771) _____

12. ''he talked, as usual, *upon* indifferent subjects'' (1791) _____

Holt, Rinehart and Winston, Inc.

Name _____

7.14   Grammar: Conjunctions

In each of the following excerpts from EMnE texts, the italicized conjunction would not be used, at least in this context, in PDE. Give the equivalent conjunction in PDE.

0. "it was concluded that King Richard . . . should have all things honorably minist'red unto him, *as well* for his diet *as also* apparel." (1569) "for his diet as well as his apparel" or "for both his diet and his apparel"

1. "Owen Glendower kept [Edmund Mortimer] in filthy prison, shackeled with irons, only *for that* he took the king's part and was to him faithful and true . . ." (1569) _____

_____

2. "and, *for* the time shall not seem tedious, / I'll tell thee what befel me" (a. 1595) _____

_____

3. "Thou rememberest / *Since* once I sat upon a promontory." (1594–95) _____

4. "Tell me where is fancie bred, / *Or* in the heart, *or* in the head?" (1596) _____

5. "They will set an house on fire *and* it were but to roast their eggs." (1597–1625)

_____

6. "Baptista Porta . . . will by all means have the front of an house stand to the South, *which how* it may be good in Italy and hotter Climes, I know not, in our Northern Countries I am sure it is best." (1621–51) _____

7. "Henry Percy offered . . . to free the Queene of Scots out of prison *so as* Grange and Carre . . . would receive her at the borders." (1635) _____

_____

8. "No man therefore can conceive anything, *but* he must conceive it in some place." (1651) _____

9. "you have scarce begun to admire the one, *ere* you despise the other" (1672)

_____

10. "Run sweet Babe, *while* thou art weary, and then I will take thee up and carry thee" (1688) _____

11. "he whispered me in the Ear to take notice of a Tabby Cat that sate in the Chimny-Corner, which, as the knight told me, lay under as bad a Report as Moll White her self; for *besides that* Moll is said often to accompany her in the same Shape, the Cat is reported to have spoken twice or thrice in her Life" (1711–12) _____

7.15 Syntax

Reproduced here are two English translations of the gospel of St. Mark, 2:13–22, the first
from ME and the second from EMnE. For each of the categories listed in the exercise that
follows, compare the syntax of the ME and the EMnE translations. (See *A Biography of
the English Language*, pp. 277–83, for general remarks about EMnE syntax.)

ME	[13]And he wente out eftsone to the see,
EMnE	And he went out agayne vnto the see,
ME	and al the cumpanye of peple cam to hym;
EMnE	and all the people resorted vnto hym;
ME	and he tauȝte hem. [14]And whenne he passide,
EMnE	and he taught them. And as Jesus passed by,
ME	he say Leui Alfey sittynge at the tolbothe,
EMnE	he sawe Levy the sonne of Alphey sytt att the receyte of custome,
ME	and he seith to hym, Sue thou me.
EMnE	and sayde vnto him, Folowe me.
ME	And he rysynge suede hym. [15]And it is don,
EMnE	And he arose and folowed hym. And yt cam to passe,
ME	whenne he sat at the mete in his hous,
EMnE	as Jesus sate att meate in his housse,
ME	many puplicanys and synful men saten togidre at the mete
EMnE	many pubplicans and synners sate att meate also
ME	with Jhesu and his disciplis;
EMnE	with Jesus and his disciples;
ME	sothely there weren manye that foleweden hym.
EMnE	for there were many that folowed him.
ME	[16]And scribis and Pharisees seeyinge, for he eet
EMnE	And when the scribs and Pharises sawe him eate
ME	with puplicanys and synful men,
EMnE	with publicans and synners,
ME	seiden to his disciplis, Whi ȝoure maister
EMnE	they sayde vnto his disciples, Howe is it that he
ME	etith and drinkith with puplicanys and synners?
EMnE	eateth and drynketh with publicans and synners?
ME	[17]This thing herd, Jhesus seith to hem,
EMnE	When Jesus had herde that, he sayd vnto them,
ME	Hoole men han no nede to a leche,
EMnE	The whole have no nede of the visicion,
ME	but thei that han yuele; forsothe I cam
EMnE	but the sicke; I cam
ME	not for to clepe iuste men, but synners.
EMnE	to cal the sinners to repentaunce, and not the iuste.

ME	[18]And the disciplis of Joon and the Pharisees weren fastynge;
EMnE	And the disciples of Jhon and of the Pharises did faste;
ME	and thei camen, and seien to hym,
EMnE	and they cam, and sayde vnto him,
ME	Whi disciplis of Joon and of Pharisees fasten,
EMnE	Why do the discipls of Jhon and off the Pharises faste,
ME	but thi disciplis fasten nat? [19]And Jhesus seith
EMnE	and thy disciples fast nott? And Jesus sayde
ME	to hem, Whether the sonnys of weddyngis mown faste,
EMnE	vnto them, Can the chyldren of a weddinge faste,
ME	as long as the spouse is with hem?
EMnE	whils the brydgrome is with them?
ME	Hou longe tyme thei han the spouse with hem,
EMnE	As longe as they have the brydgrome with them,
ME	thei mowe nat faste. [20]Forsothe dayes shulen come,
EMnE	they cannot faste. Butt the dayes wyll come,
ME	whenne the spouse shal be taken awey from hem,
EMnE	when the brydegrome shalbe taken from them,
ME	and thanne thei shulen faste in thoo days. [21]No man
EMnE	and then shall they faste in thoose dayes. Also no man
ME	seweth a pacche of rude clothe to an old clothe,
EMnE	soweth a pece of newe cloth vnto an olde garment,
ME	ellis he takith awey the newe supplement,
EMnE	for then taketh he awaye the newe pece from the olde,
ME	and a more brekynge is maad.
EMnE	and so is the rent worsse.
ME	[22]And no man sendith newe wyn in to oold botelis,
EMnE	In lyke wyse no man poureth newe wyne in to olde vesselles,
ME	ellis the wyn shal berste the wyn vesselis,
EMnE	for yf he do the newe wyne breaketh the vesselles,
ME	and the wyn shal be held out,
EMnE	and the wyne runneth out,
ME	and the wyne vesselis shulen perishe.
EMnE	and the vessels are marde.
ME	But newe wyn shal be sent in to newe wyn vesselis.
EMnE	Butt newe wyne must be poured in to newe vesselles.

Name _____

A. Syntax of Phrases

1. Use of definite article (see especially verses 15, 18) _____

_____

_____

2. Use of *do* as auxiliary (see verses 18, 22) _____

_____

_____

3. Formation of future (what is the auxiliary in ME and EMnE?) _____

_____

B. Syntax of Clauses

1. Word order of independent clauses (see especially verse 21) _____

_____

2. Syntax of questions (see especially verses 16, 18, 19) _____

_____

_____

3. Syntax of imperatives (see especially verse 14) _____

_____

_____

4. Syntax of negative clauses (see especially verses 17, 18, 19) _____

_____

_____

Holt, Rinehart and Winston, Inc.

Name _____

7.16   Lexicon: Loanwords

I. Borrowings from Romance Languages Other than French
Spanish, Portuguese, and Italian contributed scores of words to the EMnE lexicon. Identify which of these three languages was the *immediate* source of the following words. (In some cases, the *ultimate* source is different, e.g., an American Indian language.) Because Spanish and Portuguese are so closely related, dictionaries may give both as the origin. When this is the case, list both.

0. buffalo _Portuguese_

1. cargo _____

2. cedilla _____

3. flamingo _____

4. launch (boat) _____

5. Madeira _____

6. manage _____

7. mandarin _____

8. miniature _____

9. mosquito _____

10. negro _____

11. picturesque _____

12. port (wine) _____

13. rusk _____

14. stevedore _____

15. stucco _____

16. studio _____

17. torso _____

18. umbrella _____

19. vanilla _____

II. Borrowings from Other Germanic Languages
A Biography of the English Language lists numerous EMnE loans from Dutch and German and a few from the Scandinavian languages. From which Germanic language group did the following EMnE loans come?

    A. Low or High German
    B. Dutch
    C. Scandinavian, including Swedish, Norwegian, Danish, and Icelandic

0. brackish _B_

1. frolic _____

2. gabble _____

3. hamster _____

4. hug _____

5. hustle _____

6. minx (hussy) _____

7. monkey _____

8. morass _____

9. narwhal _____

10. ogle _____

11. prattle _____

12. rumple _____

13. simper _____

14. slurp _____

15. snarl _____

16. spanner (wrench) _____

17. sprint _____

18. tern _____

19. vole _____

20. widdershins _____

21. wiseacre _____

Holt, Rinehart and Winston, Inc.

III. Borrowings from non-Indo-European Languages

In addition to those mentioned in *A Biography of the English Language*, English borrowed numerous words during EMnE from languages in Africa, Asia, and the Americas. Identify the language of origin of the following words.

0. bey _Turkish_

1. calico _____

2. catalpa _____

3. chintz _____

4. coati _____

5. cot (bed) _____

6. gopherwood _____

7. jute _____

8. kangaroo _____

9. kayak _____

10. paddy (rice) _____

11. taboo _____

12. tattoo (on skin) _____

13. umiak _____

14. wombat _____

15. yaws _____

Name _____

7.17   Lexicon: Common Nouns from Proper Nouns

A.   The following words entered EMnE from various sources, but all originated as proper nouns, as the names of places, of tribes, of people (real, fictional, or mythical). Give the origins of the words and indicate the type of proper noun from which they came.

0. agaric *Agaria, Samartia (place)*

1. amaryllis _____

2. bungalow _____

3. charlatan _____

4. clink _____

5. doily _____

6. fauna _____

7. finnan (haddie) _____

8. frangipani _____

9. gage (plum) _____

10. gardenia _____

11. gavotte _____

12. harlequin _____

13. mausoleum _____

14. merino _____

15. mocha _____

16. morris (dance) _____

17. nankeen _____

18. python _____

19. solecism _____

B.   The following words, first appearing in EMnE, originated as short forms of given names or as nicknames. Identify the shortened form or the nickname and the full form of the name.

0. dandy *Andrew*

1. davit _____

2. dobbin _____

3. grimalkin _____

4. grog _____

5. hick _____

6. jackanapes _____

7. jenny _____

8. jilt _____

9. jug _____

10. magpie _____

11. tomcat _____

12. zany _____

Name _____

7.18   Lexicon: New Words by Modification of Old Words

I. Shortened Forms

New words are sometimes formed by abbreviating earlier words. This shortening may take the following forms:

  A. **aphesis**, or dropping the unstressed first part of a word, as in *squire* from *esquire*
  B. **clipping**, or dropping the latter part of a word or phrase, as in *soap* from *soap opera*
  C. **contraction**, or omitting part of the interior of a word or phrase

All of the following shortened words first appeared in EMnE. Identify which of the processes (A–C) was involved and give the original, unshortened form.

0. char (burn) _B-charcoal_

1. fancy _____

2. fortnight _____

3. gaffer _____

4. lunge _____

5. pester _____

6. rear (back part) _____

7. quack (charlatan) _____

8. trump _____

9. twit (reproach) _____

10. whim _____

11. wig _____

II. Blends

The process is most typical of PDE, but a number of probable blends (or *portmanteau words*) first appear in EMnE, though dictionaries do not always agree on the original elements of the blend. Look up in two different desk dictionaries each of the following words that are first recorded in EMnE. If the two dictionaries agree on the original elements of the blend, simply write the elements in the blank. If the dictionaries differ, write both the suggested etymologies in the blank beside the word.

0. scrawl _scrawl + crawl_

1. chump _____

2. flabbergast _____

3. flounder (verb) _____

4. fluff _____

5. flurry _____

6. jolt _____

7. pennant _____

8. riffle _____

9. smash _____

10. twiddle _____

11. twirl _____

In what way are most, though not all, of these words semantically similar? _____

_____

Holt, Rinehart and Winston, Inc.

Stylistically similar? _____

_____

III. Back Formations

A back formation is a new word created by removing what is mistakenly assumed to be an inflectional or derivational affix from an existing word. For example, the verb *burgle* was created by removing what looked like an agentive suffix from *burglar*. That is, by analogy with such pairs as *walker* : *walk*, *bungler* : *bungle*, and so on, the relationship *burglar* : *burgle* was created. The following words all originated as back formations. For each, find in a desk dictionary the earlier form from which it was created and the apparent suffix that was removed to make the new word.

0. asp   *aspis; Greek original interpreted as English plural*

1. difficult _____

2. dishevel _____

3. fog _____

4. hero _____

5. laze _____

6. mix _____

7. quip _____

8. truck (noun) _____

9. waft _____

Name _____

7.19   Lexicon: Doublets

PDE has many *doublets*, words ultimately from the same source but borrowed at different times in different forms. Often, one member of the pair was borrowed, especially from French, during ME and then later borrowed from Latin, Greek, or another language during EMnE. By checking the etymology in a desk dictionary, you should be able to determine the second member of the doublets listed below.

0. balm *balsam (<L. balsamum)*

1. compost _____

2. custom _____

3. desk _____

4. envious _____

5. fashion _____

6. influenza _____

7. mean (average) _____

8. memory _____

9. mussel _____

10. naive _____

11. poor _____

12. priest _____

13. ray (beam) _____

14. reason _____

15. round _____

16. syrup _____

17. vow _____

18. voyage _____

19. zero _____

Holt, Rinehart and Winston, Inc.

Name _____

7.20   Lexicon: Reduplication

A.   Pure reduplication has always been rare in English, except for echoic words like *ha-ha* or *tweet-tweet*. Most of the reduplicated words in English dictionaries are loans from other languages, though EMnE saw the first of a very few apparently native formations. Identify the language of origin of the following reduplicative words; three are native to English.

1. aye-aye _____

2. bulbul _____

3. bye-bye _____

4. dodo _____

5. furfur (dandruff) _____

6. gru-gru _____

7. haha (ditch) _____

8. kaka (parrot) _____

9. motmot (bird) _____

10. papa _____

11. pooh-pooh _____

12. so-so _____

B.   Much more common than pure reduplication in English is *ablaut reduplication*, or reduplication with a vowel change (e.g., *mishmash* or *dribs and drabs*). The EMnE period seems to have been one in which the process was especially productive, examples include *fiddle-faddle*, *zig-zag*, *dilly-dally*, *flim-flam*, and *whim-wham*. All of these involve the alternation of the high front vowel [ɪ] in the first part with the low front [æ] in the second part. Another fairly common ablaut variation is between [ɪ] and [ɑ] or [ɔ]; EMnE examples include *ding-dong*, *flip-flop*, and *wishy-washy*.

Ignoring the date of entry into English, what are some other examples of ablaut reduplication in [ɪ] / [æ]? _____

_____

_____

In [ɪ] / [ɑ] or [ɔ]? _____

_____

C.   Another kind of ablaut reduplication is represented by two different words, varying in their vowels, that share similar or almost identical meanings, such as *rile / roil*, *sweep / swipe*, and *taffy / toffee*. The vowel differences are of various origins, such as dialectal differences and analogy. For each of the following words, provide another word related in meaning but with a different vowel.

0. sleek _slick_____

1. muss _____

2. poppet _____

3. saucy _____

4. snuffle _____

5. thresh _____

6. flop _____

7. hoist _____

8. blat _____

9. slosh _____

10. skim _____

11. snout _____

D.   Still another kind of reduplication, also more common than pure reduplication, is rhyming reduplication, as in *peewee* or *fuddy-duddy*. Again, the EMnE period saw many such formations, including *helterskelter*, *humpty-dumpty*, *mumbo-jumbo*, and *roly-poly*.

What are other examples of rhyming reduplication? _____

_____

Holt, Rinehart and Winston, Inc.

Name _____

7.21   Lexicon: Words from Borrowed Phrases or Other Parts of Speech

Most of the loanwords into EMnE retained their original part-of-speech category, but sometimes the part-of-speech category was changed. For each of the following, give the language of origin, the original part of speech (or phrase), and the original meaning.

0. alarm (noun) __French < Italian phrase *all'arme* 'to arms'__

1. alert (verb) _____

2. atone (verb) _____

3. auto-da-fé (noun) _____

4. caret (noun) _____

5. carouse (verb) _____

6. deficit (noun) _____

7. don (verb) _____

8. fiat (noun) _____

9. habitat (noun) _____

10. handicap (noun) _____

11. malaria (noun) _____

12. quota (noun) _____

13. veto (noun) _____

Name _____

7.22   Lexicon: Lost Vocabulary

The italicized word in each of the following sentences has been lost from the vocabulary of standard PDE (though some of the words may survive dialectally). By consulting the *OED*, determine the meaning of each word and write it in the blank that follows the quotation.

0. ''And if ye will, then leave your *bordes*, / And use your wit and show it so.'' (early sixteenth century) _jests_____

1. ''old men may love not only without slander, but *otherwhile* more happily than young men'' (1561) _____

2. ''that hot love is soon cold, that the *bavin* though it burn bright, is but a blaze'' (1579)

_____

3. ''Reason, in faith thou act well served, that still / Wouldst *brabbling* be with sense and love in me'' (1591) _____

4. ''Unto life many implements are necessary; *moe*, if we seek, as all men naturally do, such a life as hath in it joy, comfort, delight and pleasure.'' (1593) _____

5. ''and how zealously our preachers *dehort* men from them [women], only by urging their subtleties and policies and wisdom'' (1633) _____

6. ''what praise could be then due to well-doing, what *gramercy* to be sober, just, or continent?'' (1644) _____

7. ''set this house on fire with fevers and *calentures*'' (1647) _____

8. ''extending along a meadow to a *cripple* or brushwood'' (1647) _____

9. ''The *Monack*, the Musk-Rat, and several others . . . inhabit here in Mary Land.'' (1666) _____

10. ''Shrink his thin essence like a *rivèled* flower'' (1714) _____

11. ''The Major . . . was so bountiful as frequently to throw me a *tester*'' (1722)

_____

12. ''He called his *hinds* about him, and asked them . . . whether they had ever seen in the fields any little creature that resembled me'' (1735) _____

13. ''Sits in yon western tent, whose cloudy skirts, / With *brede* ethereal wove'' (1746)

_____

14. ''The public reputation is, every moment, in danger of being *compromitted* with him.'' (1787) _____

Holt, Rinehart and Winston, Inc.

7.23   Semantic Change

The italicized word or words in each of the following sentences has undergone a semantic shift since EMnE times. With the help of the *OED*, determine the meaning of the word as used in the sentence.

0. ''The whiteness of her *leer*'' (early sixteenth century) <u>face, complexion</u>

_____

1. ''The king ... kept the day of Sainct George at his manor of Greenwich with great solempnity, and the court was greatly *replenished* with lords, knights, and with ladies and

gentlewomen to a great number with all *solace* and pleasure.'' (1548) _____

_____

2. ''King Richard, perceiving them armed, knew well that they came to his *confusion*, and putting the table from him, valiantly took the bill [battleaxe] out of the first man's hand, and manfully defended himself, and slew four of them in a short space.'' (1569)

_____

3. ''the tricks that in young men be gallantness, courtesy, and preciseness so acceptable to women, in them [old men] are mere follies and *fondness* to be laughed at'' (1561)

_____

4. ''I doubt not but in this register he may find some to content him, unless he be too

curious'' (1573) _____

5. ''Or blind *affection*, which doth ne'er advance / The truth'' (1623) _____

_____

6. ''it will be acknowledged even by those that practise it not that clear and *round* dealing

is the honor of man's nature'' (1625) _____

7. ''if other things as great in the church, and in the rule of life both *economical* and

political, be not looked into and reformed ...'' (1644) _____

_____

8. ''The man therefore read it, and looking upon Evangelist very *carefully*, said Whither

must I fly?'' (1678) _____

9. ''Where unfledged actors learn to laugh and cry, / Where infant *punks* their tender

voices try'' (1682) _____

10. ''His manners, it is true, are tinctured with some strange inconsistencies, and he may

be justly termed a *humorist*'' (1762) _____

11. ''little regard is due to that bigotry which sets *candor* higher than truth'' (1765) ____

_____

12. ''The Indians ... killed and *captivated* all.'' (1768) _____

_____

13. ''A fine shirt with *chitterlings* on the bosom'' (1776) _____

_____

14. ''Such a sudden diversion of all its circulating money from trade to land, must be an additional *mischief*.'' (1790) _____

15. ''There was no affectation about him; and he talked, as usual, upon *indifferent* subjects'' (1791) _____

Name _____

7.24   Semantics: Semantic Shift in Borrowed Words

Some of the words borrowed during EMnE had undergone a dramatic shift in meaning by
the time they reached English or underwent such a shift after entering English. For each
of the following, consult a good desk dictionary to determine the language of origin and
the original meaning.

0. anecdote _French < Greek "things unpublished"_

1. biceps _____

2. coccyx _____

3. cynic _____

4. grotesque _____

5. larva _____

6. lens _____

7. parakeet _____

8. paregoric _____

9. patrol _____

10. prism _____

11. protocol _____

12. rival _____

13. satire _____

14. vermicelli _____

15. vignette _____

7.25   Dialects: Eighteenth-Century New England

Used with caution, the writings of literate but poorly educated speakers can be a valuable source of information about earlier stages of the language. James Browne was an eighteenth-century Rhode Island merchant who kept a book of his business letters. The following excerpts are from letters written between 1735 and 1738.

I. Evidence for Phonology

1. for mr *notton* [Norton]
2. take a morgidg *dead* of it
3. a *pritty* good price
4. Capt *hopkings* [Hopkins]
5. Give him a *Resate* [receipt]
6. their best *Rushey* [Russia] duck
7. to *parfection*
8. a safe *Conshius* [conscience]
9. very *Sudently* some go's up
10. I am sadley *disapinted*
11. *instidd* of the holl sum
12. you must *venter* [venture] that
13. I *Bag* you would assiste me
14. a *perticular* freind of mine
15. Give the *Baror* [bearer] a *Resate*
16. you will *obleg* yours to *sarve*
17. Befoar *fardor* orders
18. I muste have him in a *footnit* [fortnight] if *a tall*
19. Give mr mitchl a *Resate*
20. *puaswad* him to *latt* Baror have it
21. to the *naxte* Corte
22. *Consarning* the rum
23. *twantey* two hhds of molasis
24. he did not Receve *tham*
25. I would pray you to *sarch* in to the afair
26. I *sand* you heir [here] *annacounte* of whot . . .
27. sum pots and sum *kittles*
28. the *wather* is so Colde that *orsters* is not to Be Cacht
29. you shall Be no Losar By *sarving* of me
30. *Bagg* of him *anna Counte* not *ondley* of the Rum But of . . .
31. the Coffey that was *Lafte* in his hands
32. *Consarning* mr Jotham
33. I would pray you to *sarch* into the accounte
34. any *purticurler* one
35. this *misfortin*
36. your *whife* is well
37. fail not of *Bringin* of them
38. Geet me sum Beaf Cost whot it *whill*
39. which Being *intarpretid* is patience
40. desire that you *whould* send me
41. your umb[le] *sarvant*

Holt, Rinehart and Winston, Inc.

Name _____

Identify the phonological feature illustrated in the preceding phrases by writing the number of the appropriate phrases in the blank to the right.

a. Omission of preconsonantal or final [r] _____

b. Intrusive [r] _____

c. Final [ŋ] → [n] _____

d. PDE [ð] appears as [d] _____

e. Lack of phonemic /hw/ _____

f. Intrusive consonant _____

g. PDE final [jər] appears as [ər] (and assibilation probably not present) _____

h. PDE assibilation not present _____

i. Earlier [ɛr] → [ɑr] _____

j. Raising of [ɛ] to [ɪ] _____

k. Lowering of [ɛ] to [æ] _____

l. Incomplete GVS; PDE [i] appears as [e] _____

m. PDE [oi] appears as [ɑi] _____

n. Final [ə] → [i] (or [ɪ]) _____

o. False division between words _____

What are possible explanations for the following spellings?

Conshius (No. 8) _____

perticular (No. 14) _____

obleg (No. 16) _____

II. Evidence for Grammar

1. I have thoughts of what you Said to me Concerning *them* fish
2. if you will send them *direct* up here in good Order for Shiping . . .
3. Untill you had *gave* me an account of what you had Cutt
4. he will *Show it you*, if you will *bring it me*, I will give you Twenty Shillings for *so doing of it*
5. I *wonder* you had not *wrote* to me
6. brother Obadiah *is Safe Arrived*, but lost Andrew Harris, *which* died on his passage
7. You are mistaken, *them* Sails *doth* not belong to me
8. I have a Vessell at Nantucket *a whaleing*
9. I am *a going* to send to Boston for Sails
10. you may think that I have *forgott* it . . . but . . . an Article of Eleven pounds Eighteen Shillings & Eight pence is not so soon *forgott*
11. Your wife *remembers* her love to you
12. I would begg the favour of you to send me . . . an Eight inch Cable Sixty *fathom* long

Holt, Rinehart and Winston, Inc.

13. tell John Browne that there *is 21 Ox's* left at Sam: Carrs
14. I have According to your desire sent for the Negroe and he *is come*
15. the Charge *in getting of him* is about Seventeen pounds
16. as to your being Concerned in a Sloop with me you write so *Indifferent* about it, gives me Suspition . . .
17. I addmiar you *hath* not sante *them* Cowes and oates you prommosied me

Identify the grammatical feature illustrated in the preceding phrases by writing the number of the appropriate phrases in the blank to the right.

a. Nonstandard plural form _____

b. Singular measure word after number _____

c. Relative pronoun not acceptable in PDE _____

d. Pronoun direct object precedes indirect object _____

e. Nonstandard demonstrative _____

f. Nonstandard strong verb form _____

g. Singular verb with plural subject _____

h. Gerund or present-participle construction not acceptable in PDE _____

i. *To be* as perfect auxiliary _____

j. Plain adverb _____

III. Evidence for Lexicon

In the following selections, the italicized words are used in a way normally unfamiliar in PDE. Check the *OED* to find the meaning intended by James Browne and put it in the blank following the excerpt.

1. Mares will do if they are in good *Case*, they must be between three & *Advantage* & Eight years of Age _____

_____

2. it is *ticklish* times here _____

3. gett me a Jibb Stay—one hundred feet long, and five inches *bigg* _____

_____

4. for a likely *Stone* Horse that you bought of him _____

5. Eight *Tearses* [tierces] of . . . rice _____

_____

6. I will pay them in Rum, hoops, Cydar or some other *truck* _____

_____

7. I hope not to have any more *palavers* before I see the pay _____

_____

8. you write so Indifferent about it, gives me Suspition whether you are *forward* for it or no _____

Holt, Rinehart and Winston, Inc.

In the following two sentences, the italicized words are still used in the same meaning, but the phrases are nonetheless not acceptable in PDE. What is the problem?

9. I *wonder* you had not wrote to me _____

_____

10. Your wife *remembers* her love to you _____

_____

Holt, Rinehart and Winston, Inc.

Name _____

7.26 An EMnE Commentator on the Language

During EMnE, for the first time in the history of English, its speakers began to take a serious interest in their language, to describe it, and especially to try to improve it. Most of their works are solemn, plodding, and generally disapproving of the status quo as the authors see it. One exception is Alexander Hume's *Of the Orthographie and Congruitie of the Britan Tongue*, written c. 1617 and dedicated to King James I of England (James VI of Scotland). Its very subtitle, *A Treates, noe shorter than necessarie for the Schooles*, suggests the briskness, clarity, and occasional asperity that characterize this lively little work.

Hume was a Scot; hence his dialect was not that of the standard language in England. But he neither apologizes for his own dialect nor ridicules the language of the south; he seems to accept the two dialects as equally respectable varieties of the same language. There are numerous differences in Hume's northern spelling from that of PDE (and Hume himself is not always consistent), but you should have little difficulty in understanding it.

From the Introduction:

May it please your maest excellent Majestie, I, your grace's humble servant, seeing sik uncertentie in our men's wryting, as if a man wald indyte one letter to tuentie of our best wryteres, nae tuae of the tuentie, without conference, wald agree; and that they quhae might perhapes agree, met rather be custom then knawlege, set my-selfe, about a yeer syne, to seek a remedie for that maladie. Quhen I had done, refyning it, I fand in Barret's alvearie, quhilk is a dictionarie Anglico-latinum, that Sir Thomas Smith, a man of nae less worth then learning, Secretarie to Queen Elizabeth, had left a learned and judiciouse monument on the same subject. Heer consydering my aun weaknes, and meannes of my person, began to fear quhat might betyed my sillie boat in the same seas quhaer sik a man's ship was sunck in the gulf of oblivion. For the printeres and wryteres of this age, caring for noe more arte then may win the pennie, wil not paen them-selfes to knau whither it be orthographie or skaiographie that doeth the turne: and schoolmasteres, quhae's sillie braine will reach no farther than the compas of their cap, content themselfes with αὐτὸς ἔφη my master said it.

From "Of the Britan Vouales"

1. Of a, in our tongue we have four soundes, al so differing ane from an-other, that they distinguish the verie signification of wordes, as a tal man, a gud tal, a horse tal.

2. Quherfoer in this case I wald commend to our men the imitation of the greek and latin, quho, to mend this crook, devysed diphthonges. Let the simplest of these four soundes, or that quhilk is now in use, stand with the voual, and supplie the rest with diphthonges; as, for exemple, I wald wryte the king's hal with the voual a; a shour of hael, with ae; hail marie, with ai; and a heal head, as we cal it, quhilk as the English cales a whole head, with ea. And so, besydes the voual, we have of this thre diphthonges, tuae with a befoer, ae and ai, and ane with the e befoer, ea. Ad to them au, howbeit of a distinct sound; as, knaulege with us, in the south knowlege.

A. What are the PDE equivalents of the four *a* sounds that Hume discusses here? _____

_____

What is the probable difference between the English and the Scots pronunciation of the

vowel in what is today spelled ⟨whole⟩? _____

_____

Holt, Rinehart and Winston, Inc.

3. The instrumentes of the mouth, quherbe the vocal soundes be broaken, be in number seven. The nether lip, the upper lip, the outward teeth, the inward teeth, the top of the tongue, the middle tong, and roof of the mouth. Of these, thre be, as it wer, hammeres stryking, and the rest stiddies [anvils], kepping [catching] the strakes of the hammeres.

4. The hammeres are the nether lip, the top of the tongue, and the midle tongue. The stiddies the overlip, the outward teeth, the inward teeth, and the roofe of the mouth.

5. The nether lip stryking on the overlip makes b, m, p, and on the teeth it makes f and v.

6. The top of the tongue stryking on the inward teeth formes d, l, n, r, s, t, and z.

B. Comment on Hume's statement in point 6. Do you think the point of articulation of sounds like [d, l, n, s], and so on, has changed since Hume's time? Or was Hume a poor observer? Or was the articulation of these sounds different in Scots and in southern English? _____

_____

7. O, we sound al alyk. But of it we have sundrie diphthonges; oa, as to roar, a boar, a boat, a coat; oi, as coin, join, foil, soil; oo, as food, good, blood; ou, as house, mouse, etc. Thus we commonlie wryt mountan, fountan, quhilk it wer more etymological to wryt montan, fontan, according to the original.

C. What does Hume's statement ''oo, as food, good, blood'' imply? _____

_____

From ''Of Our Abusing Sum Consonantes''

1. Now I am cum to a knot that I have noe wedg to cleave, and wald be glaed if I cold hoep for help. Ther sould be for everie sound that can occur one symbol, and of everie symbol but one onlie sound. This reason and nature craveth; and I can not but trow but that the worthie inventoures of this divyne facultie shot at this mark. . . .

3. First, to begin with c, it appeeres be the greekes, quho ever had occasion to use anie latin word, quharein now we sound c as s, in their tymes it sounded k; for Cicero, thei wryt kikero; for Cæsar, kaisar; and plut., in Galba, symbolizes principia, πρινκίπια.

4. This sound of it we, as the latines, also keepe befoer a, o, and u; as canker, conduit, cumber. But, befoer e and i, sum tymes we sound it, with the latin, lyke an s; as, cellar, certan, cease, citie, circle, etc.

5. Behind the voual, if a consonant kep it, we sound it always as a k; as, occur, accuse, succumb, acquyre. If it end the syllab, we ad e, and sound it as an s; as, peace, vice, solace, temperance; but nether for the idle e, nor the sound of the s, have we anie reason; nether daer I, with al the oares of reason, row against so strang a tyde. I hald it better to erre with al, then to stryve with al and mend none.

D. What is Hume's ultimate position on spelling reform? _____

_____

14. T, the last of these misused souldioures, keepes always it's aun nature, except it be befoer tio; as, oration, declamation, narration; for we pronounce not tia and tiu as it is in latin. Onelie let it be heer observed that if an s preceed tio, the t keepes the awn nature, as in question, suggestion, etc.

E. Has assibilation occurred in Hume's dialect? _____

How did his pronunciation of *question* differ from that of PDE? _____

_____

7. And, be the contrarie, here it is clere that soundes pronunced with this organ can not be written with symboles of that; as, for example, a labiel symbol can not serve a dental nor a guttural sound; not a guttural symbol a dental nor a labiel sound.

8. To clere this point, and alsoe to reform an errour bred in the south, and now usurped be our ignorant printeres, I wil tel quhat befel my-self quhen I was in the south with a special

Holt, Rinehart and Winston, Inc.

gud frende of myne. Ther rease, upon sum accident, quhither quho, quhen, quhat, etc., sould be symbolized with q or w, a hoat disputation beuene him and me. After manie conflictes (for we oft encountered), we met be chance, in the citie of baeth, with a doctour of divinitie of both our acquentance. He invited us to denner. At table my antagonist, to bring the question on foot amangs his awn condisciples, began that I was becum an heretik, and the doctour spering how, ansuered that I denyed quho to be spelled with a w, but with qu. Be quhat reason? quod the Doctour. Here, I beginning to lay my grundes of labial, dental, and guttural soundes and symboles, he snapped me on this hand and he on that, that the doctour had mikle a doe to win me room for a syllogisme. Then (said I) a labial letter can not symboliz a guttural syllab. But w is a labial letter, quho a guttural sound. And therfoer w can not symboliz quho, nor noe syllab of that nature. Here the doctour staying them again (for al barked at ones), the proposition, said he, I understand; the assumption is Scottish, and the conclusion false. Quherat al laughed, as if I had bene dryven from al replye, and I fretted to see a frivolouse jest goe for a solid ansuer. My proposition is grounded on the 7 sectio of this same cap., quhilk noe man, I trow, can denye that ever suked the paepes of reason. And soe the question must rest on the assumption quhither w be a labial letter and quho a guttural syllab. As for w, let the exemples of wil, wel, wyne, juge quhilk are sounded befoer the voual with a mint [physical movement] of the lippes, . . . As for quho, besydes that it differres from quo onelie be aspiration, and that w, being noe perfect consonant, can not be aspirated, I appele to al judiciouse eares, to quhilk Cicero attributed mikle, quhither the aspiration in quho be not ex imo gutture, and therfoer not labial.

F. In contemporary terminology, what two different pronunciations of the words *who*, *what*, *when*, and so on, are at the bottom of this argument? _____

_____

It [the stress] may possesse the last syllab; as supprést, preténce, sincére; The penult: as súbject, cándle, cráftie; The antepenult: as difficultie, mínister, fínallie; And the fourth also from the end . . . as spéciallie, insátiable, díligentie. In al quhilk, if a man change the accent, he sall spill the sound of the word.

G. Which of the illustrative words here apparently were stressed differently for Hume from the way they are today? _____

_____

Holt, Rinehart and Winston, Inc.

CHAPTER 8

PRESENT-DAY ENGLISH

8.1 Important Terms and Names

1. acronym
2. American Academy of Language
3. American Structuralism
4. back formation
5. Black English
6. Leonard Bloomfield
7. calque (loan translation)
8. Noam Chomsky
9. A. J. Ellis
10. J. R. Firth
11. Benjamin Franklin
12. glottal stop
13. M. A. K. Halliday
14. hypotaxis
15. James A. H. Murray
16. Lindley Murray
17. *Oxford English Dictionary*
18. parataxis
19. perfect progressive passive
20. periphrasis
21. Isaac Pitman
22. plain adverb
23. Prague School
24. Received Pronunciation
25. root creation
26. Society for Pure English
27. spelling pronunciation
28. Noah Webster
29. *Webster's Third New International Dictionary*

Holt, Rinehart and Winston, Inc.

8.2   Questions for Review and Discussion

1. Summarize the movement for spelling reform during the nineteenth century.

2. What important developments in English dictionary making have taken place since 1800?

3. Why have efforts to establish a national academy in the United States failed?

4. Distinguish among (a) prescriptive grammar, (b) traditional grammar, and (c) scientific grammar.

5. What changes in the English consonant system have occurred during PDE?

6. What is the chief difference in word stress between American English and British English?

7. What part-of-speech category retains the most inflections in PDE?

8. What verbal inflection that survived into the EMnE period has been lost in PDE?

9. What has happened to plain adverbs in PDE?

10. What type of noun phrase has experienced a great increase between EMnE and PDE?

11. What type of verb phrase first appeared in PDE?

12. Which foreign language(s) has (have) contributed the most loanwords to English during PDE?

13. Why did trade names and acronyms as productive sources of new vocabulary first appear only in PDE?

Name _____

8.3   Ongoing Changes and Dialectal Variation

Many spelling errors, such as *pray* for *prey* or *vice* for *vise*, result from confusion of two different words normally pronounced the same but spelled differently. Other spelling errors, however, reveal contemporary pronunciation or dialectal variation in some way. Give the probable reason for the deviations from conventional spelling of the following italicized words.

0. "If you have more gears, you won't have to *petal* so hard going uphill." <u>The writer</u> <u>pronounces poststress intervocalic /t/ and /d/ alike.</u>

1. "Someone was passing out religious *tracks*." _____

_____

_____

2. "He couldn't move it because it *wheighed* too much." _____

_____

_____

3. "There is no *signifigant* difference between the two." _____

_____

_____

4. Off-Track *Bedding* (name of a contemporary furniture store; why is the pun possible?)

_____

_____

5. "I was *sought of* tired." _____

_____

_____

6. "Nobody ordered *lamp* chops." _____

_____

_____

7. "The town council passed an *ordnance* against drinking in the park." _____

_____

_____

Holt, Rinehart and Winston, Inc.

Name _____

8.4   Grammatical Trends

What changes in traditional usage do the following suggest?

1. ''Michigan Campus Becomes *More Wild* Than the Game'' (headline in the *New York Times*, April 5, 1989); ''The *most heavy* rainfall will occur in the north'' (PBN radio announcer, Orono, Maine) _____

_____

_____

2. Many people object to such sentences as ''Drive *slow*'' and ''Don't feel *bad*.'' Why?

_____

3. Why do many people say ''for you and *I*'' or even ''between them and *we*''? _____

_____

_____

4. ''*As far as tomorrow*, it should be a beautiful day.'' (Very common, especially among weather announcers) _____

_____

5. Perhaps nine out of ten people misinterpret the meaning of the second sentence of the Lord's Prayer (''Thy kingdom come. Thy will be done, On earth as it is in heaven.'') and read it as a future-tense construction. What does it actually mean and why is it so often misunderstood? _____

_____

_____

6. ''I didn't go because I already *saw* the movie.'' _____

_____

_____

Holt, Rinehart and Winston, Inc.

Name _____

8.5   Lexicon: Loanwords

A.   Although French continues to be the modern language from which English borrows the most heavily, other European languages have also contributed to the PDE lexicon. Because these loanwords have been in the language for a relatively short period of time, their nonnative origin is sometimes obvious in their spelling and even pronunciation (e.g., *putsch* from German or *jai alai* from Spanish). From what European languages have the following words been borrowed?

1. boxer (dog) _____
2. deckle _____
3. dope (substance) _____
4. droshky _____
5. eisteddfod _____
6. flamenco _____
7. hoosegow _____
8. mavourneen _____
9. poteen _____
10. rowan (tree) _____
11. rucksack _____
12. scrod _____
13. slalom _____
14. snorkel _____
15. soviet _____
16. spiel _____
17. sporran _____
18. wanderlust _____

B.   Each of the following words has been borrowed into PDE from a different non-European (though not necessarily non-Indo-European) language. Identify that language.

1. beriberi _____
2. cushy _____
3. haiku _____
4. mukluk _____
5. polo _____
6. potlatch _____
7. safari _____
8. swastika _____
9. wapiti _____

Name _____

8.6   Lexicon: New Words by Shortening Old Ones

Frequently used words or phrases are often shortened, resulting in a word that may replace the original or at least acquire a separate identity. Shortening may involve any of the following processes.

  A. **clipping** (including **aphesis**, or dropping off the beginning of a word), as in *mike* from *microphone* or *stogy* from *Conestoga*
  B. **contraction**, or omitting elements from the middle of a word or phrase, as in *bos'n* from *boatswain* (the result does not always have an apostrophe)
  C. **back-formation**, as in *self-destruct* from *self-destruction* (rather than the expected *self-destroy*)
  D. **blend**, as in *stagflation* from *stagnation* + *inflation*
  E. **acronym**, as in *OD* from *overdose* or *linac* from *linear accelerator*

For the following items, give the original word or phrase and indicate by letter the process by which it was shortened. In some instances, more than one of the processes is involved. You will need to consult a desk dictionary for most of the items.

0. aerosol *aero + solution; E*

1. amatol _____

2. blimey _____

3. blues _____

4. brash _____

5. bushwhack _____

6. butane _____

7. Conelrad _____

8. coon _____

9. Delmarva _____

10. electrocute _____

11. frazzle _____

12. laddic _____

13. lube _____

14. methadone _____

15. middy _____

16. mum (flower) _____

17. op-ed _____

18. ornery _____

19. ramshackle _____

20. Reaganomics _____

21. recap (summary) _____

22. reminisce _____

23. rev _____

24. Seabee _____

25. sepal _____

26. soccer _____

27. squawk _____

28. sulfa _____

29. telex _____

Name _____

8.7   Lexicon: Words from Proper Nouns

The process of making new words from proper nouns has continued in PDE. Identify the
origin of the following words, and indicate whether the proper noun is the name of a place,
an animal, a tribe, a real person, or a fictional or mythological person or creature.

0. artesian *Artois, France; place*

1. atropine _____

2. bauxite _____

3. bertha (collar) _____

4. bikini _____

5. bowdlerize _____

6. cereal _____

7. cretonne _____

8. dago _____

9. daiquiri _____

10. dobson (fly) _____

11. farad _____

12. fata morgana _____

13. ferris (wheel) _____

14. fez _____

15. gauss _____

16. hansom _____

17. hertz _____

18. julienne _____

19. jumbo _____

20. leghorn _____

21. lesbian _____

22. lima (bean) _____

23. littleneck (clam) _____

24. macabre _____

25. macadamia _____

26. martini _____

27. mazurka _____

28. paisley _____

29. sisal _____

30. stroganoff _____

31. strontium _____

32. tattersall _____

33. thorium _____

34. trudgen _____

35. tulle _____

Holt, Rinehart and Winston, Inc.

Name _____

8.8   Semantics: Recent Semantic Changes

All of the italicized words in the following sentences have been in the language for at least a century (often many centuries). All have undergone semantic changes of some type within the past few years, so recently that none of the new meanings are listed in the first edition of the *OED*, and some of them do not even appear in the second edition. The changes usually involve adding new meanings to words. In some cases, the newer meanings threaten to replace older ones. Some of the new meanings are not yet considered acceptable, but all are frequently encountered. For each word, explain what the newer meaning is and suggest the reason for the semantic change (e.g., technological innovation, euphemism, metaphorical extension, confusion between similar-sounding words).

0. The changes made are only *cosmetic*. _Metaphorical extension from beauty products to something else superficial and decorative._

1. Turn the *antenna* to the right. _____

2. From this, I *deduct* that he is angry. _____

3. Both of them have *dependency* problems. _____

4. Ellen is totally *disinterested* in tennis. _____

5. We couldn't finish because the computer was *down*. _____

6. Joel has been working with *exceptional* children. _____

7. That rest area has no *facilities*. _____

8. You should have your cat *fixed*. _____

9. It's disgusting the way he *flaunts* the rules. _____

10. The critics all gave *fulsome* praise to our production. (*Note:* This meaning is listed as obsolete in the first edition of the *OED*.) _____

11. He ran through the *gauntlet* of excuses. _____

12. There's a demonstration for *gay* rights today. _____
_____

13. She's been a *hacker* since she was eight years old. _____
_____

14. Martha was *livid* with anger. _____
_____

15. That hamburger made me *nauseous*. _____
_____

16. They bought a new electric *range*. _____
_____

17. Jobs were scarce during the *recession*. _____
_____

18. His repair service is really a *shoe-string* operation. _____
_____

19. Blutex failed in its *takeover* attempt. _____
_____

Holt, Rinehart and Winston, Inc.

CHAPTER 9

ENGLISH AROUND THE WORLD

9.1 Important Terms and Names

1. accent
2. American Dialect Society
3. American Linguistic Atlas Project
4. Black English
5. Cockney (Estuary English)
6. creole
7. dialect
8. English Dialect Society
9. General American
10. Geordie
11. Gullah
12. Krio
13. Hans Kurath
14. William Labov
15. Lallans
16. H. L. Mencken
17. nonrhoticity
18. Pennsylvania Dutch
19. pidgin
20. Received Pronunciation (RP)
21. rhoticity
22. Scots
23. Scouse
24. Sranan
25. Standard British English
26. standard language
27. Strine
28. Tok Pisin
29. Joseph Wright

Holt, Rinehart and Winston, Inc.

9.2   Questions for Review and Discussion

1. Why are most native speakers of English monolingual?
2. What are some of the factors that have made English the world language?
3. What is the difference between a dialect and an accent?
4. In what ways does standard written English differ from standard spoken English?
5. Summarize the major consonantal differences between Standard British English (SBE) and General American (GA).
6. What is the major prosodic difference between the native English of North America and that of the rest of the world?
7. List some of the differences in morphology and syntax between SBE and GA.
8. Explain why terms relating to transportation differ in Britain and the United States much more than terms in most other semantic fields.
9. Who speaks Cockney?
10. How does the English of England's West Country resemble that of the United States?
11. What historical events have contributed to the difference between Scots English and English English?
12. Summarize some of the major differences between Irish English and SBE.
13. What aspect of Australian phonology is most distinctive?
14. What nonnative influences have contributed heavily to New Zealand English?
15. What are the most important non-English linguistic influences on South African English?
16. Why is it difficult to ''map'' American dialects back to specific areas in the British Isles?
17. Why are American dialects so similar (compared to British dialects)?
18. What are the major distinguishing features of General American?
19. Which of the major dialectal areas in the United States have the most distinctive (not necessarily distinguished) accents?
20. What are some of the reasons why ''r-lessness'' seems to be declining in its traditional strongholds in the United States?
21. Is Black English a regional dialect? Explain.
22. In what aspects of the language does Black English differ most strikingly from General American?
23. Why is Canadian English so similar to the English of the United States?
24. What is unique about Newfoundland English?
25. What is unique about Western Atlantic English?
26. Summarize the characteristics that most varieties of nonnative English share.
27. Why is English still at least the second most important language of India?
28. Upon what native variety of English is the (nonnative) English of the Philippines based? Why?
29. Why is English the official language of Nigeria when it has very few native speakers of English?
30. What is unique about English in Liberia?
31. What is the difference between a pidgin and a creole?

9.3   British English

A.   The following is an actual, although abridged, letter received by an American from a friend in Britain. It contains at least nine examples of minor differences between British and American English. Identify these nine differences and state what the equivalent American usage would be for each. Do not count the lack of the possessive form in "Andrew having to have extra time" because Americans do this too. Do not count "headmaster" because many American schools have a headmaster instead of a principal.

Dear Janet,

How about Easter? That would mean Andrew having to have extra time off school and we would have to clear that with the headmaster. He gets his holidays from 28th March to 15th April.

I have to admit that I was in the States myself last May and I didn't even phone you as I meant to do. But I was only there for seven days and it was all such a rush. Richard went over to sit the professional exam so that he could work in the U.S. We even went down to Williamsburg for a day. This had been highly recommended to us and we thought it was all so pleasant and relaxed though we didn't realise before we went that it was all a tourist trap.

Thank you for the snaps. We thought they were very good ones. It was nice to be reminded of them together again. Andrew has several times started a letter to Jim but he is so lazy he never goes back and finishes them and posts them.

This is election day here. I've just been along and voted Liberal, but Labour seem likely to get in and I don't think that will solve any of our problems.

Anne

0. ~~holidays~~—vacation
_____

1. _____

2. _____

3. _____

4. _____

5. _____

6. _____

7. _____

8. _____

9. Any other things that don't seem quite right to American ears?

_____

_____

Holt, Rinehart and Winston, Inc.

B.   Although British and American speakers normally have no difficulty in communicating with each other, the natives of each region frequently accuse those on the other side of the Atlantic of having a "strange" sense of humor, of telling pointless jokes, or even of having no sense of humor at all. This misapprehension sometimes results from a difference in vocabulary, as is the case with the following joke told to me by a Scottish child.

> When the woman of the house answered the doorbell, her dog came to the door with her. The man at the door said, "That's a nice dog. What's his name?"
> "Joiner."
> "Joiner? That's a funny name for a dog. Why do you call him Joiner?"
> "Because he does odd jobs around the house."
> "Maybe you should teach him to make a bolt for the door."

Most Americans will see that there are puns involved in *does odd jobs around the house* and *make a bolt for the door*. But if they do not know the British, and especially Scottish usage of the term *joiner*, they will miss the real point of the joke. Look up the word *joiner* in the *OED* or, if available, *The Concise Scots Dictionary*. What does it mean and how does it explain the joke? _____

_____

_____

C.   British children sing a ditty to the tune of *Frère Jacques*, to which the only words are "Life is but a melancholy flower." It is broken up for singing as follows.

> Life is but a, life is but a
> Melancholy flower, melancholy flower
> Life is but a melan-, life is but a melan-
> Choly flower, choly flower.

What are the puns involved in the first, third, and fourth lines? _____

_____

Why are these not good puns for most American speakers? _____

_____

9.4   Literary Representations of Dialect: British Regional Dialect

The uniform spelling system of modern written English normally conceals the many phonological differences among English dialects. Some authors, however, use ''phonetic'' spellings that reflect, to some extent at least, deviations from the standard, whatever version of English the standard itself may be. One such writer is Alan Garner, a British author of supernatural tales for young people. His two young heroes, Colin and Susan, speak Standard British English; standard spellings are used for their dialogue. The farmer Gowther Mossock and his wife Bess, with whom the children spend their holidays, are natives of the West Country of England, and various adjustments to standard spelling are used to represent their speech.

'Well,' said Colin, 'if it's all right with you, we thought we'd like to go in the woods and see what there is there.'

'Good idea! Sam and I are going to mend the pig-cote wall, and it inner a big job. You go and enjoy yourselves. But when you're up th'Edge sees as you dunner venture down ony caves you might find, and keep an eye open for holes in the ground. Yon place is riddled with tunnels and shafts from the owd copper-mines. If you went down theer and got lost that'd be the end of you, for even if you missed falling down a hole you'd wander about in the dark until you upped and died.'

'Thanks for telling us,' said Colin. 'We'll be careful.'. . .

'And think on you keep away from them mine-holes!' Gowther called after them as they went out of the gate. . . .*

'The funny thing is,' said Gowther when the children had finished reading, 'as long as I con remember it's always been said there's a tunnel from the copper mines comes out in the cellars of the Trafford. And now theer's this. I wonder what the answer is.'

'I dunner see as it matters,' said Bess Mossock. 'Yon's nobbut a wet hole, choose how you look at it. And it can stay theer, for me.'

Gowther laughed. 'Nay, lass, wheer's your curiosity?' 'When you're my age,' said Bess, 'and getting as fat as Pig Ellen, theer's other things to bother your head with, besides holes with water in them.

'Now come on, let's be having you. I've my shopping to do, and you've not finished yet, either.'

'Could we have a look at the hole before we start?' said Susan.

'That's what I was going to suggest,' said Gowther. 'It's only round the corner. It wunner take but a couple of minutes.'

'Well, I'll leave you to it,' said Bess. 'I hope you enjoy yourselves. But dunner take all day, will you?'. . .

'I suppose you'll be wanting to walk home through the wood again,' said Gowther.

'Yes, please,' said Colin.

'Ay, well, I think you'd do best to leave it alone, myself,' said Gowther. 'But if you're set on going, you mun go—though I doubt you'll find much. And think on you come straight home; it'll be dark in an hour, and them woods are treacherous at neet. You could be down a mine hole as soon as wink'. . .†

*Alan Garner, *The Weirdstone of Brisingamen* (London: Williams Collins Sons & Co. Ltd, 1960), p. 19.
†Alan Garner, *The Moon of Gomrath* (London: William Collins Sons & Co. Ltd, 1963), pp. 11, 12, 13.

Holt, Rinehart and Winston, Inc.

Name _____

A.   1. What do the spellings *inner*, *dunner*, and *wunner* suggest about the pronunciation of contracted negative auxiliaries? Use phonetic transcription in your answer. ____

_____

2. How do Gowther and Bess pronounce *there* and *where*? _____

_____

3. What do the spellings *ony* and *con* suggest about the pronunciation of these words?

_____

4. What does *nobbut* mean? If you don't know, look it up in the *OED*. _____
From what two words is it formed? _____

5. How does Gowther pronounce the world *old*? _____

6. How does Gowther pronounce *night*?_____ What does this suggest about the status of the Great Vowel Shift in the West Country? _____

_____

7. Comment on the spelling *th'Edge*. _____

_____

B.   The preceding sample also illustrates several deviations from standard English grammar, some familiar to Americans, others perhaps unfamiliar. Supply a standard English equivalent for the following phrases.

1. *sees as you dunner* _____

2. *Yon place* _____

3. *think on you keep away; think on you come straight home* _____

_____

4. *them mine-holes; them woods* _____

5. *there's a tunnel from the copper mines comes out* _____

_____

6. *I dunner see as it matters* _____

7. *Yon's nobbut a wet hole* _____

8. *choose how you look at it* _____

9. *(it can stay theer), for me* _____

10. *let's be having you* (Hint: You can find the appropriate meaning in the *OED*, where it is labeled "obsolete.") _____

_____

11. *as soon as wink* _____

Name _____

9.5 American Regional Dialect

Because of the limitations of the alphabet, most dialect writers can do little more than hint at phonological features. It is much easier to represent in writing the grammatical and lexical deviations of social and regional dialects. In the following excerpt from Andrew Lytle's "Mister McGregor," the author scarcely hints at phonological features (use of [n] instead of [ŋ] in *-ing* endings is one exception). On the other hand, this relatively brief passage contains at least a score of grammatical and lexical items that deviate from standard written English today. Examine the passage and list these items on the lines below.

> "I wants to speak to Mister McGregor."
> Yes, sir, that's what he said. Not marster, but MISTER McGREGOR. If I live to be a hundred, and I don't think I will, account of my kidneys, I'll never forget the feelen that come over the room when he said them two words: Mister McGregor. The air shivered into a cold jelly; and all of us, me, ma, and pa, sort of froze in it. I remember thinken how much we favored one of them waxwork figures Sis Lou had learnt to make at Doctor Price's Female Academy. There I was, a little shaver of eight, standen by the window a-blowen my breath on it so's I could draw my name, like chillun'll do when they're kept to the house with a cold. The knock come sudden and sharp, I remember, as I was crossen a T. My heart flopped down in my belly and commenced to flutter around in my breakfast; then popped up to my ears and drawed all the blood out'n my nose except a little sack that got left in the point to swell and tingle. It's a singular thing, but the first time that nigger's fist hit the door I knowed it was the knock of death. I can smell death. It's a gift, I reckon, one of them no-count gifts like good conversation that don't do you no good no more. Once Cousin John Mebane come to see us, and as he leaned over to pat me on the head—he was polite and hog-friendly to everybody, chillun and poverty-wropped kin especial—I said, Cousin John, what makes you smell so funny? . . . Then I didn't know what it was I'd smelled, but by this time I'd got better acquainted with the meanen.

1. Grammatical Features

_____   _____

_____   _____

_____   _____

_____   _____

_____   _____

_____   _____

_____   _____

_____   _____

2. Lexical Features

_____   _____

_____   _____

_____   _____

Holt, Rinehart and Winston, Inc.

_____   _____

_____   _____

3. The context makes it clear that the ''speaker'' here is white and young. Make a guess as to the geographical location and approximate date when this story supposedly took

place. _____

_____

Name _____

9.6   Regional Variations in Meaning

Despite the extraordinary homogeneity of American speech, there are still extensive differences in lexicon in the various areas of the United States, especially at the colloquial level. Communication is less likely to break down if a word is totally unfamiliar to one of the speakers; he or she can simply ask what the word means. More confusing is the situation where the term means one thing to the speaker and something else to the listener. Give the usual meaning *for you* of each of the following terms. Then, by checking the *Dictionary of American Regional English* or a good general dictionary, find another, different meaning that could lead to confusion to speakers from another area of the country.

1. *bug*, as in "He's always trying to bug me." _____
_____

2. *mango*, as in "Order me a pizza with mangoes." _____
_____

3. *gumption*, as in "He needs a little more gumption." _____
_____

4. *afoul of*, as in "Guess who I ran afoul of this morning!" _____
_____

5. *alley*, as in "You must have dropped it in the alley." _____
_____

6. *wait on*, as in "I'm sick and tired of waiting on him all the time." _____
_____

7. *ambitious*, as in "The trouble with him is that he's too ambitious." _____
_____

8. *cabinet*, as in "That pig had a cabinet for breakfast!" _____
_____

9. *boulevard*, as in "You can't park on the boulevard." _____
_____

10. *cleanser*, as in "I'm looking for a better cleanser." _____
_____

11. *dope*, as in "Dope is really good on a day like this." _____
_____

12. *fall out*, as in "She almost fell out when I told her." _____
_____

Holt, Rinehart and Winston, Inc.

9.7   Written Indian English

The following selections are from the April 1, 1989, edition of *The Hindu* (International Edition), published in Madras, India. The English is fluent and sophisticated and uses an extensive vocabulary. It is clearly not a creole, let alone a pidgin. Nevertheless, there are numerous differences from what one would find in an equivalent American or British newspaper. Read the passages carefully, then identify the differences between American and Indian English in the grammatical and stylistic categories listed after the passages. In some instances the *OED* will provide clues to puzzling constructions (e.g., *berth* in "missed the berth"). *Pan masala* is a popular addictive mixture for chewing, consisting of betel and other ingredients such as spices and tobacco.

I. Political News Story

Sailing Smooth on Troubled Waters
Nothing disturbs the equanimity of the Karnataka Chief Minister, Mr. S. R. Bommai, who is already set to earn his partymen's sobriquet, "Sthitapragna", in the midst of the jams that he has been caught in from time to time.

Right now, his partymen are cross with him. It is over the manner of the expansion of his Ministry. He has added 10 more Ministers to his existing team of 11. The exercise has misfired, say his partymen who want him to make amends, sooner than later.

Mr. Bommai's latest pursuit falls into a pattern as a thankless job evoking long faces from those who have missed the berth. His party critics have however missed a point. The striking aspect of Mr. Bommai's Ministry-making is that the exercise materialised, after all. In the process, he had brought his aspirant flock to the verge of desperation and breakdown, either by design or by default.

Lucky Number
Seven long months the Chief Minister took to keep his promise, exact to the day, since he constituted his first team of Cabinet Ministers on August 14, 1988, a day after he himself was sworn in. He has a weakness for the numeral 13. He got into the "gaddi" vacated by his illustrious predecessor, Mr. Ramakrishna Hegde, on August 13 last year, with a team of 13, including himself. On March 13, 1989, he expanded his Ministry. Number 13, so it seems, is his mascot.

However he seems to have displeased more people than he has pleased. Instead of a war cabinet that the election year demanded, the Chief Minister has given himself a 'lacklustre' outfit. It need not have taken him that long to form the team that he has is the snide remark one hears in the party.

The Chief Minister has, however, promised a second expansion, within the next one month. He has dangled the carrot, understandably. The Budget session, though a short one, began on March 17, when he presented his first Budget, as Chief Minister, for 1989–90.

II. Letter to the Editor

Sir,—Whatever be the merits of the Budget presented by the Union Finance Minister, Mr. S. B. Chavan, the salaried man has been badly let down again. The salaried class has been bracketed with cigarette and pan masala. As Mr. Chavan has put it "a spoonful of sugar makes the medicine go down". The IT cut on the first slab is nothing but a spoonful of sugar. The surcharge on income above Rs. 50,000 is a cruel joke on the already overburdened tax-payer. This indirectly makes a salaried man feel that it is no use asking for an increase in pay, for an increase in pay will only mean a disproportionate increase in the tax burden.

The Budget therefore is a poor man's Budget in the sense that it makes a middle income earner a poor man.

The concession under section 80C will be only a pittance unless the scheme of deduction is changed to benefit the tax payer. The exemption limit of income could have been raised to atleast [sic] Rs. 25,000 or under Section 80C the deduction could have been raised to 100 per cent of the first Rs. 15,000 and 50 per cent of the balance. The salaried man, the most honest tax payer, now feels that he has been let down. Truly, this should not be the price for honesty.

However, the Finance Minister deserves kudos for making cigarettes, pan masala and the idiot box costlier. It is hoped against hope that this will discourage people from falling a prey to any one of these. This will contribute to the social and moral health of the economy and not to the economic health of the economy as desired by Mr. Chavan.

III. Stock Market Report

Smart Recovery in Stock Markets

A spurt in values at the fag end of the week was the highlight of trading on the Bombay Stock Exchange for the week upto [sic] March 25.

Share prices began lower and dropped further in the absence of support and offerings. Speculative support was not emerging in the initial stages due to end of account considerations. Most of the bull operators preferred to reduce their overall commitments by unloading. The decline was not heavy as bears were covering their earlier short sales. The sellers were, however, more than the buyers.

However, the downward march proved shortlived and equities staged a smart recovery on Thursday on shortcovering. Bull operators also turned aggressive buyers because of first day of new account trading. The final list showed a mixed trend.

There were only three sessions due to closure of market for two days.

IV. Book Review

Love Story

THE LAST WORDS: By Sukumar Chatterjee, Sangeeta Chatterjee, 50, Protapaditya Place, Calcutta–700 026; Rs. 50/.–

A highly independent and religious Shubhamoy, on a wandering adventure, reaches Bombay penniless and chance-meets a fabulously rich Sindhi woman. Already married, young Eva shows extraordinary interest in the well-groomed Bengali youth; but, the upright Shubho discovers the trap in time and gives the slip.

In his next phase of adventure, Shubho takes up a job in Madras and develops acquaintance with an innocent local belle, Damini. Soon their friendship blossoms into a deep love. Shubho, however, meets his villain in Damini's father who is bent on exploiting his daughter's dancing skill to grow rich. Becoming aware of her father's plot to murder her lover, a shocked Damini falls seriously ill. Forced to leave Madras, Shubho moves to Aurobindo Ashram at Pondicherry with memories of Damini and hopes of getting united with her in wedlock some day.

V. Film Review

'Pattukku Oru Thalaivan'   Tamil

A familiar plot of an innocent rustic youth going through the vicissitudes of life to face the challenges of society is retold with some humour in the first half in Tamil Annai Creations' ''Pattukku Oru Thalaivan.'' The title has little to do with the hero but Vijayakanth, as the uneducated youth in love with the MLA's daughter, steals most of the frames here where director Liyakath Ali Khan provides him his script, with veiled vulgarity, to keep the proceedings going.

The hero is considered a bungler by his parents because of his over enthusiasm to help others and not being wordly-wise. The director brings in enough scenes to show this weakness of the hero which Vijayakanth seizes avidly. The sequence where hero Arivu's father Veluchamy (M. N. Nambiar does a neat job) taking out the cow for breeding with Arivu's questions providing a few guffaws is to show the hero's poor knowledge of breeding, which

Holt, Rinehart and Winston, Inc.

even children in villages are aware of, then thank god, he knows the difference between a cow and bull as he sings along with his friends ''how can one milk a bull!''

Vijayakanth is all fire and brimstone in the second-half where the plot takes the familiar lines crashing and burning cars highlighting the climax where Rajarajan's camera makes the best use of the action. So also his lens beautifully picturising the fountain background of Brindavan for the song sequence.

Shobana is the heroine Shanti, unable to give her consent to marry Arivu because of her father's (Vijajayakumar) cunning tactics. Her gazelle like features add to the elegance of her work. Senior artist K. R. Vijaya as the mother of the hero shows the younger elements what an understanding portrayal means. There is nothing much in the S. S. Chandran—Senthil comedy.

''Ninaithathu yaaro'' (lyrics: Gangai Amaran) is a beautiful number tuned in by Ilayaraja.

VI. Cassette Review

Penchant for Speed   **Madras**

Carnatic music lends plenty of scope for innovation but it does not imply the rendering being converted into jazz or choir types of presentation. Also, respect for tradition provides an unwritten injunction that the form of the songs should be in the tempos usually adopted. The young Ganesh-Kumaresh have a penchant for speed and almost all the songs in the two volumes of their violin recital, released by AVM audio, are in the fast pace. The swaras too are so fast that the beauty of the various combinations is beyond the pale of an ordinary listener.

No doubt, their technical skill is superior, the sruti absolutely pure and such a rendering requires remarkable practice and precision. They combine perfectly and bow in a masterly manner but these plus points alone cannot be ennobling. They can be termed Mod-music. The opening Kamalamanohari of Thyagaraja itself reveals their racing style. Such a small piece does not require elaborate swaras but perhaps the youngsters expect the listeners to admire their virtuosity. The familiar Nalinakanti piece resembles an English tune. The Hindolam piece of Papanasam Sivan has an overdose of swaras, though pure, yet with a variety of unfamiliar combinations. Listening to the Sindhu Mandhari, one feels he is inside a church where western instruments are played. Both have however excelled in the Kalyani raga elaboration.

VII. Personal Advertisement

Matrimonial

Straightforward, simple, openminded lifepartner wanted for an Indian girl, 26. Preferably with profound interest in cosmology, metaphysics, psychology, philosophy and Rajayoga. With a liking for nature and adventure. With a strong belief in good and virtue. Preferably interested in the elimination of evil. Preferably below 33. Compatible person with other interests acceptable. Absolutely no bars. Write to . . .

1. Native (non-English) vocabulary items _____

_____

2. Unexpected meanings of English words or phrases _____

_____

3. Unfamiliar compounds or phrases, including hyphenation differences _____

_____

_____

4. Unexpected use or omission of definite or indefinite articles _____

_____

5. Differences in verb tenses or moods _____

_____

_____

6. Differences in punctuation _____

_____

_____

7. Unexpected incomplete sentences _____

_____

_____

8. Unfamiliar treatment of idioms or colloquialisms _____

_____

_____

9. Stylistic differences, especially mixing of stylistic levels _____

_____

_____

_____

10. Other differences _____

_____

_____

_____

Holt, Rinehart and Winston, Inc.

Name _____

9.8   Melanesian Pidgin

Melanesian Pidgin, or Tok Pisin, originated during the nineteenth century in the northern part of Papua New Guinea and has spread throughout the country and to neighboring islands. It is an important *lingua franca* in an area that has scores of indigenous, mutually unintelligible languages. Tok Pisin is sufficiently well established to have developed dialectal differences. However, because English is the language of most education, commerce, and diplomacy in the country, Tok Pisin is under constant influence from the standard language.

The following excerpt is from a Melanesian culture-contact myth. On the blanks below each line, identify the English word or phrase from which the pidgin is derived. A relatively free translation follows the passage.

Orait. Em tufela man, hir—wanfela manki, na wanfela pusi. Em

All right. _____

manki tru hir, i-gat longfela tel. I-no pikinini, i-manki tru. Orait.

_____

Em tufela i-go long bush. Tufela go wokim bigfela hol long graun.

_____

Gisim spaten, na wokim bigfela hol i-go dawn tumas. Orait.

_____

Wokim finis, tufela i-go gisim bigfela ston. Baimbai ston i-fas long

_____

ai bilong hol. Baimbai olsem dor hir. Na tufela i-go long ples

_____

bilong waitman. Tufela wetim tudark, na tufela wokabaut long

_____

nait i-go. Tufela i-go kamap long ples bilong waitman. Orait. Na

_____

tufela stilim plenti samting bilong waitman—plenti nadarkain

_____

samting. Tufela stilim machis, stilim laplap, stilim masket, stilim

_____

katlas, stilim shu, stilim tinbulmakau, stilim cher, stilim tebal,

_____

blanket oltageder sumting bilong waitman. I-no gat wanfela

---

samting tufela i-no stilim.*

Translation

Very well, [There were] these two men—one monkey and one cat. It was a real monkey, which had a long tail. It wasn't a boy, it was a real monkey. Very well. The two of them went to the bush. They went and made a big hole in the ground. They took a shovel and made a big, deep hole. Very well. When they had made it, they went and got a big stone, to fasten it at the mouth of the hole. Then it was like a door. Very well. Then they went to the European's village. They waited until dark, and then walked along in the night. They went and arrived at the European's village. Then they stole many of the European's things—many things of all kinds. They stole matches, stole loincloths, stole muskets, stole cutlasses, stole shoes, stole tinned beef, stole chairs, stole tables, blankets, all of the European's things. There wasn't a single thing they didn't steal.

With the help of the translation, you should be able to identify most of the underlying English words or phrases. Fill in as many of the rest as you can. *Na* means "and"; *-fela* (<*fellow*) is an adjective suffix for single-syllable adjectivals. *Em* is an all-purpose third-person pronoun (= *he*, *she*, *it*, *him*, etc.).

1. What is the verb suffix? _____

2. What is the possessive marker? _____

3. What does *i-* signify? _____

4. Is a distinction made between singular and plural of nouns? _____

*From Robert A. Hall, Jr., *Hands off Pidgin English* (Sydney: Pacific Publications Pty. Ltd, 1955), p. 139.

Holt, Rinehart and Winston, Inc.

Name _____

9.9   Surinam Creole

Surinam Creole, also called Taki-Taki or Sranan, is an English-based creole that is the language of coastal Surinam and a *lingua franca* for the entire country (which has two other English-based creoles). Surinam was first settled by the English, but was then ceded to the Dutch in 1667 in exchange for New York. It became independent of the Netherlands in 1975. Because of this political history, Sranan has been without significant influence from standard English for over three centuries. Hence, unlike the pidgin Tok Pisin, it is virtually unintelligible to an English speaker.

In addition to its English base, Sranan has had influence from Dutch and Portuguese. For example, in the following passage, the words *tanta* 'aunt,' *omu* 'uncle,' and *erken* 'recognize' are from Dutch (*tante*, *oom*, *herkennen*, respectively). The word *sabi* 'know' is from Portuguese *saber*; *pikin* 'children' is ultimately from Portuguese *pequeninho* 'very small,' but it is widespread in English pidgins around the world (cf. English *pickaninny* from West Indian pidgin). *Fesa* 'feast' could be from Portuguese *festa*, but could equally well be from English *feast* or Dutch *feest*.

This Sranan excerpt is much more difficult to read as an ''English'' text than the Tok Pisin passage. However, with the aid of the translation, you should be able to identify a number of the underlying English words, especially in the first three sentences. Fill in as many as you can.

Mi papa no lobi mi moro. A no lobi mi mama tu. A no lobi mi

My papa no love me more. _____

mama pikin tu. Me tanta dati, fu mi mamasey, a no lobi srefsrefi.

_____

Famari fu papasey di e seni suku pikin gebroke a e yagi. ''Meki

_____

den suku masra efu go na lansigron! Mi no ben opo fraga seni

_____

kari no wan sma!'' Wan leysi wan famiri seni kari en fu kon na

_____

wan fesa. Ma di na wan omu fu Nelis ben erken na lutu fu na

_____

famiri dati, sobu fu di den no ben de trutru famiri, en ati teki faya.

_____

''Mi dati no bay famiri! Mi no sabi fu san ede den piki ebi poti na

_____

wi tapu!'' Nanga dati a tori kaba.*

_____

*From Jan Voorhoeve and Ursy M. Lichtveld, eds., *Creole Drum: An Anthology of Creole Literature in Surinam*, trans. Vernie A. February (New Haven: Yale Univ. Press, 1975), pp. 260, 261, 262, 263.

Holt, Rinehart and Winston, Inc.

Translation

My father doesn't love me anymore. He doesn't love my mother either, nor does he love her children. My aunt on my mother's side, he can't stand her at all. He sends away his own relations when they come to ask for something. "Let them look for a man or go to the alms-house. I have no flag at the mast inviting people to come and fetch something." Once a member of the family invited him to a feast. But because one of Nelis's uncles had recognized this branch of the family, so that, as far as he was concerned, they were not really family, he became angry. "I did not buy family. I don't understand why they cause us this trouble." And that was that.

1. What is the negative marker? _____

2. What is the undeclinable first-person singular pronoun? _____

3. What does the word *a* mean? _____

4. Many pidgins and creoles include reduplicated words; the Tok Pisin passage had *laplap* 'loincloth.' One example in this Sranan passage is *srefsrefi*. The root of a second reduplication is an English adjective. What is it? _____

Holt, Rinehart and Winston, Inc.

Acknowledgments

Excerpt from *A Bowl of Bishop* by Morris Bishop, copyright © 1954 by Morris Bishop. Used by permission of Doubleday.

Photograph of the Beowulf manuscript, folio 190r of BW MS. Cotton Vitellius A.xv, courtesy of The British Library.

Excerpts from Cecily Clark, ed., *The Peterborough Chronicle, 1070–1154* (Oxford: Clarendon Press, 2nd ed. 1970).

Excerpts from Kenneth Sisam, ed., *Fourteenth Century Verse & Prose* (Oxford: Clarendon Press, 1921).

Excerpt from Henry Sweet, ed., *The Oldest English Texts;* Early English Text Society O.S. 83 (1885; repr. 1966).

Excerpt from Henry B. Wheatley, ed., *Alexander Hume: Of the Orthographie and Congruitie of the Britan Tongue;* Early English Text Society O.S. 5 (1870; repr. 1965).

Photograph of *Mandeville's Travels* from top portions of Bodley Rawlinson manuscript D.99, f.8v, courtesy of the Bodleian Library, Oxford.

Excerpts from N. F. Blake, ed., *Middle English Religious Prose* (York Medieval texts [Edward Arnold], 1972).

Excerpts from Rolf Kaiser, *Medieval English: An Old English and Middle English Anthology* (1961 impression); Proclamations of Henry III; William Caxton's Prologue to Chaucer's *Canterbury Tales.*

Excerpts from *The Works of Geoffrey Chaucer, Second Edition.* Copyright © 1957 by F. N. Robinson, Editor. Used with permission of Houghton Mifflin Company.

Photograph of Roger Williams' letter to the Providence Town Meeting courtesy of the Rhode Island Historical Society.

Excerpts from April 1, 1989, issue of *The Hindu* (International Edition).